READER'S COMMENTS

"I had read the author's first book, "THE TANNING BED MURDERS" and wanted to find out what happened to NORA WALLACE. So I had to get the second book. "NORA" is a much faster paced book than the first book. It was so exciting and held my interest. I finished it in two days. I'm an avid reader. I love mysteries. This kept me captivated throughout the book. It is well worth the money and is 'G' rated if you wish to give it to a young reader who is a mystery buff. I can't wait for the next offering from this author."

~Claire James, "Avid Reader", Springfield, VA

From the eyes of another cop: "John Eisler has done it again! He has woven several separate criminal activities and investigative procedures into one outstanding story. Unlike TV Cops and CSI Investigators, Eisler's characters like real officers, work a group of cases at one time. Some cases have a direct impact on another. Others cases ending but opening another search for different offenders. "Nora" has a surprise ending much different from most police tales. Sometimes, the guilty punish themselves."

~ Dick Boultinghouse, Retired Soldier, Cop, International Police Instructor

"A great story! Sometimes I thought the other investigations overshadowed that story about Nora Wallace. The chase was a long

one. I thought Nora cheated Jake in the end.. She cheated him of his victory of arresting her. There was "No Book em Dano."
~ *Mike O'Donnell, Las Vegas, NV*

"I like a good read when I retire for the night. I found myself going to bed early for this read."
~ *Reader, Oregon*

"The author has written a great book! I worked with the author in Jordan training Iraqi Police Officers. John is very knowledgeable with more police experience than most police officers will ever see. You can see his experience and background in the book. I look forward to his next book. Keep it up John!"
~ *Randy Stensass, author of: "A HORSE CALLED H BOMB", WY*

"John Eisler sets his novels in the U.S. and in my neck of the woods, Northumberland, U.K. That's not the only attraction though: his plots, description of characters and locations keep you engaged on every page. There is always a surprise twist at the end and "Nora Wallace" is up there with the best! A real "Page Turner."
~ *Geordie Girl, Northumberland, U.K.*

"Another multifaceted mystery by John Eisler. A great read for taking one's mind off the day. The writer's vast experience with real life confidence men (and women) shows through in the characters he has created for this series. If you like mysteries, buy this one!
~ *L. Friskoop, Nebraska*

"I like Eisler's writing – easy flow and interesting from page to page. John has taken his police training and experience and put it to good use in this story. I read John's first book and found it equally fascinating and entertaining."
~ Joseph H. Race, "Jose Mango" Author, Saipan, MP U.S.A.

"Reading your stories makes me feel like I am in the scenes due to your complete descriptions. The colors, sounds, and smells that you portray are sensory blasting. I could smell the ocean in England, taste the food in Idaho and feel the chilly air in Canada all without ever having been there.
~ Donna Cooley, Fairfield, CA

"I thoroughly enjoyed the book. Just my kind of reading. I was held captive by this book from the moment I read the first page. Please write another."
~ TOP, Pinehurst, NC

A Jake Lowry Mystery

The Coeur d'Alene Murders

John Eisler

ISBN: 1456439146
ISBN-13: 9781456439149

Library of Congress Control Number: 2010918707

CHARACTERS

Jake Lowry: 57, 6', Born in Vacaville, California, retired California cop, retired USAF S.E.R.E. instructor, married 30 yrs, no children. Bachelors Degree in Criminal Justice from Chapman University, Masters Degree in Psychology from St. Mary's University, Doctorate from University of San Francisco. Currently employed as a Detective, Kootenai County Sheriff's Department, Coeur d'Alene, (Cd'A) Idaho. Lives in an old house on former meat processing and dairy farm in Kingston, Idaho.

Elizabeth Lowry: 48, 5'10", Born in Camas Washington, Bachelor's Degree in commercial art from Sacramento State University. Sculptor, oil painter, interior designer, currently manages an art collective in Coeur d'Alene, Idaho.

Bruce David: 44, born in Cd'A, Idaho. Graduated from Lake City High School. Has a Bachelor's Degree in Criminal Justice from Lewis & Clark State College. Detective in Kootenai Sheriff's Department. Bruce is normally called by his last name only.

Gunter Lenca: 29, born in Berlin, Germany immigrated to Cd'A in 1985 with his family and sister Morgan. Gunter is a new Detective in Kootenai County and has recently graduated from North Idaho College with an Associate's

Degree in Criminal Justice. Gunter was previously Jake Lowry's patrol partner.

Morgan Lenca: 32, born in Berlin, Germany. Immigrated to Cd'A in 1985 with her family. Former Office Manager and 'Girl Friday' for Ken Kunkle. Morgan has an Associate's Degree in business from North Idaho College. She is multilingual. Speaks and writes German, French, Russian and English flawlessly. She is a recent hire as the Detective Division's Secretary.

Wodhouse McNair: 30, born in Arlington, Virginia. Moved with her parents to Fairchild AFB when her U.S.A.F. father was transferred there. As a teenager, she fell in love with the Pacific Northwest. Her father's favorite author was P.G. Wodhouse. He vowed that his first child would be named after him. She attended Spokane Community College. Received an Associate's Degree in Criminal Justice. Was hired by the Kootenai County Sheriff immediately after graduation. Her nickname is "Woody." Woody has also recently been promoted to Detective. She is partnered with Gunter Lenca.

Zack Corker: 46, born in Arlington, Virginia. Patrol Sergeant in the Kootenai County Sheriff's Department.

Jay Bass: 38, born in Post Falls, ID. Graduated from Lake City High School. Has an Associate's Degree in criminal justice from North Idaho College. Lead evidence technician at Kootenai County Sheriff's Department.

Sherry Lee: 32, born in Pinehurst, ID. Graduated from Wallace Junior/Senior High School. Has an Associate's degree in criminal justice from North Idaho College. Currently enrolled in a Bachelor's degree program at University of Idaho, Cd'A campus. Evidence technician at Kootenai County Sheriff's Department.

Ron Wong: 36, born in Nha Trang, Vietnam. Immigrated to the U.S. in 1969. Has a Bachelor's Degree in forensic science from Lewis & Clark State College. Evidence technician at Kootenai County Sheriff's Department.

Clyde Kunkle: 62, born in Lexington, Nebraska, moved to Cd'A in 1938. Married Carole Rushbrooke of Coeur d'Alene. Operated a sawmill during the heyday of northwest logging. Expanded the sawmill and opened a mining supply company. He bought shares in the Bunker Hill and Sunshine Mines. Sold them when the silver boom ended in the Silver Valley. He served on the Coeur d'Alene City Council from 1952-1960. Maintains the family compound on the west shore of Lake Coeur d'Alene.

Rebecca Kunkle Lenca: 29, born in Cd'A, Idaho, graduated with a Bachelor's Degree in Music from University of Idaho in Moscow. Sister of Ken Kunkle (now deceased). Married to Gunter Lenca. Rebecca and Gunter now reside in Ken's former custom-built ranch house on the shore of Lake Coeur d'Alene. Rebecca has assumed control of Ken's property management corporation. Has limited outside interests other than the family mill, charities and falconry.

Consuelo Gonzales: 24 5'7" born in Chihuahua, Mexico, graduated from Lake City High School. Works as the maid and cook for Gunter and Rebecca. Her mother, Maria, is Clyde Kunkle's cook and maid. Her father Roberto is Clyde's gardener. Consuelo has plans to become an interior designer. She takes evening and weekend classes at North Idaho College.

Husam Al Nageeb: 43 born in Amman, Jordan. Husam originally worked for Clyde Kunkle at his lumber mill. Maintaining his equipment. Ken Kunkle hired him away from Clyde to maintain Ken's 'Big Boy Toys.' Upon Ken's death, Husam was rehired by Clyde. Clyde has also sponsored Husam's family to allow them to immigrate to Idaho. They are due at any time.

Michelle Keller: 25, born in Pinehurst, Idaho. Graduated from Kellogg High School and North Idaho College. Former Dancer at Showgirls. Now employed as the Office Manager at Ken Kunkle's old firm. Prior frequent associate of Ken Kunkle.

Amadeus Vecchio: 35, born in Vancouver, British Columbia. Nickname 'Ammo' Sergeant in the Kamloops, British Columbia Detachment, Royal Canadian Mounted Police. 'Ammo's detachment investigated the first murder committed by Nora Wallace.

Robert Forbes: 39, born in Whitley Bay, England. Police Inspector, Whitley Bay Police Station. Nickname 'Robbie.' Robbie served as an International Police Officer with the

United Nations in Bosnia. Was assigned as the team leader of the English Police Team assigned to assist Jake and David in the search and apprehension of Nora Wallace.

CHAPTER ONE

The phone ringing at 2 A.M. is never a good omen. I don't have any kids so I know it won't be the call all parents dread at this hour of the morning. I'm a detective with the Kootenai County, Idaho Sheriff's Office so I may be the one making that dreaded call later this morning. "Jake Lowry here. Who's calling?"

"Jake this is Sergeant Corker. Sorry to wake you at this hour, but we have a real doozy on our hands. The Watch commander told me to get you and Detective David here ASAP."

"Where's here Sarge?"

"On the shoreline beside Ken Kunkle's old house. We have a dead body. The Watch Commander thought we should get you two on this before anyone screwed up the crime scene. We've called out the evidence team and they're enroute also. How long will it take you to get here? I know you live in Kingston."

"I figure about ten minutes to throw on some clothes and thirty minutes driving time. It's thirty-two miles from my house to COSTCO. I buy gas there for my personal vehicle and reset my odometer when I refuel. You said you've called David. He should be there before me since he lives close to Dalton Gardens. Tell him I'm on the way."

"Will do. We've secured the scene and aren't letting anyone enter until you get here. A private security company's guard discovered the body while doing routine patrol. He called 911. One of our patrol deputies responded. He froze the scene and advised me. The Watch Commander thought there might be some connection and told me to wake you guys. This was because you and David worked the Kunkle homicide."

"Got it Sarge. I'm dressing as we talk. I'll be there in thirty. There shouldn't be any traffic on I-90 westbound at this hour so I can run right at the speed limit. Bye."

As I dressed, I thought; i*t's been almost two years since Nora Wallace murdered Ken Kunkle. Nora committed suicide in Northumbria, England almost one year ago. What possible connection could there be between those crimes and this dead body? Although Ken's house does sit in an isolated spot on the edge of Lake Coeur D'Alene, it's now inhabited by Gunter and Rebecca Lenca. They've been married for six months. Both thought that it would be a shame to sell the house since Ken had put so much effort into the design and construction. The setting at lakeside is remarkable. Rebecca thought long and hard about moving into her dead* *brother's house, but in the end felt it would be a fitting tribute to have it still occupied by a member of the Kunkle family. Gunter on the other hand took an awful lot of kidding from both David and I about being adopted by Clyde rather than marrying Rebecca.*

Hey that's enough rumination! I'll leave Liz a note and call her if I have time later this morning.

I jumped into my unmarked detective's vehicle and quickly got onto I-90 westbound. I ramped the speed up to seventy-five miles an hour. Which was the speed limit and headed for 'Fourth of July Pass' toward Coeur d'Alene. I grabbed the microphone and advised dispatch that I was in service, 10-8, enroute to the crime scene. I didn't specify the exact location to hopefully prevent the media from descending on the scene prior to my arrival.

As soon as I finished the call to dispatch, Detective Bruce David, my partner, came on the air to advise he was also enroute. Detective Bruce David does not normally use his first name and simply goes by 'David.'

Detective David and I have been partners for over two years. The partnership began soon after I joined the Kootenai County Sheriff's Department as a 'Road Dog'. I had a long and interesting career as an Oakland California Police Officer. I retired and moved to Kingston, Idaho to enjoy the fruits of my retirement. I, and my beloved wife, Liz live on what had been a beef processing operation in Kingston. The original owner was one of three brothers who owned quite a bit of property in Kingston. Kingston is now only a wide place in the road with two gas stations, two bars, and a restaurant called the Hilltop that serves wonderful hamburgers and on the weekend good prime rib. The North Fork of the Coeur d'Alene River makes a turn at Kingston and then runs by the Cataldo Mission which is the oldest wooden building in Idaho. Just up the river about one mile is the Enaville Resort and Restaurant. It is housed in what in times past was a hotel, and brothel. The most used name for the establishment is "The Snake Pit." No one is sure if that moniker refers to the former occupants of the brothel or has some other obscure connotation.

Growing tired of not matching wits with criminals and also missing the joy of arresting them, I applied with the Kootenai County Sheriff's Department and was hired.

When Ken Kunkle was brutally murdered by being forcibly restrained in his tanning bed, I, and my patrol partner, Gunter Lenca, answered the dispatch call to cover the deputy assigned to the scene. My handling of that case got me promoted to detective. David and I've been partners ever since.

Gunter Lenca met Rebecca Kunkle while assisting in the Ken Kunkle homicide. Over time their relationship blossomed. They had a fantastic wedding at the Kunkle Compound shortly after the entire team returned to Idaho from England where they were pursuing Ken's murderess. Nora Wallace committing suicide ended that tragic situation.

Gunter has now also been promoted to detective and has been teamed with former deputy Woody McNair. *I wondered if the flashing lights and noise would wake Gunter and Rebecca. I imagine that would depend on the actual location of the dead body.*

The speed limit over 'Fourth of July Pass' is sixty-five. I turned on my "P.R." lights and kept the speedometer at seventy-five.

I guess turning on my P.R. lights is for my conscience only since there's no one on the road right now. They call them P.R. lights because it improves public relations when an emergency vehicle goes speeding past. Most folks probably say to themselves, "They're probably late for donuts."

I crested the top of 'Fourth of July Pass' and stared the descent into the Coeur d'Alene Valley. Lake Coeur d'Alene was shimmering in the bright moonlight. I took the Sherman Avenue off-ramp and started down that street until I came to the turn that would take me to Ken's house.

I should stop thinking of that house as Ken's house. It's Gunter and Rebecca's house now and is a happy place. It wasn't a happy place the first time I entered. You never forget the scent of burned flesh. Ken had been cooking in that tanning bed for three days. O.K. Jake. Gunter and Rebecca's house. Happy place!

As I approached the lakeshore I could see the inevitable flashing lights of the sheriff's patrol units and ambulance.

I wonder if law enforcement and emergency medical personnel received some type of subliminal thrill from those flashing lights. Obviously there was no one that required notification that they were there. No speeders or illegal left turn criminals. They were at the scene and flashing lights were unnecessary. This was probably a topic for someone's erudite research paper. But for the moment, I turned off my lights and coasted to a stop on the lakeside roadway.

David was already there dressed in his Tyvek bunny suit and nitrile gloves. He really looked ridiculous in the red and blue flashing lights. Much like an out-of-place lab worker. Jay Bass was stepping out of the driver's side of the evidence vehicle. Ron Wong and Sherry Lee were already dressed in Tyvek. Sherry had her video camera on her shoulder and had started filming the lake shore area surrounding the crime scene.

I opened the trunk of my car and extracted a Tyvek bunny suit and multiple pairs of blue Nitrile gloves. Just as I'd zipped up the suit, Gunter Lenca walked up. He looked very sleepy and had the proverbial 'bed head.'

"Jake what's going on?"

"Well sleepy head I see that the lure of flashing emergency lights roused you from your bed. At the moment, all I know is that we have a dead body leaning against the rock wall that surrounds your property. Apparently a 'Rent-a-Cop' from a private security company spotted him during his routine patrol. We're just now entering the crime scene. Do you want to stick around or are you just curious?"

"No. I'll go back and tell Rebecca what's going on. I'm sure you can handle this."

"Thanks for the vote of confidence!"

With that remark I turned to the evidence team and David and said, "Shall we begin? Sherry you go in first. Sweep everything with your camera we'll want the broadest view we can get. Ron, I see you have a digital. We'll hold back so you can get detailed shots. Jay, you'll be the "Finder' for everything we decide is evidentiary. David, you're the "Note Taker." That'll allow me to move freely among you as you do your respective jobs."

Sherry started walking toward the body that was sporadically illuminated in the flashing lights. From a distance it appeared as if the man had simply sat down and leaned back against the dry-stacked rock wall. The victim appeared to be completely dressed in a long sleeved shirt and long trousers. He was wearing deck shoes but no hat. That was unusual in the Coeur d'Alene area. Ball caps worn conventionally or with the bill facing to the rear was almost a local custom. Seeing a male without a ball cap was unusual. Many females also adhered to this custom. Most wearing the cap with a pony tail sticking out of the hole in the rear. Sherry's video light swept left to right and seemed to be almost like a pendulum in its regularity. Jay had a stack of small plastic triangular markers that were numbered.

Occasionally, Sherry would stop her progress and ask for Jay to mark either a footprint. cigarette butt or small bit of fabric. As she paused, David would make notations and Jay would place a marker. The progress was extremely slow and the team would stop and discuss what had been observed and its potential for future use as evidence. As they got about five feet from the body, they saw a large group of footprints in the sand. There were prints with a distinctive tread and also small footprints that would imply that there had been a small child or female around the body. Jay returned to the evidence van and brought some molding rubber to make molds of the prints. This process stopped any further movement for the rest of the team.

As they paused, Doctor Lionel Hardcastle, the county coroner arrived. I explained that they were trying to preserve the footprints surrounding the victim. Dr. Hardcastle had worked with the entire team during the investigation of Ken's murder and was cooperative.

Jay announced that it would be just five minutes until the rubber molds were set. Once they were set, they could continue their progress into the scene. Ron changed the lens on his camera and set it on a tripod so he could take detailed long shots of the victim before he was moved. As he looked through the lens he let out a gasp.

"Jake come have a look through the view finder. I've put on a telephoto lens and I think you want to see this. Sherry focus your video light on the victim's chest so it'll give Jake a better view."

I moved over to the tripod and squinted through the camera's viewfinder.

"Ron, you're right that is unusual. It looks like there is an awl stabbed into the area of the victim's heart. Doc have a look."

I turned to the team and said, "If this is the cause of death it will be a classic case of a man being murdered in Coeur d'Alene with a traditional Coeur d'Alene. I'm sure I don't have to conduct a history or etymology lesson for the team do I?"

Ron said, "I thought that etymology was the study of bugs."

"No. Sorry it is the study of the origin of words. I'll continue with the lesson. When the French fur traders came to this area they dealt with the local Indians. They were a combination of Coeur d'Alene, Spokane, Kalispel, and Kootenai tribes. The fur traders thought that the Indians were such shrewd traders they said it was like having the heart of an awl. Over time that has been translated to be: an awl through the heart. There's a jeweler in Coeur d'Alene on Northwest Boulevard, by the name of Cheryl Burchell. She creates unique jewelry that depicts the awl through the heart. I have a tie tack made by Burchell depicting the awl through the heart. Liz gave it to me for Christmas two years ago. Apparently our victim has suffered at the hands of one or more criminals who are intent on duplicating that term. This case may turn out to be very complicated."

Jay said, "The molds have set so I'll retrieve them and we can continue toward the body. I'll bet you're really anxious to do a close examination now."

I replied, "Not any more now than before. Violent crime has always fascinated me and this case will be no different."

The team advanced toward the body with Dr. Hardcastle trailing behind. Once Sherry & Ron had taken their pictures, I motioned for Dr. Hardcastle to examine the body so he could make an 'Official Pronouncement' that the victim was dead. That having been done, I stepped up to the body and closely examined the awl. It had a wooden handle with a round metal cap on it. It appeared to have been driven through the victim's shirt at a downward angle directly over his heart. The victim was a Caucasian male who appeared to be in his late twenties or early thirties. He had on navy blue trousers a black 1 ½" wide leather belt with a silver colored buckle and burgundy deck shoes with white soles. Neither his clothing nor his shoes were remarkable. There was an irregular bloodstain on the left side of the shirt, three inches in diameter below the awl.

Dr. Hardcastle commented, "If the awl pierced his heart, he may have bled to death internally. That's why we don't see a lot of blood on his shirt. I can tell you more when I conduct the autopsy."

David and I said simultaneously, "Let's roll him over and see if he has any identification."

David said, "We should be so lucky. The only dead bodies that have I.D. are on TV on Law & Order or CSI. We usually end up having to roll their prints, run their picture and hope for an I.D. Well! The god's are smiling on us. He has a wallet in his back pocket. It's in his left rear pocket so we can assume that he was left-handed. Well Howdy! He even has a driver's license. Not only that but an Idaho driver's license. Our Victim's name appears to be..... You're not going to believe this, Doctor Lawrence Matile! I thought his face looked familiar. This is the veterinarian that Nora Wallace worked for. Remember he's the person who led us to Nora's leather straps in his Post Falls office.

Sherry piped up and said, "If my memory serves me correctly, he drove a white Mercedes 250. Maybe we should have our uniformed deputies look around the area for his car. Mercedes aren't that unusual in this neighborhood, but if they find a white 250 they should run the license plates. I don't remember that he lived around here."

I added, "Sherry you're right. Remember, I rode with him. You and David followed in David's car when we went to his office to look at the straps that Nora had fabricated. You know it seems almost wrong to refer to her as Nora now since she was called Roberta when she worked for Dr. Matile. How does that expression go? 'It just gets curiouser and curiouser!' When the phone rang at 2 A. M., I said to myself that those early morning calls are never good news. It looks like David and I'll be making that 'Much-dreaded Advisement' later this morning. David wasn't his wife's name Heidi?"

"Yes. That's right! It's been almost two years since we interviewed him but you still remember that much detail. It's remarkable. When you stimulate my sagging memory bank, I can bring up those kinds of details but if we were doing a pop quiz, I wouldn't have been able to recall her name. I'll go talk to a uniform and ask for additional units to come sweep the area for our victim's car."

I turned to Jay, Ron, & Sherry, "If you folks are finished, I don't think there's anything more we can do now. Let's have the ambulance crew come in and load the body. Dr. Hardcastle would you and Ron ride with the body so we can protect any evidentiary items for the chain of evidence? I assume that you'll be taking him to the county morgue. We'll have one of our uniformed deputies drive your car to the morgue. Jay I see you have placed only six evidence triangles around the crime scene. Let's discuss what you think is evidentiary. Then you and Sherry can collect what you have marked."

Jay replied, "That sounds like a deal. Let's start with # 1 and proceed in numerical order."

#1. I saw was a small piece of white material that looked as though it had been torn. It might be part of a handkerchief or possibly a shirt or blouse. The rest of the shoreline looks fairly clean so this seemed out of place.

#2. Is the remaining butt and filter from a cigarette. Depending on the sensitivity of the case we can send this for DNA testing. There is a national DNA registry so we might get a match for the smoker. Naturally, this butt might be days old and have no bearing, but again it seemed out of place.

#3. Is the first treaded footprint that I cast into a moulage or as they are more commonly referred to; a mold. We could see from our vantage point outside the immediate crime scene that the victim was wearing deck shoes. Although they usually have a distinctive tread, they don't have the deep groves we observed.

#4. Is the second molded footprint that appears to be much smaller in size than the treaded print. This print looks as though it might belong to an athletic shoe. In the old days we'd call it a tennis shoe.

#5. Looks as though it is a finger torn from a latex glove. It might be one of those latex coverings that you place over an injured finger to keep it dry. Unless it was violently torn off the finger, we might be able to turn it inside out and recover a fingerprint.

#6. Is the most interesting! This looks to be a black nylon or ballistic cloth sheath for the awl that's protruding from the victim's chest. It doesn't have a belt loop so it may have just been the holder if the awl was kept in a tool bag or box.

I took a minute to consider the information that Jay had produced. I manifested one of my irritating mannerisms and placed my right index finger alongside my temple as if trying to push the information into my brain. After that pause, I looked at the team and said, "Comments, observations, opinions anyone?"

David spoke quickly, "Jay I agree with your observations and concur with your diligence. We may be overreaching for evidentiary items. Having the tests conducted may impact our division's budget, but I for one, would rather err on the side of being overcautious rather than err on the side of frugality."

Not hearing anymore comments, I said, "Jay you know the drill. We go into the 'Tag it and Bag it Mode' now. I wholeheartedly agree with David. Again you've done an excellent job. We'll be here interviewing the rent-a-cop if you need any assistance just give us a shout."

Turning to David I said, "Partner, let's go talk to our witness."

David said, "The first uniformed deputy kept him in the back seat of the marked unit to make sure that he didn't overhear any of our discussions and he also didn't have his observations contaminated by talking to anyone else. Where do you want to talk to him?"

I replied, "Let's invite him into the front seat of my unmarked. You'll sit in the back seat after you introduce yourself and bring him over; I think that will put him at ease. We will feel him out first to see if he's a 'wanna-be' or if he's satisfied with his career choice as a private security officer. If we see that he's prone to be 'badge heavy' and a frustrated 'wanna-be, we can invite him to our office and give him the 'Honored Colleague Treatment.' This guy may know more information that he realizes. We want to extract every pertinent detail from him no matter which interview technique we employ."

David walked off to retrieve the witness and returned to my car in less than a minute.

"Detective Lowry, this is Officer Garrett Reeves. He's the private security officer who first spotted our victim. Officer Reeves has made some extensive notes while he was waiting for us to process the crime scene. He has offered to share his notes with us or we can conduct an oral interview while he refers to his notes. I'll sit in the back while you get the basics from Officer Reeves."

I stepped out of my vehicle and walked around to the passenger's side of the car. I solemnly took Officer Reeve's hand and gave it a firm handshake. I opened the door and asked Reeves to have a seat.

"Officer Reeves, may I call you Garrett?"

"Yes sir."

"First of all my partner and I want to thank you for your diligence. We seldom get qualified witnesses in any of our cases. I can't remember when we've had a witness who had made notes of his observations. What I'd like to do right now is get the basics from you and then we'll establish a time certain for you to come to the detective division so we can make copies of your notes and conduct an extensive interview. As you well know, later this morning we'll be making an 'Advisement' to the victim's family. That could take some time to identify exactly whom we should notify and how to contact them. First of all when you spotted the victim how close did you go to the body before you decided that he was dead?"

Reeves pulled a mini double AA cell flashlight from its holder on his belt and shined it on his notebook. He flipped pages with a flourish and then tapped the page. "I spotted the body at zero one thirty hours. I was on routine patrol in my assigned area and operating my marked emergency vehicle. As I drove my vehicle down Lakeside Road I was using my spotlight to illuminate the beachfront. This is a location where trespassers frequently go to lie on the beach and smoke dope. I shone my light along the stonewall and saw the body against the wall. I alighted from my vehicle and illuminated my flashlight. I walked toward the body advising him that he was trespassing and had to leave immediately. When he didn't respond, I stepped up to him to attempt to awaken him. I imagine that I was within two feet of the body when I spotted the ice pick in his chest and saw the blood stain."

I asked, "May I see the sole of your boot?"

Reeves lifted his boot. I could see that the sole was a deeply treaded sole that appeared identical to the print that Jay had molded.

I said, "Garrett, we'll ask you to go directly from here to the Sheriff's Department on Government Way so that our evidence technicians can make a mold of your boot sole. We lifted a print close to the body and feel that it might be a print of your sole. This would eliminate our search for an owner. You're aware of how we eliminate as many persons as possible at the outset of the investigation. This'll significantly reduce our investigative tasks."

"Of course, I'll take them off right now. I've a back-up pair of rubber Wellingtons in the trunk of my unit. I keep them there in case I have to wade into water and would get my boots wet."

"That would be excellent! If you'll give Detective David your keys he'll go to your unit right now and retrieve your Wellingtons. That way we can release your boots to the evidence technicians here at the crime scene right now. That'll allow us to keep a tight chain of custody on the boots. You know how important that is. I'm sure that we'll be able to release your boots to you when you come to the station later today."

"Don't worry sir; I've two spare pair at my residence. I try to be prepared for any possible emergency. When exactly do you think we should set up the appointment for later today? I can be there any time you say. I normally work the graveyard shift at Alpha and Omega Security. Although I'm scheduled to report for duty at twenty-four hundred, I try to get there before twenty-three thirty hours. I can grab some sleep when I leave here and be at your office anytime."

I took a minute to think of all the remaining steps that had to be taken prior to David and me finally arriving at the Sheriff's Department. After the pause and the finger to my forehead, I said, "Garrett, I think that if you went home and got some sleep and planned on being at our office on Government Way at fifteen hundred hours we'd only keep you for about an hour. That is unless you'd like to have an escorted tour of the Sheriff's Facility. If you want to do that, it'd take a total of two hours and we'd keep you until seventeen hundred. How does that sound?"

"I'd really appreciate the tour sir. I wasn't aware that benefit was offered."

"Well we don't normally allow full access to civilians, but in your case since you are a fellow law enforcement officer, it'd be Detective David's and my pleasure to show you around and introduce you to some of the other members of the sheriff's team. O.K. we'll plan on you being at the Department at fifteen hundred and I'll set up the tour for you. I'm sure that if the Sheriff isn't otherwise obligated, he'd love to meet you."

David returned with the Wellingtons. Garrett took off his boots and gave them to Sherry Lee. Sherry gave him a receipt and placed them in a large paper grocery bag.

"I'll take these to the lab and make a mold and compare that mold to the one we made out here. I should be done before noon."

I said, "Officer Reeves is coming to the Department at fifteen hundred hours, after we copy his notes and conclude his interview, Detective David and I are going to give him a tour of the entire facility. Would you speak with Mr. Bass and tell him to expect Officer Reeves, Detective David and I around sixteen-forty five for a tour of the crime lab."

"Will do Detective. We have a very interesting specimen we're examining with Thin Layer Chromatography that Officer Reeves may be interested in."

Reeves said, "I'm sure it'll be very interesting. Thank you Miss Lee."

I stepped out of the driver's door and walked around to the passenger's side and opened the door so Reeves could put on his Wellingtons. I shook Reeves hand and repeated the appointment time. Reeves made a note in his notebook and saluted both of us as he walked to his Alpha and Omega Security vehicle.

As soon as he started the vehicle and left the area, Sherry grabbed me by the arm and with eyes that expressed incredulity, asked, "What in the world just happened? You're going to give this rent-a-cop a tour of the facility and you want us to do the twenty-five cent tour of the crime lab! What'd this guy say in your vehicle? Does he have the keys to the kingdom or something?"

Before I could answer, David added, "I heard you say that we extend this benefit to other law enforcement officers. Reeves is just a rent-a-cop."

"I know he's a rent-a cop and you both think I went overboard, but Reeves is a dangerous person. You see how methodical he is about notes and having spare Wellingtons in his trunk. Did you hear him say he has two spare pair of boots at his residence? You know how the arson investigators always make sure that they video the crowd at a fire. They do that because arsonists love to watch their work and they return to the scene of the fire. Well some psychopaths also like to be deeply involved in their crimes. Much like criminals who abduct small children involve themselves in the search for the missing child. It's not a far stretch to imagine that Officer Garrett Reeves may be the murderer of Dr. Matile. This provides him with the best cover in the world to be close to the inside track of this investigation."

"Jake, you're something." David said. "I'm figuring Reeves is a nice guy with a tendency to be a little over precise. You're thinking he may be a psychopath. I guess I better re-think my opinion until either you or I'm proven correct. So what do we do now?Is this Departmental tour a dodge to see how screwed-up he really is or are you being nice to our star witness?"

"The tour is to soften him up a little and appeal to his sense of belonging to the 'Brotherhood of the Badge.' By treating him like an equal and not referring to him as either a civilian or rent-a-cop, he'll feel that he's one of us. This may cause him to let his guard down a little. I may be wrong. If I am, then this charade won't hurt one bit. We'll do the 'Dog & Pony Show' for him. I'll try to have the sheriff meet with him. But only after we brief the sheriff on our purpose of doing the tour. To answer your question about star witness, he truly is the only witness we're aware of at this time. So being nice never hurts."

"As far as what we do next, I'm thinking that it's time to go give the sad news to the Widow Matile. This will be a hard one to do. Remember we met her at the Veterinarian's office after Nora escaped. When we provided the explanation for Dr. Matile's involvement in attempting to bring

Nora to justice. Heidi Matile seemed like a nice person, but even though she seemed nice, we can't rule her out as a suspect. You know the old adage. 'Most folks are killed by immediate family or at least relatives.' Until we know better, we'll walk a tight line when we do the 'Advisement'. Of all the questions we ask of a spouse, the toughest is; "Where were you last night?" or "Where were you during the time the coroner estimates the victim was murdered?" Those questions usually inflame the person being questioned. I try to leave those until the very last minute of the interview."

David suggested, "Possibly we should ask Woody to accompany us, since having a female officer along occasionally makes the 'Advisement' easier"

"Good idea! I'll call dispatch on my cell and ask them to wake her. She can meet us at the Department. We'll have to check records to verify if the Matiles still live at the same address. We don't want to knock on the wrong door at that early hour. That'll give us time to freshen up, make computer entries, brief Woody, and see when Dr. Hardcastle has scheduled the autopsy."

David asked, "While I was getting Reeves' Wellingtons did you hear from Dispatch or any of the uniformed deputies about finding Dr. Matile's car?"

"No I haven't. Maybe we should put in a call to see if anyone's had success. If we know the location of Matile's car it might give us more critical information to discuss with Mrs. Matile. I'm going to call dispatch on my cell and discuss having a marked unit drive past Matile's residence and office just to verify that his Mercedes isn't sitting out in plain sight at either location."

I punched the proper number on my cell speed dial for dispatch. "Dispatch, this is Jake Lowry. We're at the crime scene and had asked for marked units to drive around the area looking for the victim's white Mercedes 250. Has anyone called in with a hit?"

"Sorry detective. No luck yet. We've three units driving in an expanding circle around the crime scene. Actually the circle is slightly lop-sided since the lake is on one side of the expanding circle. At last report they're ten blocks away from the scene and no white 250 Mercedes has been spotted."

"In that case, dispatch call off the search and send one unit to the victim's residence and one unit to the victim's office to see if the vehicle is parked there. We have the address information in the contact file so we don't have to disclose names over the open line. Once we hear from those two units, Detective David and I are going to the widow's house to make the 'Advisement'. We'll stand by for your call on my cell."

"O.K. Detective. Consider it done. We'll get back to you the moment the units have completed their assignment."

I turned to David and commented, "I assume you heard my side of the conversation. We'll wait for the units to do their job. The sun is coming up. It must be getting close to five. That gives us two hours to get to the office and put the results of our investigation so far in the computer. I'm really anxious to speak with Dr. Hardcastle about his preliminary examination of the body. He said that if the awl pierced the heart of Dr. Matile he might have bled to death internally. I'm curious if that type of death was painfully slow or very fast. You have to wonder if the killer knew what the body's reaction would be and planned the murder for a specific effect."

"Just the thought of that makes me shiver. Do you believe that the killer was so cold blooded that he or she knew enough about anatomy and physiology that they planned the murder to cause pain and suffering to Dr. Matile?"

"We'll just have to wait and see what Dr. Hardcastle has to say during the autopsy. Meanwhile shall we mount up and head for the office? I've a lot of thoughts running through my head and I want to get them down on paper. To be more specific in the computer so it can check my spelling and grammar."

"O.K. we can roll. Dispatch will call on your cell Jake. If they find the car you call me on my cell. Otherwise, we'll roll into the office and start our reports."

The drive to the Kootenai Sheriff's Department on Government Way went quickly. We were seated at our computers in less than fifteen minutes. I called dispatch on the internal line to advise we were in the office. Dispatch said neither marked units had seen the victim's vehicle at either his office or residence. We began our reports and in no time had entered our reports into the departmental main frame.

Dr. Hardcastle called to advise the autopsy was set for nine o: clock.

David said, "If we're going to make the 'Advisement,' we'd better get a move on."

I replied, "I checked with dispatch and verified the Matile's address. I've done some soul searching and decided that you should make the 'Advisement.' Heidi and I seemed to create a bond when we were briefing her at Dr. Matile's office."

"I know you are joking. Woody hasn't shown up yet. So even though we need to hustle, we should wait until she arrives."

Woody arrived, as David was making the statement,

"Sorry I'm late guys, I ran into a little traffic outside. Apparently the press got wind of our dead body. They're bunched at the public and employee's entrances screaming questions at anyone entering or leaving."

"Well that tears it! Now we'll have to stonewall the press and should probably call the sheriff at home to advise him that the circus has started. Woody, you and David go out the employee's entrance carrying briefcases. I don't care if they're empty. That should draw the press away from the door. Fumble with responses and fumble loading your cases into the trunk. Buy some time. I'm going to try calling the sheriff to give him an update. Once the sheriff is briefed, I'll join you also with a briefcase and we can head for Mrs. Matile's residence."

I called the sheriff's cell phone and was advised that it was out of service. I next called his home phone and got a busy signal. I decided I would ask dispatch to notify me when the sheriff went into service on the radio. That being done, I exited the employee's entrance to a considerably smaller crowd than Woody and David had experienced. I walked quickly to David's car and got in the rear seat. Woody was already seated in the front passenger's seat. Once the door closed, David walked to the driver's side and started the car. He backed slowly out of the parking space and carefully drove on to Government Way.

"I'm turning left to head for Fernan Lake. The Matile's have a nice house on the north side of the lake. I'm dreading this more than any prior 'Advisement' I've done. I can't remember any occasion where I've had prior contact with a person to whom I'm bringing the bad news."

Woody and I both agreed. The car was silent for the remainder of the drive.

David stopped in front of the Matile's house. The three of us walked slowly to the ornate front door. I rang the bell and waited with some apprehension. About one minute passed with no response so I knocked on the door loudly. We allowed another minute to pass. Again, no response.

I said, "We've no reason to believe that Mrs. Matile is in danger, nor do we have a reason to make a forced entry into the residence. There are a thousand reasons why she isn't answering the door. She may be out of town or may be a very sound sleeper. At this juncture, I suggest we do some more intelligence collection. Let's go by Dr. Matile's office and see if perhaps Mrs. Matile went into the practice early. If not, possibly we can get a look at Dr. Matile's appointment book"

"Jake we're going to have to cook up a story for Matile's staff. We can't advise them of his death without first advising his wife. What're you going to say if Mrs. Matile isn't in the office?"

"I'm tossing that ball to Woody! Woody what are you going to say?"

"Don't toss that ball to me. I have no idea what to say. I agree with David. We simply can't tell the staff that Dr. Matile is dead prior to advising his wife. I hope you're joking."

"I'm joking! If we don't see Heidi Matile when we go in, I'm going to tell the staff that we have an allegation of animal cruelty that we've been assigned to investigate and wanted to ask Dr. Matile personally to accompany us to the scene. We'll explain that if he's not free, we have an animal control officer standing by to meet us at the site. We'll rely on him for the initial observation and then ask Dr. Matile to appear as an expert witness. That way we can ask about his schedule for a future consultation. I think that'll work."

We arrived at Dr. Matile's office in Post Falls and entered as a group. Heidi Matile wasn't in the office. I went into the animal cruelty explanation and sold the story convincingly. The receptionist pulled up Dr. Matile's schedule on her computer screen and apologized that Dr. Matile was not there at that time. She explained that he was in the office by seven thirty every morning but today he was attending a conference in Boise. She offered to try to reach him on his cell phone if it was important.

David asked, "Doesn't Mrs. Matile also normally come in with the Doctor?"

The receptionist said, "Mrs. Matile has a meeting this morning at the Coeur d'Alene Resort. She's a member of the Susan G. Komen Walk against Cancer Committee. Heidi won't be in until after lunch. This is her favorite charity and she spends a great deal of time with other committee members planning for the walk. Last year they raised over fifty thousand dollars for cancer research. Detective you should know the Chairperson of the committee. She's married to one of your detectives, Rebecca Lenca. She was formerly Rebecca Kunkle."

To say that I was astounded is an understatement. David and I'd been so busy trying to do the right thing that we had missed an obvious step. How were we to know that Gunter's wife and Heidi Matile were on the same committee? As a matter of fact Liz had vaguely commented about attending a breakfast meeting at the Resort the previous evening. Unfortunately, I had only half listened because her comments were during the sports section of the evening news and I wanted to know who had won the U.S. Open.

I thought: "I've got to start listening more effectively. Liz has a busy schedule and she wants to share her day with me. I'll work on this starting today. Now I better send Liz a text message to see if she, Rebecca and Heidi Matile are at the same meeting. I'll try to show real concern and attempt to hide the fact that we're primarily interested in Heidi Matile. This is definitely not the way she should learn of her husband's death."

I started the text and took my time with the composition. I felt it was a feeble attempt to make up for last night's failure to listen attentively. I knew the Liz might be deeply involved in committee business and did not anticipate a speedy reply. I turned to David and said, "I texted Liz to see if Heidi Matile is also at the meeting. We probably could have asked Gunter early this morning if we knew where this case was going. I don't anticipate a rapid reply to my text. We might as well head back to the office."

Both Woody and David agreed and we walked back to David's car.

"Well partner I think you sold the animal cruelty story effectively so the office staff isn't suspicious. How do you plan on catching Heidi? We don't want her to get back home and have the press contact her. You know no matter how strongly we try to seal the leaks in the department, someone always leaks victim's identity to the press. If that happens we might be able to transfer to animal control after the sheriff rips us thoroughly."

"Actually, I'm counting on Liz to text me. Then I'll ask when they anticipate the meeting ending. Once we get a ballpark time, I'll suggest lunch if that is plausible. If not, we'll just happen to be in the Resort when the meeting breaks up. With Woody assisting us and Rebecca's and Liz's shoulder to lean on this 'Advisement' might go better than expected."

"Jake it seems to me like you are backing down from this duty. That's not like you."

"I'm not backing down; I'm really trying to make this go as easy as possible. I do admit that I dread and positively hate 'Advisements.' To put a positive spin on this, I'll feel much better if Heidi has a number of other females around to help her through this ordeal."

"Hey my phone just buzzed. Maybe it's Liz. I must be psychic. It's Liz. Heidi, Rebecca, and Liz are there with seven other females. The meeting was a breakfast meeting and should end around ten thirty. That shoots a big hole in my scam to be at the Resort for a lunch meeting. It looks like we'll just have to be at the Resort around ten thirty. I'm texting Liz back to tell her thanks for the update. I'm sure she'll be going to her office at the Art Collective immediately after the meeting."

"If we bump into them as the meeting breaks up we can do the 'Advisement' and offer to drive Heidi home and call a family members to stay with her. David you can drive her car. Woody and I'll put her in with us. That way Woody and I can answer her questions and Woody can still be a shoulder to lean on."

David commented, "Sure you put Heidi in MY CAR and I'll probably have to drive some beat-up wreck to her house. It looks to me like we've some time on our hands. We can get back just in time for the autopsy. We should have a pretty good idea of the gross findings from Dr. Hardcastle's physical examination. We'll know more about the killer's motives."

Dr. Hardcastle was just beginning the autopsy as we arrived at the morgue. He'd made the initial "Y" cut to the chest and begun dictating the procedure thus far.

The three of us put on gowns, gloves, shoe covers and entered the procedure room.

"Doc, we're here and see that we're barely on time. Have you made any important observations that we need to know or are you just in the initial stages?" David asked.

Hardcastle replied, "This is the initial cut. I saw nothing of significance when we removed Dr. Matile's clothing. I've secured the clothing for release to your evidence techs. I've already released the awl to Jay Bass. He said he'd process it for prints and DNA. I'm ready to lift the "Y" and begin examining the interior of our victim. Are you detectives ready?"

We all nodded agreement.

Dr. Hardcastle lifted the "Y" and continued with his running commentary. "This autopsy is being conducted on a white male, approximately forty years of age. The subject has been identified to me as Dr. Lawrence Matile. The subject is five feet eleven inches tall and weighs one hundred and seventy two pounds. He appears to be in good health and gross observations of his extremities reveal no bruises, cuts, or contusions. The subject appears to have well defined musculature. I personally observed and removed a metal awl pushed into the subject's chest directly above the heart. That awl left a puncture wound one half of a millimeter in diameter in the left chest cavity above the fifth rib. As I examine the chest cavity I see that the awl nicked the upper edge of that rib. The awl penetrated the heart and there is a copious amount of blood pooled in the chest cavity. The heart is of normal proportions and no abnormalities are observed."

Hardcastle continued with the examination and narrative for almost two hours. Not finding any unusual data. He concluded the examination stating that the cause of death was the awl piercing Dr. Matile's heart. The two hours consumed by the autopsy caused us to miss Heidi Matile leaving the Coeur d'Alene Resort after her meeting. Jay Bass returned to the morgue to collect the clothing just as the autopsy was completed.

I asked, "Shall we leave from here and go to Matile's house or stop by the department and brief the sheriff? I wasn't successful in trying to call him and dispatch hasn't notified us that he is on the air,"

Woody and David both opted for briefing the sheriff first.

I called Mrs. Nelson on my cell to arrange a meeting with the sheriff. Mrs. Nelson said that the sheriff was in and available. I advised that we'd be there in fifteen minutes.

Mr. Nelson waved us into the sheriff's office the minute we arrived.

David took the lead, "Sheriff, we have had a homicide adjacent to Gunter Lenca's house. We're sure you remember that this was formerly Ken Kunkle's house. The victim was Dr. Lawrence Matile. Just to jog your memory, Dr. Matile was Nora Wallace's employer. He led us to the straps made by Nora that were identical to the strap that confined Ken in the tanning bed. The three of us agree that these events may well be coincidental, but the proximity to Ken's old house and the victim make us suspicious that this murder has more to it than just coincidence."

I added, "The interesting thing about this murder is that Dr. Matile was stabbed through the heart with an awl. No other injuries, no sign of a struggle, and we're waiting on the toxicology report for any presence of drugs in his system. We wanted to brief you first. Woody encountered the press when she came into the department this morning. We wanted you to be up to speed. We're taking Woody with us to do the 'Advisement' to Heidi Matile. We were going to catch her as she left a meeting at the Coeur d'Alene Resort, but the autopsy took longer than expected."

The sheriff said, "Again, you seem to be on the ball on this case. Woody, I appreciate your acting as a feminine voice in the 'Advisement.' They're always tough and anything our office can do to assist Mrs. Matile we'll offer to do. Please extend my condolences to her and offer our continuing support. You all better hit the road before the press gets wind of the victim's identity. I don't want the widow being called by some reporter to ask how she is handling the death of her husband."

Woody said, "I'll drive this time."

Morning traffic was light from the Sheriff's Department down Government Way to Appleway and then left to Fourth Street, right on fourth and left on east I-90. Woody took the Sherman Avenue exit and turned left toward Fernan Lake. There were still young deer feeding in the quiet yards of this small pocket of civility and upscale homes on the edge of the lake. Woody stopped in front of a multi-level house that had used brick facing and a well maintained front yard. This time, the three-car garage was open and a white Mercedes 250 and an older red Mercedes 190 SL were parked in the garage. There was a Silver UTV and a golf cart parked in the third spot. A lawn maintenance truck with the door sign stating that this was Kootenai Lawn and Landscaping was parked in the circular driveway. The sound of weed whackers and lawn mowers could be heard from the back yard.

"I guess that folks don't cut their own lawns here. They also must not sleep late either since it looks like the front lawn has already been done." Woody said.

I led the way to the ornate, hand-carved, front door and rang the bell. We could hear the sounds of classic rock music coming from the house. Soon after, footsteps approached the door. Heidi Matile answered the door in a spandex leotard and tights with beads of sweat glistening on her brow and a towel draped over her shoulders. Her obvious shock at seeing David, Woody, and I standing there was apparent!

"Detective Lowry, Detective David, what on earth are you doing here at my door at this hour? If you're looking for Larry, he's in Boise at a conference. Is there a problem at the office? I'm afraid I don't recognize the young woman with you. Have we been introduced?"

Woody replied, "Mrs. Matile, I'm Detective Woody McNair. No, we haven't been introduced and no, there isn't a problem at your husband's office. May we come in?"

"Of course, of course, excuse my manners! I was just doing my morning fitness routine. I had a breakfast meeting at the Coeur d'Alene Resort that put me behind schedule. After all the delicious food they served, I felt I'd better not miss my workout or it would all go immediately to my hips. May I offer you something to drink? I have cold water, iced tea, coffee, or soft drinks. I guess I should say 'Pop' but I just can't get into that habit. 'Pop' was someone's father where I grew up. I guess it's a local anomaly here to refer to soft drinks as 'Pop.' I'm chattering. I guess to cover my apprehension about having three detectives in my living room this morning. May I ask why you're here?"

Woody replied, "Mrs. Matile, there's no easy way to tell you this news. Your husband, Lawrence, was murdered last night. We're so very sorry for your loss and the three of us are here to help you deal with this shocking trauma."

"Larry was killed last night in Boise? How? Why? Why did this happen?"

I stepped closer to Heidi Matile and gently took her arm, "Mrs. Matile, perhaps you should sit down. Dr. Matile wasn't in Boise last night. He was killed just two miles from here on the shore of Lake Coeur d'Alene. His body was found leaning against the rock wall of the house formerly owned by Ken Kunkle. We can't answer your questions about why he was killed and please be assured that the entire staff of the sheriff's department is focused on attempting to answer that question and all of the other questions you just asked."

Heidi Matile's face suddenly blanched and she seemed to stagger. My hand on her arm steadied her. I gently helped her to sit on the butter soft leather sofa.

David said, "Mrs. Matile, we know you're shaken. Is there someone we could call to come and be with you? Perhaps your parents, a brother, or sister live here in the area?"

"My parents are deceased. I do have a sister who lives in Post Falls. She works with Lawrence and me at the vet's office."

As Heidi said that her voice cracked. She sobbed and tears began to flow. Woody quickly took a seat beside Heidi. She placed her arm around Heidi's shoulder.

Woody asked, "Mrs. Matile, may I call you Heidi? If you'd give us your sister's name, we'll call the office and ask her to come be with you. We were at the vet's office earlier looking for you but we didn't tell the staff about Dr. Matile's death. They believe that we were looking for Dr. Matile to assist us with an animal cruelty case. We know there are a thousand questions swirling through your head right now. Please feel free to ask us anything that comes to mind. Naturally, there are some questions we won't have the answers to and some of your questions may invoke questions from us."

Heidi gave Woody her sister' name. Woody excused herself to walk outside to call the vet's office on her cell phone.

Heidi seemed to get a grip on her emotions. She took a tissue from an ornate box on the coffee table and wiped her eyes. When she'd answered the door she had a white towel draped over her shoulders. She had muffled a few sobs in that towel. Her posture straightened and she appeared to collect herself. As she assumed this posture, she looked directly at David and me.

"O.K. I think I'm in control now. First I want to ask, how can you explain how Larry was in Coeur d'Alene last night rather than in Boise? I personally drove Larry to the Spokane Airport day before yesterday to catch an early flight to Boise. He was due to arrive back in Spokane at five this afternoon. I'd planned to meet him. We have dinner reservations at Anthony's in Spokane tonight."

I replied, "Heidi, we can't answer that question. We learned that Dr. Matile was supposed to be in Boise when we went to his office this morning. I can say that I was called from bed at two A.M. this morning. So the entire team is in the very early stages of our investigation. A private security guard on routine patrol spotted Lawrence's body. He called 911 and the investigation started from that call. Rest assured that we'll immediately look into that question of why Lawrence was here in Coeur d'Alene rather than in Boise."

Heidi said, "Oh! I have so many questions running through my head! Lawrence was scheduled to make the keynote address at the conference. He'd worked on that speech for an entire month. The topic was: Large Animal Care in a Suburban Practice. He'd done some cutting edge research and consulted with many other veterinarians in the local area. He was quite excited about the prospect of meeting other vets from the Northwest."

David asked, "Heidi, do you know into which hotel Lawrence was booked? That would help us to determine when he checked out. That is, if he checked out. You said you took Lawrence to the airport. What airline did he use to fly to Boise? We'll check to see if he changed his return reservation to come back to Coeur d'Alene early. We hate to bombard you with these questions, but since you believe that Lawrence should still be in Boise, the mystery deepens as to why he was here in Coeur d'Alene last night."

"I'm so confused! I can't imagine that Larry was up to something. We've had a very good marriage. I also can't imagine that he'd voluntarily miss the keynote speech. He had worked so very hard on that speech."

"Heidi don't jump to conclusions. There are many questions that have to be answered in this case. Nothing will be gained by making assumptions or beginning to question the life you and Dr. Matile had together." As Woody said this she wrapped her arms around Heidi's shoulders and pulled her close to provide both verbal and physical reassurance.

A ringing doorbell and persistent knock at the front door interrupted any more possible dialogue. I rose from the armchair in which I was sitting and walked to the front door. A tall, willowy, natural redhead with striking brown eyes rushed past me into the living room and shrieked, "Heidi!"

Heidi rose from the sofa and held out her arms, "Emilee, thank you for coming! I've horrible news! These detectives have just told me that Larry was murdered last night."

Emilee said, "What do you mean? These detectives were at the office early this morning asking for Larry to help them with an animal cruelty case. If they knew he was murdered why did they tell us such horrible lies? You! You're detective Lowry aren't you? You're the one who said that you wanted Larry to help you with the animal cruelty case. You and this other man, I don't know his name were at the office almost a year ago too. Murdered you say. How? Why? Where? This is horrible! Heidi, are you safe? Do you want to come over to my place for a while? You know I have plenty of room and you're always welcome."

I stepped in between Heidi and Emilee. "Ma am, I'm afraid that we did tell a small white lie this morning. We were actually looking for Mrs. Matile. We wanted to make sure that we were the first to notify her of Dr. Matile's murder. Both the print and electronic media are ruthless in pursuing news stories. You and the staff were most helpful in advising us of Heidi's whereabouts so that we could complete our mission and protect her from being even more shocked than she is now. Your offer to have Heidi come over to your place in Post Falls is a good idea. I'm not implying that she's in any danger that we're aware of, but the shock of losing Dr. Matile has just started. Heidi appears perfectly fine now, but the total effects of the shock are insidious and can be very devastating. If you'll be kind enough to provide us with your full name and address in Post Falls, we'd be most grateful for your assistance. Heidi, Woody will accompany you to your bedroom to assist you in packing a few items to take to Emilee's. While you're doing that we'll fill Emilee in on the few details that we know."

Heidi and Woody left the room.

I turned to Emilee. "We've heard Heidi call you Emilee, but we do need your full name and address for our case files if you don't mind. I apologize for our rocky start earlier this morning, but on many occasions, officers have to bend the absolute truth to accomplish our mission."

Emilee responded, "My name is Emilee Lukin. I reside at 898 Farm Garden Road, Post Falls Idaho."

"Ms. Lukin do you have a middle name, and may we have a phone number?" David asked.

"My middle name is Tish. My phone number is (208) 512-0000."

I commented, "That's both an unusual name and phone number. How did you get that number? I had a friend that had a four zero phone number. He simply asked if that number had been assigned and they said no. So he had that number for years. Did you do the same?"

"As a matter of fact I did. I use my cell phone for all voice communication. When Heidi and Larry moved to Idaho, Larry asked me to come here and work in his practice. I'd studied veterinary medicine in England while I was abroad and had no particular destination in mind when I returned to the U. S. Idaho sounded great with all of the outdoor activities and the four seasons. Coeur d'Alene sounded particularly attractive with the lake and mountains so close by. I'm an outdoor activities freak. I love swimming, boating, riding ATV's, shooting, bike riding, and hiking."

I commented, "Do you have time to enjoy those pursuits Emilee? When we were at Dr. Matile's practice it seemed to be a very busy place. Where did you study veterinary medicine in the U.K.? I don't detect any English accent when you speak."

"I spent four years in Europe mainly in the U.K. I tried to assimilate the culture, but not mimic the accents. Most of the professors at Oxford were 'Veddy British' and looked down their noses at foreign students. We sort of created a clique to protect ourselves. Most of my classmates were British, but there were students from Pakistan, India, Germany, Thailand, Newfoundland, and three Americans. I was fortunate to be accepted into the program. The selection process was very tough! I'd served as an unpaid intern in three different vet's offices all three years while I was in high school. I had many letters of recommendation and good work performance evaluations from the three vets I had worked for. Oxford required that I attach a thousand word dissertation discussing the future of veterinary practice in the two years following completion of the course if I were selected. When I was asked to come to Oxford, I had to defend my dissertation to the interview panel. They were ruthless!"

David said, "That does sound like a grueling process. Was this just for foreign students or did all the students have to comply with that process?"

"Actually they were harder on the British candidates. Their dissertation was to discuss the future of veterinarian medicine for the next five years and they had to do it in two thousand words. The foreign students all agreed that our interview was a piece of cake compared to the British students. The classes were all challenging but the laboratories were very challenging. We would go to large farms and treat cows, horses, goats, sheep, tons of sheep, and then they would bring in ducks, geese, chickens, rabbits, dogs, and cats to the university clinic. I was there during the 'Mad Cow Scare.' We had a widely varied clinical exposure."

Woody and Heidi returned. Both were rolling suitcases. Woody also had a soft duffle over her shoulder.

Heidi said, "We're ready if you are Emilee. I've packed enough clothes for five days. Woody was very stern about what I should pack. She assured me that I could come back home to get more clothes if I needed them. Detective Lowry should I ride with Emilee or take my own car?"

"We'd prefer that you ride with Emilee. Both of your cars are distinctive and very easily recognized. If you stay with Emilee for five days that'll give us time to really focus all of our efforts on the case and we'll hopefully have a better idea of the killer's motivation by then."

David took Heidi's rolling bag and the duffle from Woody's shoulder. He led the way to the front door and+ out to Emilee's car. I cautioned Heidi to make sure that all doors and windows were locked and walked around with her to make a last minute check. After everyone walked out the front door, Heidi locked the deadbolt. She got into Emilee's car.

We entered Woody's car and followed Emilee as she drove onto I-90 heading west toward Post Falls.

CHAPTER TWO

After we had gotten Emilee and Heidi safely to Emilee's house in Post Falls it was time for lunch. We stopped in Famous Willie's Barbecue for some brisket and Cole slaw. Famous Willies had previously been the Donut House. The change was good for everyone's waistline.

After lunch we returned to the sheriff's department just in time for Officer Reeve's arrival at fifteen hundred hours. I had made brief calls to make sure that everyone was ready for the 'VIP Tour.'

David brought Officer Reeves to Interview Room number one.

I started the interview. "Officer Reeves, you know we have to 'tag' the tape before we start the interview. Do you have any objection to this interview being recorded?"

"No sir! I understand that this is standard police procedure. Go right ahead. I have no objection to your recording the interview."

"O.K. Here we go! My name is Detective Jake Lowry of the Kootenai County Sheriff's Department. Present in the room are Detective Bruce David also of the Kootenai Sheriff's Department and Officer Garrett Reeves of the Alpha and Omega Security Service. Garrett would you please state your full name and spell your last name for the record?"

"My name is Garrett Jack Reeves. R-E-E-V-E-S. I live at 53 Mississippi Street, here in Coeur d'Alene. I'm employed as a uniformed officer at Alpha and Omega Security Service. My normal duty hours are from twenty four hundred until zero eight hundred hours Wednesday through Sunday. I'm assigned to patrol sector six. That sector encompasses southeast Coeur d'Alene from Lake Coeur d'Alene to Interstate Ninety and west to Northwest Boulevard. I also cover Fernan. Is that all the information you require to properly 'tag' the tape?"

I answered, "Garrett that's excellent! The way we'll start is to allow you to refer to the notes you made immediately after you discovered the victim this morning. We'll just let you describe your actions in a narrative style. Once you've done that, Detective David and I may have some specific questions for you. I really doubt that, as your notes and recollection this morning were outstanding. Why don't you begin?"

With a great flourish Reeves reached into his shirt pocket and produced his black leather notebook. Looking at his notebook he began "I reported for duty at twenty three twenty hours on the night in question. I inspected my marked unit prior to beginning my shift. The initial hour and one half of my shift was without merit, just routine patrol. At zero one thirty hours I was in the lower southeast section of sector six. That is the area along Lakeshore Drive and borders Lake Coeur d'Alene. I observed a white male adult, or as we say in police jargon; WMA, apparently seated along a rock wall. This is an area known to me to be frequently used by transgressors who lie on the beach and smoke dope. I alighted from my marked patrol unit illuminated my flashlight, approached the WMA and ordered him to evacuate the immediate area. I cautioned him that he was trespassing and had to leave immediately. Receiving no response I approached closer.

When I was about two feet from him my light reflected off the ice pick stuck into his left chest. I immediately notified Alpha and Omega Dispatch of my findings and requested that they notify your department. I established a secure perimeter by moving my marked unit to screen the victim's body from open view from Lakeshore Drive and established a stationary position as close as possible to the victim but still not interfering with the immediate crime scene. Upon arrival of the first deputy, I advised him of my findings. He placed me in his marked unit and I made the notes to which I am now referring. I believe that this is the sum total of the information that I have that is pertinent to this investigation. I will also add that I surrendered my uniform boots to Evidence Technician Sherry Lee to compare the tread to those of the molds you made at the crime scene. Is there anything else you need Detective? I've tried to provide only the pertinent information that will support your investigative procedures."

I sat very still for a few moments pondering what David and I had just heard. I thought to myself, *I'm not sure of this guy. Is he a fruitcake 'Wannabe' or a poster child for Obsessive Compulsive Disorder? Many of the things he says and does reflect the OCD mannerisms. It is possible that he is a very competent private security officer who has all his ducks in a row.*

"Garrett, your narrative has been very complete. I can tell you at this time that your boot imprints did match those that were molded two feet from the victim's body. The print match allows us to identify you and verifies your spoken narrative on the events leading up to your notifying Alpha and Omega of your discovery. If it would be possible we would like to make photocopies of your notebook to include in our evidence file. We'd be most appreciative if you could release your entire notebook for inclusion in the file. I'm aware that the leather-bound notebooks are expensive, but I see that you use the removable inserts, so we could just take the insert and photograph the cover for the file. I'll call one of the evidence techs to do the photocopy and take the picture."

"No need detective, I have others in my locker at work. If keeping the integrity of the notebook will aid your case, keep it. When the case is over I'll call in to evidence and collect it."

I called evidence and asked for a tech to come to the detective division to pick up the notebook. I turned to David and asked, "Well partner, do you have any additional questions for Officer Reeves? If not, why don't you take him toward the sheriff's office for his interview?"

David said, "I don't have any questions and will be glad to take Garrett down to see the sheriff. Will you be joining us or should we just continue with the tour?"

"No, I'll join you in a few minutes. I have to take care of a personal issue right now and I'll be right down."

David and Garrett Reeves left the detective division. I took out a pair of blue nitrile gloves and placed Garrett's leather notebook in a paper evidence bag. When Sherry Lee walked in the door, I said, "Sherry, I've bagged Officer Reeve's leather notebook. Would you make out a receipt? We'll pick it up when he gets there for the tour. The reason I bagged the notebook is I want it processed for DNA. If we get DNA from the awl or cigarette, I want to compare Reeves' DNA to those samples. Can you possibly get DNA without destroying the leather cover?"

"We might get slight discoloration, but I have seen identical notebooks in a police supply catalog. If we need to return the leather cover, I can order one and I'm sure he'll never know we switched."

"Great! Do that. I think this opportunity is too good to pass up. What are you going to show him on the chromatograph?"

"Actually we're going to show him the difference between thin layer chromatography and gas layer chromatography. We have some standard samples of unusual items that display quite well. It's a routine part of our "Dog & Pony Show" when we have schools and other visiting groups come through the lab. We'll then show how we lift fingerprints using super glue fuming. That's usually a showstopper. Why? Did you have something else in mind?"

"No. I had nothing in mind and I appreciate your cooperation in this 'VIP Tour.' David and I still haven't figured this guy out. We don't want to alienate him if he'll prove to be valuable, but we also aren't eliminating him from the 'Persons of Interest File.' His boot print did match the mold we made at the crime scene. In our interview he did say he got within two feet of the victim. We need more exposure to him but we'll not focus exclusively on him just yet. We'll still work on developing more investigative leads. I'm going to catch up to David and 'Officer Reeves' at the sheriff's office. We'll be down your way soon."

I caught up with David and Garrett just as they were entering the sheriff's office. The sheriff was extremely cordial and shook Garrett's hand warmly. He gave a brief synopsis of the sheriff's duties; the charter of the department in general; and asked if Garrett had any questions. The entire process took about fifteen minutes. Garrett left the office beaming. Next stop was the evidence laboratory. Ron and Sherry walked him through the basic principles of evidence processing. Jay Bass was standing by at the Chromatograph and did an extensive briefing of the value of what had become, by now, an almost archaic piece of lab equipment. He inserted the samples and then showed the resultant readouts and explained what they indicated to a technician.

David, Garrett, and I then went to the civil division. Mary Gale, the supervising deputy, explained that one of the two primary jobs that a sheriff's department was tasked with was serving 'Civil Process.' She explained that historically in English Law the sheriff had to serve subpoenas and warrants. This has not evolved much over time, although private citizens can serve subpoenas involving civil court cases. If it is a criminal matter then that duty falls primarily to the sheriff. In modern times with the evolution of police forces inside cities, the police now serve warrants as do many Federal agencies.

The next stop was the detention division. Garrett said, "I've read that in many sheriffs' departments that this is the way to become a deputy. You start as a detention officer then go to the academy and then you go on patrol. I sure see a lot of detention officers here. Are they fully sworn deputies?"

The Detention Captain, Dwayne Evans, who was conducting the tour smiled and said, "Officer Reeves you've done some homework. Yes. That's one method of becoming a fully sworn deputy. We have career detention officers and we have officers who are on the track to become what we jokingly call 'Road Dogs.' Those are fully sworn deputies who are assigned to Patrol Division. Both Detectives David and Lowry were once 'Road Dogs.' They didn't start in detention though. You can compete and become a sworn deputy without doing time in the jail. Is that your career plan to first work in detention and then become a sworn officer?"

"I've put in my application in Nevada to work in Winnemucca. I have a friend there and he's working the jail but the sheriff there allows him to do 'Ride-Alongs' with the sworn officers. Due to the great distances, the sheriff thinks the presence of another person in the car helps to increase officer safety. It's easier to get hired in Nevada than here. I want to get some road experience under my belt before I try to transfer back to Coeur d'Alene. I'm still young and think I can make a valuable contribution to law enforcement."

"That's admirable Garrett. It sounds like you've a solid career plan. I hate to speed up this process, but David and I've some leads to follow-up on and it is getting late. We'll walk you back to the lab to collect your boots and then walk you out. We're sure that we'll be seeing you soon. Thank you for the cooperation on this case. The next time you visit, we'll tour Communications, Crime Analysis, and then drop in the Gang Unit. They're working a special project right now and apologize for not being able to host you on this tour."

"Wow! That'll be swell! I can't tell you how nice it's been to do this tour. Usually regular police officers treat private security officers like dirt. You guys have been so kind! I can't thank you enough. If there's anything you need from me, or if there's anything I can do to help with this case or any other case you've got my home and cell number. You can always leave a message for me at Alpha and Omega."

Garrett collected his boots and a receipt for the notebook from evidence. He was walked to the door and given warm and sincere handshakes.

We returned to the detective division and our desks.

"O.K. Jake what was the deal with the 'personal matter' that kept you from walking Garrett down to the sheriff's office?"

"I wanted to brief Sherry to test Garrett's notebook for any trace DNA. If we get any useable DNA from the cigarette butt that we collected at the crime scene, or from the awl, I want to compare Officer Garrett Reeves' DNA. As far as I'm concerned he's still very high up on our 'Persons of Interest List.' Shall we sit down for a few minutes and discuss today's events. I know we've both put in a very long day, but I need some time to bounce off some thoughts on you."

"O.K. I don't have a private life. Particularly since I have abandoned Capone's as a recreational destination. I'm not sure that they'll not declare bankruptcy with the loss of my business. For sure, my bank account shows a difference in my balance and my head sure appreciates the lack of hangover headaches. I'm walking in the evenings and may even take up jogging. Jake you've been a very bad influence on my lifestyle. So let's talk. I'm really interested in hearing your take on Reeves and any other part of this very convoluted case at this early stage."

"Partner, I don't really have a solid take on Reeves either. He's a real conundrum! At this juncture, I think he's OCD and a potentially scary 'Wannabe.' We need to do an extensive work-up on Officer Garrett Jack Reeves. This may either cause him to be even higher up on the 'Persons of Interest File' or eliminate him all together. The second conundrum is Miss Emilee Tish Lukin. Can it be merely a coincidence that Miss Lukin also studied veterinary medicine at Oxford University? Why didn't Dr. Lawrence Matile mention that Nora Wallace or Roberta Archer, as she was then called, worked at his practice and his wife's sister, Emilee, had both trained at Oxford University? We now know that Nora didn't study there, but Emilee allegedly did and he didn't mention that. It's not as if he wasn't aware of the fact. We discussed Nora's credentials and he provided her personnel file so we could do our further investigation. I think we're back to "curiouser and curiouser" in this case."

"I agree on Reeves. He's a sack of unanswered questions. As far as Emilee Lukin goes, the guy who could answer most of our questions is lying on a slab in the morgue. I'm thinking right now that we should call it a day and go home. Maybe if we sleep on these questions we'll have some answers in the morning."

CHAPTER THREE

"Jake, I hope you slept well last night. I don't think I even turned over once. I slept like a baby. I don't think I had a dream. I'm refreshed and ready to roll. How about you?"

"David my boy, like you, I slept the sleep of the pure. Dreams come and go in my sleep but nothing of any significance that I remember. If you're ready then you're backing up waiting for me. Let's hit it."

We booted up our computers and began typing. It took almost an hour to enter the data from yesterday's activities. After the hour was up, we then began tapping into search engines.

"I'll do all the work on Dr. Lawrence Matile and Heidi Matile. David if you'll concentrate in Emilee Tish Lukin. I think it may be time to call Ammo Vecchio in

Kamloops, Canada. His Detective Onions has family and connections in the U.K. If we can get them doing liaison with Oxford that'll save us some time on looking at any correlation between Emilee, Oxford, and Nora Wallace. If that doesn't work, I'll call Inspector Forbes in Northumbria. Between the two options, I'm sure we can get the information we need. We'll get Morgan working on the things she does so well. I'll ask her to do a complete work-up on Officer Garrett Jack Reeves. I'll also ask her to do a limited work-up on Alpha and Omega Security. By covering all bases, I think we'll have a jump on this case."

Taking their time to exploit the benefits of Internet search engines was slow and laborious work. I had spoken to Morgan Lenca and she had borrowed a laptop from the narcotics unit. This allowed her to work on two computers simultaneously. David and I set eleven thirty as a target time for the three of us to come together to discuss progress and also to brainstorm ideas for additional searches based on the results thus far achieved.

David called Ammo Vecchio at the Royal Canadian Mounted Police Detachment in Kamloops. "Ammo, Detective David in Coeur d'Alene, Idaho. I'm calling for a favor, maybe a few favors. I'll give you a quick rundown on the case Jake and I are working. Night before last Doctor Lawrence Matile was murdered by having an awl plunged into his heart. He was found propped up against the wall of the house previously owned by Ken Kunkle. To further refresh your memory. Dr. Matile was the veterinarian that Nora worked for. The murder of Dr. Matile and his placement next to Ken's house, which by the way is now owned and occupied by Rebecca Lenca and Detective Gunter Lenca. Yeah! That's right! He finally popped the question. They decided that since Ken had put so much effort into customizing the house that it would be a shame to let anyone else have it. When we informed Mrs. Heidi Matile of the murder, she called her sister Emilee to come over. It turns out that Emilee also works at Dr. Matile's veterinary practice. Now for the corker! Guess where Miss Emilee Tish Lukin received her training?"

Ammo made random guesses and wasn't even close. Finally in exasperation he said, "O.K. David, I surrender! Where did Miss Lukin receive her training? Here in Canada possibly and that's why you've called?"

"Nope! Miss Lukin was trained at Oxford University. That's why we're asking for favors. Is Detective Onions still assigned to your detachment? He is. Great! Would you ask him to contact his relatives in the U.K. and also to tap into those police contacts he used to both assist in Ken's murder investigation and for the assist he gave us in pursuing Nora. Obviously we need some more international assistance. Ammo, Jake and I'll be ever in your debt. I'll email all of Miss Lukin's vital statistics within the hour."

"David, it'll be our pleasure to again assist. This'll be some small payment for the grand treatment we received from Clyde Kunkle and your sheriff. Detective Onions has a light caseload at present. I'll get him on the Internet to the U.K. immediately after I get your email. We'll make phone calls early tomorrow morning to get Detective Onion's contacts rolling. As soon as we get results I'll let you both know. I'll say that at the moment, I agree with yours' and Jake's take on this case. I can't believe that this murder and body placement is a coincidence."

"It's good to hear that you agree with our appraisal. Thanks again for the assist."

David disconnected and turned his attention to his computer. The first order of business was to email Ammo all the information he'd collected on Emilee Lukin. He had copies of her Idaho driving license, her Idaho Health Department veterinary license, and a small article from the Coeur d'Alene Magazine describing Emilee's involvement in rescuing abused animals. While he had been talking to Ammo, I had been very busy at my computer. I rose from my desk to go to the printer to collect the results of my searches.

"David, I have the results of three different search engines. Although there are minor differences in the final product, the results are remarkably the same. I know that talking to Ammo consumed a great deal of your time and then sending him the basic facts on Emilee Lukin really cut into your search time. I haven't talked to Morgan yet but she's been keeping both computers humming. We're approaching the eleven thirty hour, so if you'll print the final work of your limited engine searches, we can go to the conference room and see how we have done thus far."

I walked across the detective division bullpen to Morgan's office and knocked lightly on her open door. "Are you in a position to stop what you are doing and meet with David and me in the conference room?"

"If you would give me a few more minutes, I can be there. I have an active name search running at the moment and should have the final results in about five minutes coming off the printer. If we can delay, this might paint a more complete picture of both Officer Reeves and Alpha and Omega."

"David and I'll be in the conference room spreading out our results for you to examine. Come in when you have the results. I know I shouldn't ask, but you did make three copies of everything didn't you?"

"Jake, I'm offended that you'd even consider that issue. Of course I made three copies. See you in five minutes."

We proceeded to the conference room and began to spread our printed material on the table. We were making three stacks. There was not a preponderance of paper to sort. Both David and I had consolidated the search engine results into a minimum number of pages. Within the promised five minutes, Morgan arrived and fell into the sorting procedure. Once the papers had been placed in three stacks, all three of us took a seat and began to read. It took twenty minutes for us to read the search results.

Morgan finished first and said, "I'm done how are you boys doing? I'll go first. Garrett Jack Reeves is a real piece of work. This is his third security job. His two previous employers simply state that he left their companies to seek a more challenging position. Both of you know that is 'politically correct terminology' for 'he was allowed to resign rather than being fired.' One company is located in Ketchum, Idaho and the other is in Provo, Utah. I got limited information from the two respective Sheriff's Departments in both locations and they have nothing in their files. Official state records show that he was, and still is a licensed security officer. I have a personal call in to an insurance underwriter friend of mine. I want to see if he can check to see if Reeves was bonded and if so, if there is any comment in the bonding file."

"Garrett Jack Reeves is an only son. His parents are deceased. He pays his rent on time, has a clean credit report, owes ten thousand dollars on a 2000 Ford Escort, and has his clothes, particularly his many uniforms, cleaned at a dry cleaner on south Third Street here in Coeur d'Alene. He occasionally orders merchandise from the Home Shopping Network. Works out at the health club on Appleway and is known there as a 'Geek' for constantly ogling female members. He doesn't hit on or verbally pester them, but seems to make them uncomfortable with his constant penetrating staring. I can't find any indication of a female connection in his life or history. He sporadically goes to a Unitarian church in Spokane. He receives his mail at a commercial rented post box. Not at the post office. So far he hasn't received any magazines or packages in plain brown wrappers. He has five pistols registered in his name. 2 -.40 caliber Smith & Wesson semi-auto pistols; 1 -.357 caliber Colt revolver; 1 - .9 mm Glock; and 1 - .22 caliber North American Arms mini revolver. It's my guess that he's always carrying. If nothing else, he has that North American Arms mini somewhere on his person. He has only has one credit card, a Visa card that has a four thousand dollar balance. He pays slightly more than the minimum required monthly payment. He has a checking account with a $ 340.22 balance. No moving violations and no criminal record."

"Alpha and Omega Security is owned by Mr. Roman and Mrs. Sharayah Breen, a married couple who are alleged devout evangelicals and hire only 'Christian' employees. They're solvent and have an impressive client list. The owners have been married for twenty-two years and this is their third business venture. The first was a donut shop in Boise that did very well and was sold for a handsome profit. This donut shop is still in business and continuing to prosper. It's located close to the capitol and apparently our legislators like donuts. The second venture was a self-storage business in Ketchum, Idaho. Apparently this is where they met Officer Reeves. He was working for a security company there. He moved up here shortly after Alpha and Omega opened its doors. He's their senior officer as far as longevity goes, although no officers have assigned rank in the company. The husband, Roman, does perform security patrol on regular occasions. The wife, Sharayah, does the bookkeeping and manages the office. Roman handles the client contact and sales aspect of the business. They pay basic minimum wage to most of their employees and at the moment, have no armed officers authorized. They do basic physical plant security and contract to do neighborhood patrol in both gated communities and some exclusive neighborhoods. That's what I've got so far. Is there anything else you want done on these two targets?"

I asked, "Morgan what perfume does Sharayah Breen wear and does Reeves bathe regularly? If you have those answers we're golden!"

"O.K. Smart guy! You told me to do a complete work-up. I did it. Your snide remark seems like you're satisfied. Am I correct?"

"As usual, you're astounding! Morgan, I'm totally satisfied. David any comments?"

"Only that after Morgan's report I think I'll just leave and go out in the back yard, eat worms, and die. The measly amount of info I collected pales by comparison. Emilee Tish Lukin was born in Las Cruces, New Mexico forty-two years ago. She is the eldest of two daughters. We know that Heidi Matile is her sister. Their parents are deceased from natural causes. She graduated high school in Las Cruces and attended Junior college there for two years. Her passport is valid and expires on July 27th of next year. There's no mention of any suspicious affiliations in her state department file. She has a solid credit rating; both a checking and savings account at Panhandle State Bank. Checking account balance is $ 5,610. 38. Savings balance is $20,276.18. She owns outright a 2008 Subaru Outback. She had three credit cards. One Visa, balance is $300.00 even. A MasterCard, zero balance, and an American Express card linked to Costco. She pays the balance each month. She lives in the condo we followed her and Heidi to in Post Falls. Makes her mortgage payments by electronic funds withdrawal monthly. Mortgage balance: $89, 000. The condo is worth about $200,000. So she has built up a large equity. I'm waiting for Ammo to verify her U.K. education. That may take us some additional time for those answers. That's it so far."

"I'll jump in now. Dr. Lawrence Matile was an only son. His parents were both medical doctors. They are deceased. He attended Loyola University for his Bachelor's Degree. He attended the University of California at Davis for his degree in Veterinary medicine. He met Heidi Whatcott Lukin while attending UCDavis. Davis has a very liberal, liberal arts program. Locals call the city of Davis; 'The People's Republic of Davis.' Apparently Davis is second only to Berkeley, California in being a sort of 'Hippie

Paradise.' Davis P.D. has no record on either Lawrence or Heidi. When Dr. Matile's parent's died they left him a sizeable inheritance. They jointly have six major credit cards and pay the balance on each card monthly. Their home in Fernan is worth two million dollars. They have a fifteen-year loan at five percent. The balance on the mortgage is slightly under one million. Dr. Matile is a member of the local Lions, Rotary, and American Legion. His membership in the Legion is honorary based upon his father's military service and Dr. Matile's financial support of their many charitable programs. Heidi is also a member of the Rotary, Kiwanis, and Susan G. Komen Association. She volunteers one day a week at the local animal shelter. Dr. Matile provided free medical care for any injured animal brought into the shelter. Apparently he was very seriously opposed to euthanasia if it could be avoided. They own both Mercedes in the garage outright. Dr. Matile was a member of the Hayden Lake Country Club and played golf there regularly. He had a twelve handicap. Heidi does not play golf but does participate in club activities. They both have valid passports. State Department has no file other than the passport applications.

They have three accounts at the U. S. Bank in Post Falls. One is a joint checking account with a $13,000.88 balance. The second a business account for the practice with a balance of $22.4765.00. The third is a savings account with a balance of $88,990.33. I have not been able to look at any stocks or bonds they may possess. I have copies of their credit card expenditures for the past six months ordered and they should be here by tomorrow. Heidi is the sole beneficiary of Dr. Matile's one million dollar life insurance policy and sole beneficiary of his five hundred thousand dollar accidental death policy. That wraps up my search engine work. Shall we discuss what we've just learned?"

Morgan spoke first, "My stomach thinks my throat has been cut. May we discuss this over lunch? Of course, lunch will be on you two stalwart gentlemen."

David said, "I'll second the lunch idea! Of course, Jake will be treating since it's his case as the detective assigned as primary investigator."

"O.K. you two! I have some Top Ramen in my desk. We can get some hot water out of the break room and slurp while we talk. Seriously, let's go get some Pho at Pho Thanh. Then we can really slurp while we discuss our findings and make a tentative plan of where to go next."

Morgan said, "I've heard of Pho but have never eaten it. Is there a restaurant close by where we can get it?"

David piped up, "Morgan you're in for a treat. Jake introduced me to Pho some time ago. I've become a real fan. Jake and I keep spare hand towels in our cars that we use as bibs so we don't get stains on our shirts and ties. We'll lend you one to make sure your blouse stays unblemished. Who's going to drive? Jake, you or me?"

"I'll drive. I have four towels in my car so we can be sure to keep Morgan's clothes clean. It's after one o'clock so the crowd will be gone. We can get a rear table and not have to worry about eavesdroppers."

CHAPTER FOUR

During the drive to Pho Thanh, I explained the protocol for eating Pho to Morgan. She advised that she was adept at using chopsticks and loved chicken in any form. We arrived and I ordered for the three of us in Vietnamese.

Morgan said, "Jake you surprise me. I think you've been hiding your talent under a bushel. I didn't know you spoke Vietnamese."

"I don't. I can order food in Vietnamese and do some limited counting. I know a few other phrases, mostly socially unacceptable but that's the extent of my linguistic abilities. When I was in 'The Nam' I picked up quite a bit but it has slid out of my memory bank since I don't practice much. Liz and I eat here occasionally but that's not enough to keep me current on the language."

The food arrived and after some added chat, hands-on demonstration and the tucking of hand towels into the tightly buttoned collars of our respective shirts and blouse we began to eat. As we ate we discussed our findings.

David spoke first, "It appears to me that we need to keep looking at Garrett Reeves. He's a conundrum in many aspects. Heidi's also still a serious person of interest in my mind. A million and a half is a very good motivator for murder. Of course, she may not see even the half million. There are tons of court cases on determining that murder is not accidental death. She'll need some very strong juice to win that case against the insurance company. I can't comment on Emilee yet I'll hold off until we hear from Ammo. The fact that Emilee and Nora were in the U.K. at the same time and may have met in or around Oxford University is a real problem in my mind."

Morgan between spoons of broth and slurps of noodles said, "First of all this is delicious! As far as my thought process goes, I agree with David. We need to really look deeply at all three folks. DNA may narrow that field when we get lab results, but inheriting a ton of money, a viable veterinary practice, and a grand home with substantial equity could motivate me to commit murder particularly, if I thought my spouse was running around on me. We have to remember that Matile was allegedly in Boise at the time he was murdered here in Coeur d'Alene. Jake you didn't mention if you were able to track Dr. Matile's movements from Boise back to Coeur d'Alene. Was that an oversight or are those results not yet available?"

"That was an oversight on my part. I should've said that I've both Boise P.D. and ISP working on his movements. We may know more when we see his credit card bills. The ISP commander in Boise has a source in the Embassy Suites in Boise that was Dr. Matile's destination lodging. His speech wasn't delivered at the conference. The venue had a catastrophic air conditioner malfunction and the conference ended one day early. Apparently there will be a protracted lawsuit brought by the Northwest Veterinarian's Association against the conference venue for failure to provide for those eventualities. I'm still seeking information about how and when Matile returned to Coeur d'Alene."

David said, "Well then that cooks it. We're in agreement on our focus on these three persons of interest. We'll just have to wait for the lab results to see if our focus narrows."

The meal finished, we returned to the sheriff's office. We'd just gotten seated at our desks when the phone rang.

David answered, "Detective David here how may I help you? Ammo! You have results already. That's great! I'm going to put you on speaker so Jake and Morgan can listen and I won't have to repeat anything. Stand by for one second."

Ammo began, "This initial information is sketchy, but very interesting. Miss Emilee Tish Lukin did attend Oxford University. She received a degree in veterinary medicine from Oxford. She did attend some classes with Rori at Oxford. The same professor that allegedly wrote the letters of recommendation for Rori also wrote letters for Emilee. This second inquiry may well have stirred the pot at Oxford. They're making sounds about an internal investigation of the professor. It seems he may have extracted personal favors in exchange for positive letters. We know that doesn't pertain to this investigation, but we'll keep you advised. Detective Onions has his contacts working additional leads and I'll get back to you as soon as we have additional information."

I shouted, "Ammo, as usual we're indebted to you and your team. Please give Detective Onions our personal thanks."

Morgan commented, "Rather than sit here twiddling our thumbs, I'll call the lab to see if they have DNA results yet?"

Both David and I agreed that was an excellent idea.

Morgan rose from her chair, walked to the fax machine and extracted two pieces of paper. "Here are the lab results. I'll make copies so we all can read at the same time. The lab said they've sent the results to the main frame so that portion of our report is accomplished."

She handed David and I each a copy of the two-page report. We settled down to read the results.

After we'd read the report, I took the lead in the discussion. "If we ignore the gobbley gook of scientific double speak and concentrate on plain English I think we have some work to do. Shall we discuss the items in the same order that we collected and numbered them? The torn piece of material doesn't contain any DNA so we are left with what the lab implies may be a portion of a finely made garment that contains Egyptian cotton and silk. This is not your run-of-the-mill fabric combination and warrants holding on to in the event we find a matching garment.

The filter tip and butt of the cigarette is second. The DNA doesn't match the Victim, Heidi, Emilee, or Garrett. Sadly it also doesn't match anyone in the National DNA Registry. So we have an unknown person close to the crime scene who smokes. The lab is also of the opinion that this filter was discarded very recently. Apparently if it had been exposed to a couple of days of sunlight it would show signs of deterioration. So we can surmise that our killer or his or her accomplice is a smoker.

The first treaded footprint we know matches Officer Reeves' boots. The second treaded footprint matches a female sport shoe size eight. Currently there are three manufacturers placing that tread on their shoes. Nike, L.A. Gear, and an obscure Chinese brand called 'Zats.' Zats are sold in discount supermarkets and Hispanic Bodegas. We can also assume that the Nikes and L.A. Gear shoes were manufactured in China.

Item number five the piece of latex we guessed might have been torn from a rubber glove or was one of those finger protectors if you are trying to keep a finger dry. The lab's guess is a latex glove. Again we struck out. There is a partial fingerprint on the inside of the latex but not enough to classify. If, and this is a big if, we get a good suspect, they may be able to match the loops and ridges inside the latex. As it now stands we don't have enough to look for a match.

Finally we come to the murder weapon, the awl and what we opined was the carrier. The awl and the black nylon sheath have traces of both cellulose and leather fiber that the lab suggests may be quite old. Again they are posing possibilities for us to examine. Cellulose is the scientific speak for wood. They suggest that this awl may have seen a previous life as a leather or woodworking tool. No prints were recovered and there was no DNA other than Dr. Matile's. If we make a huge jump in assumptions we may also be of the opinion that the killer wore the latex gloves when he or she stabbed Dr. Matile.

We now come to the most interesting part of this laboratory report: The toxicology report. Based on those results we now know that Dr. Matile had cocaine and a very powerful hypnotic drug in his system. He had Rohypnol, commonly called 'Roofies' in his system. As we all know, 'Roofies' are more commonly called the 'Date Rape Drug.' They render the victim almost totally unconscious and they have little or no memory of what has transpired. It doesn't appear that Dr. Matile was a habitual user of cocaine, but that issue will require further investigative work. We can, at this juncture, make another leap in our assumptions and render a 'Hold Close-In-House Only Opinion' that Dr. Matile was given a 'Roofie' and then brought to the lake edge and stabbed to death. This shows us a number of things that we must now consider. Number one: The killer or killers are pretty sophisticated. They have access to both cocaine and 'Roofies.' In our modern world that doesn't require too much sophistication. They moved Dr. Matile to that position without tracking up the sand at the lake side. The one print we recovered was probably a mistake. Something we all know: even the smartest crooks make mistakes.

We've possibly made a serious mistake in not expanding our crime scene search over the wall into Gunter and Rebecca's yard to look for additional footprints or scuff marks from the killer or killers dragging or carrying Matile to his final resting place. I'm not sure that we can now go back and recover any substantial evidentiary items, but

I'm calling Jay Bass right now and making arrangements for his team to meet us at Lenca's to do an even larger crime scene search. David, grab your 'War Bag' I'll grab mine. Morgan. We're sure you'll be back on the two computers expanding your exploitation of multiple search engines. Let's roll!"

CHAPTER FIVE

David was driving and I sat quietly in the passenger's seat. Although I was quiet, my mind as racing. *O.K. Jake, you've made a really dumb 'Rookie' mistake. You assumed that the crime scene was on the beach at lake side and did not expand the search for additional evidence beyond that spot. It's only been two days but you have no idea of the number of people that have trampled up the beach and possibly Gunter and Rebecca's yard to see what they could see of the murder scene. Going back now is a long shot and anything you and the team collect or assumptions you make will be suspect. You probably should have come with David only. Then and only then, if you saw that the beach was still intact called Jay and his team to come. This is your second 'Rookie' mistake. You've got to slow down boy and start thinking like a good cop. You have the experience and training. Put it to work.*

David glided through the afternoon traffic and pulled up into the driveway of Gunter's house.

"I'm sure we can park here and start our search from this vantage point. I know the owners. Here comes Jay and Sherry. They can park behind us and we still won't block any traffic or Lenca's access to their garage."

"I suggest that we approach the beach from the roadway as we did on our initial collection effort. If we see that the beach is tracked with prints we call any further efforts off and tuck our tails and leave. I'm not overjoyed that I made this bonehead error initially. I'll not make excuses, but it was a 'Rookie' error. Any idiot could see that Dr. Matile did not fly to that spot. We should have stepped over the wall to look for additional evidence. I'll bite the bullet and brief the sheriff in the morning"

"Jake don't beat yourself up. It was three A.M. and we weren't functioning on all cylinders. Jay, Sherry, what do you think?"

Jay answered, "Jake, you are not the only one who made a mistake. My whole team did. We got 'Target Fixation' and fell down on the job."

As they were berating themselves, the team approached the lake side. The beach was covered in footprints.

I groaned and said, "O.K. let's stop right here. Jay, Sherry, I apologize for bringing you out here. David and I should've come first and checked out the area. There's nothing we can do here that'll aid our case. Anything we see now has been contaminated beyond belief. Let's wrap up the day and try to do better tomorrow."

CHAPTER SIX

The day dawned bright and sunny. I was out of bed, feeding horses and birds before six. I jogged a mile and a half up French Gulch road and did wind sprints for the mile and a half back to the house. I was puffing as I walked up the driveway to the house. The horses nickered at me as I walked past the lower pasture. Liz was in the kitchen toasting English muffins when I entered.

"You're up early Mrs. Lowry. Do you have another breakfast meeting today?"

"No. After last night's discussion, I thought I might pamper you a little to help you get through the day. One of my clients brought me in some homemade orange marmalade. So I figured a couple of eggs over easy, an English muffin, some marmalade, and a nice cup of decaffeinated tea would start your day off on a better note. This way when you go in to the sheriff this morning and throw yourself on your sword, at least your stomach will be full. Of course, that'll add to the blood and gore but I'm sure he's used to that."

"Oh my beloved and so considerate wife! You've touched my soul with your deep concern. I'll shower and be right out."

The drive to the sheriff's department was uneventful but again my mind was racing as I drove over 'Fourth of July Pass.'

I need to do something extra nice for Liz. She has gone the extra mile for me lately and I don't think I have reciprocated. It was so sweet of her to make the effort this morning to put me at ease. It's never easy for anyone to admit they've made mistakes. I now have to go into the sheriff's office and admit that I, not only made the 'Rookie Error' of not expanding the crime scene search, but I also failed to exhibit adequate leadership at the crime scene. I've beat myself up all last night. I'm going to go in bare my soul and see if this causes the sheriff to lose faith in my skills. If he allows me to continue as a detective and most particularly as the lead detective on this case, I make this promise to myself that he won't be disappointed.

As I drove into the employee's parking lot, I saw Woody and Gunter standing beside their cars.

"You folks are hitting it pretty early aren't you? What have you got on tap?"

Gunter answered, "Dispatch got a call of shots fired on the east end of the lake. There are three uniforms on the scene and we're the first team rolling. The Watch Commander is in with the sheriff doing the initial briefing.

The Watch Sergeant, Sergeant Corker, was in one of the three responding units. Cd'A Police are doing back up and helping with establishing the perimeter. You'd better hustle inside. Cause you and David may be the next team to roll. The crime scene's one block from my house."

I grabbed my briefcase and hustled into the detective division bullpen. David hadn't yet arrived. I dropped my case on my desk and continued through the building to dispatch.

Speaking to the dispatch supervisor, I asked, "What do you have going?"

"Shots fired about a block from Gunter's house. Neighbor called it in on 911. No responsible seen. Five shots heard. We had a marked unit in the area and they rolled to the caller's address. We sent two other marked units and asked Cd'A P.D. for back up support. We've one detective team enroute. When the Watch Commander comes out of the sheriff's office we may step up our response. We've got the evidence team standing-by. That's all we've got right now. Are you and David ready to roll?"

"David wasn't in when I breezed through the bullpen. He may be in now. I'll go check and let you know in one minute."

I rushed back to the bullpen and met David coming in the door.

"Partner, dispatch has a 'shots fired call' one block from Gunter's house. It may not be connected, but this is really curious. We haven't had any activity in that area since Ken's murder. Woody and Gunter have already rolled toward the scene. The Watch Commander is in with the sheriff and dispatch says we may be the next team designated to roll."

"I left my 'War Bag' in my car from last night so I'm ready."

I said, "Me too. Of course, if we aren't sent, then I'm going in to the sheriff's office to confess my stupidity. The longer I delay, the worse it seems in my head. I didn't get a whole lot of sleep last night. There's one positive side to this mistake. Liz fixed me a super breakfast this morning. Since I leave much earlier than she, I usually have to fix my own breakfast."

"Oh! The agony! It must be so tough. I fix my own breakfast every day unless I go out to eat on the weekend. You're not getting any sympathy from me."

The banter stopped as both the sheriff and Watch Commander walked into the division. Both had very grim faces. The sheriff spoke first.

"David, Jake, we have a situation close to Gunter's house. Dispatch got a 'shots fired call.' By good fortune, we had a patrol unit close by. Sergeant Corker and another unit got to the scene in four minutes. The Captain, here, called Coeur d'Alene P.D. to assist in establishing a perimeter. So far no suspicious activity has been observed. I want you boys to roll and I'm sending the evidence team with you to look for victims. Be careful get your vests on before you leave the parking lot. Proceed slowly but we need to restore order in that area as we've already gotten five calls from panicked residents. By the way Jake, don't sweat the Matile crime scene blunder. We all make mistakes in our career. I'll call this one yours. You do good work. Keep it up. You boys be careful!"

I let out a huge sigh of relief and shook the sheriff's hand. "Thank you sir. I'm so sorry. I assure you that this won't happen again. I learned a valuable lesson from this mistake. I may make others, but it'll be a long time coming. Thanks again. We're rolling."

Both of us took our own cars to the scene. A mobile command post had been established about two blocks from the area. Sergeant Corker and a Sergeant from Cd'A P.D. had a street map spread over the hood of Sergeant Corker's car. They had marked 'X's' on various intersections. Sergeant Corker was speaking on his hand-held radio as we pulled up.

"You guys switch over to the 'Mutual Assistance Channel.' We're operating on that channel so we can coordinate with Cd'A P.D. This is Sergeant Robinson from Cd'A P.D. He's the Watch Sergeant. We've marked the intersections that block all vehicular traffic from leaving the immediate area. The reporting party told our first deputy on the scene that she heard five distinct shots about forty minutes ago. We had a perimeter established within six minutes after the call. So unless the shooter was doing a 'Drive-by' and kept driving, we can assume he or she is still in the area. We've gotten multiple calls about five shots but they all place them at the same time."

"No additional complaints of dead bodies or calls for medical assistance. Of course, Gunter is jumping out of his skin wanting to go to his residence. Apparently Rebecca is there alone. Consuelo and Husam left early this morning for their day off. Gunter has called the house and Rebecca's cell phone and hasn't gotten an answer. What do you think?"

I responded immediately, "Gunter and I will take one car. We'll go directly to his house and establish that Rebecca's O.K. Once that's been done we'll start a decreasing concentric circle moving units from the outer perimeter toward the center of our established scene until we find a victim, see evidence of bullet holes, or determine that we've trapped the shooter inside our perimeter and arrest him or her. I'll call Gunter. David will go to his location to relieve him."

Gunter and David made the switch and Gunter arrived at the Command Post. He and I discussed our tactics. It was decided that I would drive. Since Gunter had keys to the house he could make a rapid entry into the house while I positioned the car at the front door to act as a shield. Sergeant Corker and Sergeant Robinson agreed with the plan. Sgt. Corker suggested that they use a marked unit to 'Show the Flag' by allowing the neighbors peeking out of their windows to see the presence of a sheriff's unit in the area. Sgt. Corker offered the use of his car. Everyone agreed. Gunter and I checked our equipment and entered the marked unit.

I drove very quickly to Gunter's house and pulled into the circular drive so that the passenger's door was closest to the front door. Gunter slid out the door drawing his weapon as he did. He quietly opened the door with his key and slipped inside. I, with gun also drawn, was on his heels. We used hand signals to indicate our proposed movements. As we cleared each room in the single story ranch house we were moving toward the fitness room. We could hear loud music coming from that room. Gunter silently opened the door and let out a sigh. Rebecca was pedaling furiously on the exercise bike with earphones in her ear and the loud-speakers pounding out a B.B King Blues song at ear shattering volume. He holstered his gun and motioned for me to do likewise.

As we stepped into the room Rebecca let out a gasp of surprise.

"Gunter, Honey, what are you and Jake doing here? Oh no! Did someone call to complain about the music? I know I play it too loud, but I can't get the feeling of the music through these tiny ear buds. So I play the speakers and put the ear buds in my ears and that really lets me feel the music. Am I in trouble?"

Gunter replied, "Yes you are! First of all I have been trying to call you both on the house phone and your cell. You didn't answer either. We have a 'shots fired call' in the area. I was worried."

"Oh Honey, I left the cell in my purse in the bedroom. I guess I couldn't hear the phone across the room. I'm sorry! Is everything O.K.?"

I said, "Gunter lets go back to the CP and start compressing the crime scene circle. I'll call Sgt. Corker on his cell and brief him that it's all clear here. I love happy endings. Rebecca, I'm glad you're safe. Keep your head down and lock your doors when we leave."

"Jake you know that I used to shoot with Ken. Gunter and I occasionally go to the county range to keep my skills sharp. Gunter is very understanding about my love of target shooting. I don't hunt. I love animals too much."

"Rebecca we don't need another potential unknown gun in this crime scene. Arm yourself but only shoot if someone forces entry into the house. Get your cell phone and keep it in your pocket at all times until we notify you that it's all clear."

"O.K. Jake. I understand."

Gunter and I returned to the CP and reviewed the plan with the two Sergeants. They decided that all vehicles would start toward the center of the area simultaneously. Moving slowly and would stop every fifty feet as they drove toward the center. They would scan every vehicle on the street and the fronts of all houses for signs of bullet holes or broken windows. Sgt. Corker radioed the signal for the tightening of the circle. As each vehicle stopped they would give a brief 'No Signs Seen Report'. Five minutes had passed with no positive results from any vehicle.

David came on the radio. "I have an Alpha and Omega Security vehicle partially blocking the street. The driver's door ajar and there's no one in sight. I'm going to sit tight until I get cover to approach the vehicle."

I answered, "Sit tight. I'm enroute. This way we can still maintain our secure perimeter."

David and I slowly approached the Alpha and Omega vehicle. I took the driver's side and David the passenger's. As I peered into the rear window I saw Officer Garrett Reeves lying on the floor of the vehicle. He appeared to either be asleep or dead. I signaled to David to look into the vehicle. David cautiously peered into the rear window and shrugged his shoulders in the universal 'I don't know gesture.'

I quietly said, "I'm going to open the rear door. I know you've got my back but stay loose." I carefully grasped the door handle and as quietly as possible lifted it. As I swung the door open, Reeves swiveled onto his back quickly and started screaming, "Don't kill me! Don't kill me! I was just trying to make you stop! I didn't even aim at you! I fired into the air."

As his eyes focused he saw that it was me and gave a loud gasp.

"Detective Lowry. Thank god! I thought it was the killer. I saw him skulking around Detective Lenca's house. I hollered at him to freeze. He had a big knife and started to run away. I pursued him in my unit. After about two blocks, he stopped. I exited my vehicle and he turned and started coming at me. I drew my back-up weapon and fired into the air to deter him. I didn't have any spare bullets so I tried to secure myself in the rear of my unit to elude him. I must have dropped my hand-held radio when I started the pursuit so couldn't notify dispatch or call 911. I'm glad someone called it in."

"Garrett, before I say anything, I am going to have to advise you of your rights. Officer Reeves, you do not have to answer any of my questions. Anything you do say can and may be used against you in later court proceedings. You are entitled to the counsel of an attorney and if you can't afford an attorney, one will be appointed for you at no expense. You have a right against self-incrimination. I'm sure that you know each of these rights by heart but it is important that you verbally acknowledge to me that you understand each of the rights I have explained to you. Is everything I have said clear to you and do you understand what I have just said?"

"Detective Lowry, why are you advising me of my rights? I am an officer of the law and in the execution of my duties tried to apprehend a suspect who I believed was committing or about to commit a crime. My efforts to verbally restrain the offender were unsuccessful and in pursuing him I employed my marked emergency vehicle. When the suspect threatened me with great bodily harm, I discharged my back-up weapon to deter him from that intention. I don't see that I have violated any law or ordinance and my actions don't warrant a 'Miranda Advisement'."

"Officer Garrett, although you have made a powerful verbal case for your actions, I still haven't received a verbal affirmation of your understanding of my rights advisement. We can't proceed until that occurs. If you don't understand your rights, I have no recourse but to stop our conversation and place you under arrest for illegally discharging a firearm in a residential neighborhood. Neither I, nor my partner, Detective David, standing here beside me, want to do that, but at the moment our hands are tied. We have a number of units from the sheriff's department and Coeur d'Alene P.D. that have responded to multiple emergency calls of shots fired. Your spontaneous exclamation, when I opened the rear door of your unit, has solved the source of those shots. We must now determine if there was sufficient legal justification for your actions. Until that has been done I have to assume a crime has been committed. Again your spontaneous exclamation has disclosed you discharged the firearm. I will again ask you do you understand the rights I have explained to you and do you at this time desire the assistance of legal counsel? I must ask you to provide me with a verbal acknowledgement of your understanding and a verbal statement of your desire to continue to speak with us or request legal counsel."

"O.K. I understand my rights. I don't want legal counsel and I want to continue to talk to both of you. Is that O.K.?"

"That's perfect. Now Garrett, It's my understanding that no Alpha and Omega Officer is licensed to carry a firearm. Is that correct?"

"I'm not licensed to carry, but in this town if you don't have at least a back-up you're crazy. I have my North American Arms mini-revolver in an ankle holster at all times. If the Aryan Nations are in town, I carry one of my 40 calibers in a shoulder holster. Roman knows I do that and doesn't say anything. He carries a Glock 9 mm. all the time. Most of our officers carry. It just makes sense."

"Garrett I'm going to ask you to step out of the unit and submit to a search at this time. Before you begin to exit your unit, I'm going to reach down and remove your ankle holster and the weapon I see in it. This is both for your safety and ours. I'll ask you now do you have any other weapons on your person? Any knives, razor blades, hypodermic needles, or any other potentially hazardous item that may cause injury to Detective David as he does the search?"

"I have a folding Buck knife in its sheath on my duty belt. I'm not a drug user and would not have any hazardous items on my person during duty hours. Did you guys find my hand-held radio at Deputy Lenca's house when you responded? I'll be in big trouble if I've lost it."

David performed the search as I removed the stainless steel mini-revolver from the ankle holster and verified that it contained five, recently fired .22 caliber shells. The revolver had been modified. They had removed the small factory grip. A larger grip that swiveled had been added to provide better control when the weapon was fired.

I called for an evidence tech to come to our location. I also advised Sgt. Corker that we're 'Code four' with one in custody.

The search did yield a folding Buck knife on Garrett's duty belt and a container of pepper spray. No other potentially dangerous items were observed. David asked Garrett to unbutton his uniform shirt so he could loosen his ballistic vest and feel under the vest for any hidden items. That having been done, he handcuffed and placed Garrett in the back seat of my car.

I notified dispatch that we had a suspect in custody and were enroute to the department. I asked Sgt. Corker to thank Cd'A P.D. for their assistance. David said he'd ride with me to the department as a security measure. Gunter and Woody went 10-8 back in normal service. We asked one of them to drive David's car back to the department. As we drove, David and I were silent in a conscious effort to allow Garrett to attempt to provide further amplification on his story.

Rather than take Garrett into the department through the sally port and book him through the detention division, we walked him in through the employee's entrance and directly to the detective division. I gave David a hand signal with one finger and David escorted Garrett into interview room number one. While David got Garrett settled, I set up the recording devices in room number two. Once that was done I walked into room number one and said nonchalantly, "Lets move over to room number two."

I started the interview, "Officer Garrett, I have already advised you of your rights. To make sure that you have had time to consider my advisement, I'm going to repeat that advisement. You have the right against self-incrimination. That means you do not have to talk to Detective David or to me. You have the right to an attorney. If you can't afford an attorney, one will provided for you free of charge. If you decide to talk to us, anything you do say can be taken down and used against you in court. Those are your rights. Do you understand them?"

"Yes sir."

"Do you want an attorney?"

"No sir. I want to tell you my side of the story. As I said before, I'm innocent. I was just performing my duties as an officer for Alpha and Omega. That suspect turned and I was sure he was going to attack me with that knife."

"Garrett, before you say anything more, you know we have to tag the tape. This interview is being recorded. Do you have any objection to that recording being made?"

"No sir. You can record anything you want."

"Here goes. I am Detective Jake Lowry of the Kootenai County Sheriff's Department. Also present at this interview is Detective Bruce David also of the Kootenai Sheriff's Department. The person being interviewed is Officer Garrett Jack Reeves. Officer Reeves you have been advised of your rights and waived those rights is that correct?

"Yes sir. I want to talk to you. I said before, I'm innocent."

"O.K. Garrett, let's review the events that brought you here. We'll let you do the same narrative that you did in my vehicle. Begin with you observing the alleged suspect."

Garrett repeated his narrative. It was a perfect repetition of the narrative he had provided in my car. So prefect in fact, it seemed as if it had been rehearsed. Each point was in the exact same place as he had articulated in the first telling.

I asked, "Garrett, will you slow down and be very specific about the suspect's description again. We're going to bring in a police sketch artist to see if we can create a good photo to distribute to ours and Coeur d'Alene's officers."

Garrett took a deep breath and said, "The suspect is described as a WMA about 30 –35 years of age. He was between five feet ten inches and six feet tall He initially had on a balaclava but removed that as he ran. He was wearing a black coverall and black running shoes. He was wielding a knife that I estimate to be over one foot in length. That's the best description I can give. When I secreted myself in my unit, I didn't see in which direction the suspect fled."

"Thanks Garrett. Your description is complete as usual. We still have to deal with the issue of you carrying a concealed weapon and discharging it in a residential area. You must be aware that shots fired into the air must come down someplace. This endangers innocent citizens. As we previously discussed, no employees of Alpha and Omega are authorized to be armed. This means that you were functioning outside the established contract that the company operates under. This tacitly moves you into the position of a private citizen and removes you from security officer status. Committing that act is presently a misdemeanor and we can issue you a citation rather than book you into jail. If and this is a big if, anyone was struck by one of your bullets as it fell to earth or if anyone's property was damaged such as a broken windshield or hole in their roof then this would immediately become a felony."

"David and I have discussed this issue and it is our inclination to issue you a citation and release you. Naturally, we're obligated to notify Alpha and Omega of your activities. The action they take is solely dependent upon them. We've seized your pistol and holster. The weapon will be fired for ballistics purposes. It'll be the district attorney's decision after trial to either release it to you or have it destroyed."

Jake prepared the citation and made the standard caution as he handed it to Garrett.

"Garrett, your signing this citation isn't an admission of guilt. It's an agreement that you will appear in arraignment court on the designated day. At that time the judge will ask for a plea. If you plead not guilty, a trial date will be determined. At trial you can present a defense. It's my recommendation that if you plead not guilty that you secure the services of an attorney. Are my instructions clear and do you understand what I've just said?"

"Yes sir. I will plead not guilty."

David removed Garrett's handcuffs and walked him to the front desk. He returned back to the bullpen and sat at his desk.

"Jake lets discuss Officer Garrett. I'm even more confused than I was after our first interview. Do you think there really was a mysterious suspect? It just seems too pat a story for my taste. The description was specific but would also fit most males in the area. I'm having trouble with the suspect removing his balaclava as he ran. It's warm, but not that warm. A real suspect that had run for two blocks might think he had escaped, and tried to appear 'normal' moving through the neighborhood. Although Garrett was adamant about the 'large' knife, a twelve-inch knife isn't that big. You could put that in your pocket and not make too large a bulge. I'm back to 'curiouser and curiouser"

"Oh ye of little faith! How can you doubt Garrett? You're thinking his story is too pat?

Partner, I'm thinking that Mr. Reeves may be the poster child for 'Fruit Cake of the Year.' The thing I'm trying to decipher is whether he's trying to further integrate himself into the investigation or throw us completely off track. I'm going to ask the D.A. for an early trial date. I gave Garrett only fifteen days to appear rather than the usual thirty. I'm anxious to see whom he hires or if he thinks he can defend himself. If he doesn't hire a shyster, then I think we can discount him as a potential suspect and place him in the 'Fruitcake File."

CHAPTER SEVEN

I talked to the D.A. and explained the situation with Garrett Jack Reeves. David and I drove over to Alpha and Omega and shared our initial report with them. Roman Breen was visibly upset. Sharayah said that she'd call Garrett immediately and fire him. I asked her not to do that. "Mrs. Breen although Garrett violated your procedures, you probably shouldn't dismiss him until after his arraignment or subsequent trial. We can't tell you how to run your business, but Garrett is a 'Person of Interest' in an ongoing case and we'd like for him to remain in the area for a while. If there's a way you could utilize him in the business we'd be most appreciative."

Sharayah said, "We do have an isolated warehouse post where we could assign him. He would have to work very hard to get in trouble there. If that'll help you we'll do it."

"Thanks so much! It'll really help Detective David and me so very much."

We left the Alpha and Omega office and drove to lunch. It was Friday and Capone's fish and chips were some of the best in the city. David had a nostalgic look in his eyes when we entered. Both waitresses and the waiter greeted him by name as we entered.

"David, it seems like you lost some friends when you changed your life style. Did you ever eat when you were in here? Or was your visits focused solely on sampling the micro-brews?"

"Of course I ate. I was a connoisseur of the fine food here as well as the micro-brews. Not only are the fish and chips good, the chili is also fantastic. Remember I'm single. I'm also not a real good cook. If I want a good meal, I eat out or sponge off friends. I can name all of the better eateries for a twenty-five mile radius around our fair city. I can also name the last time my partner invited me to his house for a meal. Do you want a specific date and the meal we ate?"

"No. I get the picture. Your subtlety isn't lost on me. Liz and I'll make sure to have you over soon for a good home cooked dinner. Does that make you happy? Other than catering to your stomach, where do you think we should focus our efforts now? I'm thinking that we have let the time and manner by which Dr. Matile arrived back here slide. My calls to the airlines at Spokane airport have not been returned. We also need to see if a local charter or a conventional airline may have flown him back."

"Shall we start at the Coeur d'Alene airport? We're here and it's a short drive. Once we confirm that he did or didn't fly into Coeur d'Alene we can concentrate on Spokane. Since phone calls aren't working, maybe a little personal visit can reap results."

David drove north on Fourth to Appleway, turned west to Highway 95 and turned north. The drive to Coeur d'Alene Airport took fifteen minutes due to the mid-day traffic. Coeur d'Alene Airport is a small operation that caters to private pilots, contract airlines and helicopters. The operations terminal is also small and unpretentious.

I walked up to the clerk behind the counter and asked if the airport manager was available. She picked up the phone and said, "Robert, there's some cops here to see you. I told you not to do it, but you just wouldn't listen. Now you're gonna have to pay."

We hadn't shown our badges or identification cards and I'm sure that we aren't famous, I looked at her quizzically and said, "Ma am, what made you decide that we're police officers? I am Detective Jake Lowry and this is my partner Detective Bruce David. We're with the Kootenai County Sheriff's Department. Also while we're on the subject, what exactly did Robert do that you warned him against?"

"Actually I was kidding. I always say that when we have police officers come in here. It gets them stirred up and also embarrasses Robert. When he comes out of the back office, he'll begin apologizing immediately even before he knows who you are or what you want."

As this was being said a tall, grey-haired, middle-aged man with a red striped shirt and grey slacks appeared around the corner. He had on horn rimmed glasses and a broad smile.

"Gentlemen, I'm Robert Parrish, the airport manager. Please ignore the remarks my secretary made a moment ago. She's a would-be comedienne. She always does this when officers of the law come to the counter. What may I do for you? I assume you're officers. You just have that look."

"Actually Mr. Parrish, we're detectives with the Kootenai County Sheriff's Department. I'm Jake Lowry. This is my partner Detective Bruce David. Our needs are simple. We'd like to review the passenger manifests for all flights arriving at this airport for the past week. We're currently working a case that has presented us with a slight conundrum and a quick look at your passenger manifests would possibly solve that issue for us. I'm not sure if you remember, but Detective David and I flew out of here not too long ago with some other folks on a Gulfstream chartered by Clyde Kunkle. We know you have the ability to handle both domestic and international passengers. So we must assume you have pretty tight control on who flies in and out of your airport."

At the mention of Clyde's name, Mr. Parrish's eyes contracted slightly and his smile widened.

"Mr. Kunkle, Of course, I remember. If my memory serves me correctly, you folks flew to England. Yes. I do try to keep a tight rein of arriving and departing passengers. Some of the private pilots think I'm too controlling. They just want to buzz in and buzz out willy-nilly! I won't put up with it. I make sure they file both a flight plan and list all passengers. I'll have Mary Catherine pull up that data on the computer and we'll print you a copy. It'll just take a minute"

Parrish turned to Mary Catherine and asked her to print the manifests. She made some quick entries on her computer and the printer started humming. Six single spaced pages of paper emerged and she handed them to Parrish. Who, in turn, handed them to me.

I took three sheets and handed David three sheets. We reviewed the names listed and I didn't find Dr. Matile's name on my three sheets. David looked up and gave me thumbs down to indicate he had no luck either. I asked both Parrish and Mary Catherine if this was the complete listing for the past week? Both said it was. They were adamant that the list they provided was a listing of all passengers and was accurate and complete.

We thanked them. Took the lists and put them in our briefcase and got back in our vehicle.

"Jake, I guess our next stop is Spokane International Airport. I don't think we can get there prior to the close of business this afternoon. So we'll have to schedule that for first thing tomorrow morning."

"Partner, you're one hundred percent correct. I have a name and number for the Airport Director, Neal Sealock. He grew up in the S.E.R.E Family. His dad and I served together at the USAF S.E.R.E. Schools in Reno and at Fairchild AFB. Maybe if I contact Neal first, he'll grease the skids for us with the multiple airlines that operate out of there."

I dialed Neal's number and he answered on the second ring. We did a short bit of reminiscing and then I sprung my request on him. Neal was very cooperative and provided us with the names and contact numbers so we could make the appropriate contacts in the morning. I turned to David and gave him the 'Thumbs-Up Signal.'

We returned to the sheriff's department wrapped up the day by making our computer entries and called it a day.

CHAPTER EIGHT

It just wasn't in the cards for me to get a full night's sleep. It was a three A.M. call this time. At least I got an extra hour sleep. It was Sgt. Corker, the Watch Sergeant again.

"Jake, it's Sergeant Corker again. I'm beginning to get a complex waking you so early in the morning. We have another dead body. Captain Nearing thought you and David should respond to the crime scene."

"Sarge, why is this body special?"

"Jake this is tough, but Captain Nearing met the victim at Clyde Kunkle's house when you were working Ken Kunkle's murder. The victim's name is Cameron Haynes. He was brought to Clyde's house by Woody McNair. We haven't notified Woody yet. That'll be a tough 'Notification.' As a point of interest, Haynes was killed by being stabbed in the heart with an awl. There was a note pinned to his chest by the awl. Two murders with an awl don't make a serial killer, but it sure is odd."

"I'm dressing as we're talking. What's the body's location? I hate to ask so many questions, but have you notified David? Please don't tell me that the body is near Gunter's house again."

"Jake you're either psychic or you're the serial killer. The victim is in the same spot as Dr. Matile. He was also leaning against the wall. I can't swear that it's in the exact same spot, but it's pretty close."

"Sarge, please call Gunter and ask him to roll out of bed and to make sure he arms himself and verifies that his house is secure. Who discovered the body?"

"We got an anonymous 911 call telling us to check Dr. Matile's crime scene for another dead body. Dispatch sent a marked unit. Deputy Litsa Karina found the body. She immediately notified me, called for backup, and established a large perimeter. Jake, I think you have a good intact crime scene. Captain Nearing told me to call you, David, and to wake up the Evidence Team and start them rolling. I'll call Gunter to make sure he and Rebecca are O.K. I'll send a marked unit to his house for external security. Maybe that 'Rent-A-Cop' was telling the truth about the prowler."

"Sarge, I'm rolling code three on this one to make sure the crime scene stays intact. Expect me in thirty. Please ask David to hold everybody out of the crime scene until I arrive."

I finished dressing. Jumped into my car and turned on the emergency lights hidden behind the grill. There was no need for a siren at this hour. I only encountered one car enroute to the crime scene. The driver pulled way to the right and I breezed past with no trouble. Again, as I approached the crime scene it was illuminated with red and blue flashing lights. I guess some things never change.

Sergeant Corker was at the end of Gunter's driveway. Gunter was standing beside Corker's car dressed in a white "T" shirt and jeans. He had a black nylon holster clipped to his waistband and a five-cell flashlight in one hand. I parked on the side of the road and walked over to meet them.

"Sarge, Gunter, how's it going? Gunter I thought you would be in the house with Rebecca. Didn't the Sarge tell you of my request? As much as I really doubted him perhaps Garrett Reeves was telling the truth about the mysterious prowler. I wanted to make sure you and Rebecca were safe. You know it's no coincidence that we have a second body outside your house. We all know two bodies don't make this a serial killing, but we can see a pattern evolving."

"Jake, Rebecca is inside and armed. Prior to me coming outside, I checked all the doors and windows. I also did a walk-around of the house. I didn't see any tracks or scuff marks close to the house. I didn't expand my walking area to make sure that I didn't contaminate the crime scene."

"Man, I'm pleased you were so considerate! After my screw-up on the previous crime scene I need all the help I can get. If you want to go back inside with Rebecca its O.K. If you want to assist David and me we'd appreciate all the help we can get. These early A.M. calls are getting old. Additional eyes can give us a much-needed perspective."

"I'll stay. Rebecca will be fine. I pity anyone who tries to enter without giving the security word we decided on prior to me coming outside. If that happens, we'll have a third body here in the area. This one won't be killed by an awl through its heart, but from multiple holes throughout the body."

David and the Evidence Team had been standing by during this conversation and indicated that they were ready to begin processing the scene. I followed my previous protocol and assigned each member specific tasks. The addition of Gunter gave us one extra set of eyes and I had him hang back as an overseer to check our work and make suggestions if he thought we might have missed a step.

We began with Sherry leading the way with the video camera and doing full video coverage. Ron followed with the digital still camera. Jay and I then followed with us both agreeing on items we felt were evidentiary. David made the notes and the processing went slowly as we each did our jobs.

Jay and I stopped our progress as we saw the first item that stimulated our interest.

Jay intoned, "Item number 1 is a black nylon sheath that appears to have held the awl. This appears to be a duplicate of the same sheath we found at Matile's murder."

Nothing else was visible until we got within one foot of the body. Once there, we saw the note impaled on the victim's chest by the awl. Jay asked if we should stop our progress until Dr. Hardcastle arrived and made the 'Pronouncement'? I agreed and asked Sherry and Ron to do a very close focus on the note so we could attempt to read it without going any closer to the body. Sherry asked for Gunter to shine his five-celled flashlight on the note to amplify the video camera's light. With that additional light, we could read the following in block letters:

"NORA GONE? THAT'S A FOLIE-A- DEUX"

It appeared to be signed in a flowing script with the name:

'Fahn Quai'

I said, "Well folks, it seems like we have another literate killer. I can translate the 'FOLIE-A DEUX.' It's a French expression that loosely translates as: 'A Shared Delusion.' The signed name sounds either Chinese or at least Oriental to me. Anyone have a clue?"

No response was forthcoming from the group.

I then said, "Well, we all know that Nora is dead. David and I personally witnessed her body being pulled out of the North Sea in the red Jaguar. We attended her autopsy and heard the English Doctor pronounce her cause of death as drowning. So we must now try to determine what the killer or killers mean by the 'Shared Delusion' comment."

Dr. Hardcastle arrived and apologized for being so slow to respond. I motioned for him to come in following our tracks and make the 'Pronouncement'. He approached the victim and checked his vitals. Within seconds, he stated that the victim was dead. This gave us carte blanche to continue with the processing. Jay took a large piece of clear plastic sheeting and taped it over the awl and note to protect it from further damage. David and I moved the body from the wall and laid it out flat. David patted the body, feeling for anything in his pockets. He felt a lump in the right rear pocket and extracted a wallet.

Asking Gunter to again employ his five-cell David flipped open the wallet and said, "We're in luck again. The driver's license confirms Sergeant Corker's identification. The victim is Cameron Haynes. Jake, this is gonna be a really tough 'Notification.' I don't know how close Cameron and Woody were, but we do know that he and she had a couple of dates. Gunter, you and Rebecca probably saw them more than Jake and I. Was their relationship serious or just casual?"

"We did fly his hawk, 'Titiana' five or six times when Rebecca was flying, 'Thor.' We also had meals with them three or four times. Woody seemed to like Cameron, but I didn't detect any deep affection on either Cameron's or her part. They joked and chatted but in a very light vein. I'm sure it doesn't matter. This'll be the hardest 'Notification' you'll do in your career. Maybe we should talk to Rebecca.

She'll have a better insight into that relationship. You know how guys are. We're blind to those subtleties."

"Good idea! Once we finish here, if it's O.K. with you, we'll ask for Rebecca's point of view. You'll have to go in first. I don't want to end up looking like Swiss cheese because I didn't say the right security word."

"David, Maybe I'll let you go first and tell you the wrong word just to see if Rebecca is as good a shot as she says she is."

"Gunter, you're too kind! Thanks!

Once they removed the wallet and positively identified the victim, I suggested they step over the rock wall and try to detect any tracks on Gunter's lawn. They had seen no footprints at all in the sand and it didn't appear that anyone had attempted to obliterate any tracks they may have made. Again, Sherry led the way. Immediately, they saw deep depressions in the grass. The footprints were small. I stopped the progress and asked Jay if it were possible to create a mold of the depressions in the grass?

Jay said, "This isn't going to be easy. What Ron and I'll try to do is set the depressions by spraying hair spray heavily over the area. This'll act just like spraying a woman's hair. It'll set the prints and then we can use a lightweight casting solution to attempt to lift the print. Due to the texture and irregularity of the grass itself, we won't be able to get reliable tread marks. We'll do as many as we can to hopefully come up with good molds for comparisons. One problematic issue is that the sun is coming up and as the dew disappears the depressions will disappear. We're going to have to work fast to preserve what we have. I think rather than just Ron and I doing the casting, we're going to enlist all three of you to assist. Ron and I'll do the hair spray. Sherry, you do the mixing of the solution. David you act as the solution carrier. Jake you hold the solution David brings. By then I'll be ready to pour. If we do a 'Daisy-Chain' it'll speed up the process and maybe we can preserve these depressions."

"I'm going to say at this time, from my observations thus far, the footprints look very similar in size to the depression we lifted at Matile's scene. From the depth of the depression in the damp grass, it looks like the person who made these prints was either very heavy or carrying a heavy weight. That weight may have been Cameron's body. If you remember, the print at Matile's scene was pretty deep in the sand also. Although we all saw that, it just didn't register that the one small print, which we all said may have been a female's athletic shoe, might have been carrying Matile's body."

"Jay, you're right on target. This second murder is sharpening our skills. I apologize for not being sharper at the Matile crime scene. I hope we don't have additional killings to further sharpen my skills."

No other items of evidentiary value were selected. They were able to collect a total of twelve prints. Jay commented that with that number of possibilities, the chances of good comparisons were increased. The team continued around Gunter's house all the way to the hard surface of the lake side road. The prints disappeared at the road surface. There were no tire or shoe impressions visible on the paved road.

"I guess this is the end of our evidence collection efforts team. Gunter, David and I'll go interview Rebecca while you three pack the evidence. Jay, you've already called the mortuary wagon. When it arrives call us on the radio. We'll do the same thing this time we did last time. Dr. Hardcastle and David will ride in the wagon to protect the chain of custody. We'll have Sherry drive Hardcastle's car and Ron drive David's. O.K. guys, let's go see Rebecca. Gunter what is the security word in case Rebecca shoots you? We want to be able to make sure we're not additional victims."

"The security word is, "Thor." That's Rebecca's owl's name and we decided on that before I came outside. I'll go first and make sure you Ninnies are safe."

Gunter went to the front door and rang the bell three times. He eased open the door and shouted, 'Thor.' Rebecca it's me honey! Jake and David are with me. We need to ask you some questions."

Rebecca slid from behind the wall dividing the living from the dining room with a large black semi-automatic pistol held in both hands. The pistol was pointed at the floor, but capable of being brought to a lethal point in microseconds. As she saw that it truly was Gunter, David, and I she broke into a wide smile, raised her left hand in a greeting and easily slipped the semi-auto into her waistband.

"Can't you boys come to visit at a more decent hour? Two 'O-Dark Thirty Mornings' in less than a full week aren't what I'd call acceptable social graces."

"Honey, we've some sad news. I know you're not aware of what's been going on outside, but we have another dead body leaning against our wall. Unfortunately, the victim is another person we know. The victim is Cameron Haynes, Woody's friend. He's also been stabbed in his heart with an awl. This time there's a note attached. The awl was stabbed through a note that said: "Nora Gone? That's A Folie-A-Deux." It was signed by a name we don't understand: 'Fahn Quai."

"I'm sure you know that 'Folie-A-Deux' is French for a reference to a 'Shared Delusion.' The signature sounds Oriental. I have a Chinese to English dictionary maybe we can find those words in there."

Rebecca walked over to the living room bookcase and extracted a hard cover book. "Would you spell the name for me so I can see if it's in here?"

I said, "The first word is F-A-H-N. The second word is Q-U-A-I."

Rebecca said, "The book says that Fahn stands for: 'White.' It goes on to say that it may be colloquial as in white rice. The second word Quai stands for: 'Devil.' And also for 'Ghost.' This may also stand for Demon. The commonly used term though is "White Devil." So your signature stands for "White Devil." That sounds really mysterious! Boys, it sounds like you have a killer who knows both French and Chinese. That just doesn't sound like your 'normal run-of-the-mill' killer. If there is such a thing."

I absorbed this latest bit of information and my brain went into overload I stood in Gunter's living room and thought: *I'm completely mystified by this latest development. I'm sure that Garrett isn't that well schooled in languages. Now we have someone or some group of people with some loyalty or misplaced respect for Nora that's taking revenge. The issue that my team and I are now faced with is how serious are the killer or killers and who will be their next target?*

David said, "Folks, this is becoming very serious! We've got some weirdo or group of weirdoes sending us messages about a dead woman. Jake, Inspector Forbes, and I attended Nora's autopsy outside of Newcastle, England. She drowned in the North Sea inside the Jaguar. We had Detective Onions of the RCMP do a work-up on Nora. We didn't discover any siblings and her parents are past middle age. I'll call Ammo to ask Onions if he can liaison with his friends in the U.K. to do an even more thorough work-up on Nora and her parents. Jake, you should call Inspector Forbes and bring him up to speed. Although the murders are being committed here in Coeur d'Alene, there seems to be a strong U.K. connection"

"David, we're sharing a mutual thought wave here. I'm calling Robert right now in Northumbria. This is very spooky. I've no clue about the potential suspect or suspect's identity. Vengeance is a strong motivator. But the question we need to answer is who is being motivated."

Gunter asked, "After Nora's autopsy, to whom did you release the body? Did her parents claim her?"

"Yes they did. They were pretty taciturn about the procedure, said little, signed the forms, and showed no real emotion. Had a local funeral director actually pick up the body and said they'd made arrangements with a crematorium. Inspector Robbie Forbes handled the procedures. We were just observers. Clyde instructed us to offer the parents any assistance they might need. The father was quite obviously in charge. The mother just said yes and no at the appropriate time. David and I were ready to make an offer but the issue never came up.

Nora's parents arrived at the morgue in their personal car and spent no more than fifteen minutes with us. Once the forms were signed, they shook everyone's hands and left. No tears, no recriminations, no offer of sympathy extended to the Wickley family for their loss. They just left, we presumed to return to their house."

Rebecca added, "When Jake briefed us prior to the team loading on the Gulfstream to return here, both Dad and I felt that perhaps Nora was a product of her parent's lack of emotion that just went bad."

"I remember that the entire team had a long discussion on the return fight about the effects of nature versus nurture when we discussed Nora's propensity for violence and greed. If I remember correctly, Rebecca you said it was nurture. Maybe we need to have our friends in the U.K. do a more thorough work-up on Nora's parents and any known associates to see what the controlling elements of her behavior may have been. A thorough work-up may also disclose former friends that may have immigrated here to Coeur d'Alene. That may be our most promising lead in developing a potential suspect."

"Jake, my memory says that you were strongly on the nature side of the discussion. Based on recent developments, have you changed your position?"

"Partner, we can continue this discussion at a much later time. Right now let's return to the crime scene and allow Gunter and Rebecca to go back to sleep. Gunter how does that sit with you?"

"A few minutes of quiet will do Rebecca and me good. It's so late that I have to shower and get ready for work. Which one of you is going to do the 'Advisement' for

Woody? Remember this is your homicide. I was just out there to assist. I DO NOT WANT TO BE THE ADVISOR on this case. Woody and I've been detective partners for a little over a year. Prior to that we were both uniforms assigned to the Kunkle family's protection team. I've got too much invested both emotionally and physically to shatter our relationship. I'm tossing the ball to you so fast that it's almost magical."

"Both David and I agree. This'll be a very tough 'Advisement.' When you get to work bring Woody by immediately. We'll do a team 'Advisement' I've been thinking that we'll use Morgan to assist us."

Rebecca said, "That is a great idea! I'll also be there to assist if you think that'll help."

"Rebecca that would be a great help. You and Woody bonded during our investigation of Ken's death. You also quite obviously, became better friends while flying birds, as did Cameron. Your being there during the 'Advisement' would be an immeasurable benefit."

"I'll finish getting dressed and follow Gunter in to the office. That way we can be sure to get to Woody before she learns of Cameron's death from someone else."

"David, you should get in the ambulance with Dr. Hardcastle to protect our chain of evidence. I'll get a uniform to drive your car to the morgue. I'm heading for the office. I'll give the sheriff a heads-up on Cameron and share our 'Advisement Plan' with him. He might want to also be there to extend his personal condolences."

CHAPTER NINE

I called the sheriff at home. "Sheriff, Detective Lowry here. We've had another homicide. The victim is a friend of Detective McNair's. Gunter is bringing Rebecca in to assist with the 'Advisement.' David and I also plan to ask Morgan to come in to the office to help. We really don't know how close Woody was to the victim, but we're trying to plan for a 'Worst-Case-Scenario"

The sheriff said, "Jake you're calling early. That means you have bad news for me. Tell me the specifics son and try to be gentle. I had a bad night. Election time is approaching and I'm being dragged to small political gatherings to answer citizen's questions about our mission and how we're going to deal with the budget shortfall. I can only say that we're going to work harder and smarter so many times.

The problem is that we have mostly the same group of folks attending all these functions and they are getting tired of my 'Harder and Smarter' responses. They're really pressing for specifics."

"Sheriff, I'm afraid that this news has the potential to deeply affect a member of our department. The victim was stabbed through the heart with an awl. David and I are internally calling it a 'Coeur d'Alene Murder.' The victim is Cameron Haynes. Detective McNair and he have been friends for quite a while. He was a falconer like Rebecca Lenca. The victim was posed against the wall of the Lenca house just like Dr. Matile. This time there was a note. The note was attached to the victim by having the awl stabbed through it. The note said, "**Nora Gone? That's a Folie-A-Deux**" that was done with block letters. It was signed in script by '**Fahn Quai**." We know that '**Folie-A-Deux**' means '**A Shared Delusion**'. Rebecca had a Chinese- English Dictionary. We'll need a more definitive definition but the rough translation of '**Fahn Quai**' is '***White Devil.***' Or '***White Ghost***' We haven't gotten any further on Matile's homicide but I'm going to contact Inspector Robbie Forbes in Whitley Bay and ask him to do a very thorough work-up on Nora's family to try and identify any close friends that may have immigrated. David is also going to bring Sergeant Vecchio up to date and ask him to get Detective Onions to exploit his U.K. resources."

"When are y'all going to do the 'Advisement'? I want to be there. If Woody needs time off it'll be no problem. Whatever we can do to help her, we're gonna do it. This is gonna be rough."

"I wholeheartedly agree! Two tough 'Advisements' in a row, makes me wonder why I came out of retirement. I've asked Gunter to contact Woody the minute she shows up here in the department. Rebecca is coming in with Gunter. I quickly briefed Morgan and asked her to assist. I think the two women will soften the blow. Your being there also will show Woody that we all care. Again, I have to say that we may be preparing for the worst and hoping for the best. Do you want to come down with me or shall I call you after we've done the 'Advisement'?"

"I'll come in. This'll shake up the troops if I'm seen walking around. They'll start dusting, cleaning, and looking for 'busy work'. The phones will ring off the hook trying to guess which division I'll show up in next. I'm enroute in five minutes."

The sheriff arrived in the Detective Division at the same time that Gunter, Rebecca, Woody and David arrived.

Woody asked, "Something is up. If it's bad news you might as well tell me right now. Morgan is looking at me like I'm a wounded bird. What's happening?"

I stepped forward. "Woody, you know the most unpleasant part of our job is doing 'Advisements'. It's my duty to tell you that your friend Cameron Haynes was murdered last night. His body was found posed in the same position and at the same location that Dr. Matile's body was found. We're here to provide any support and assistance you may need."

Woody was visibly shaken. Rebecca and Morgan were standing on either side of her and gently took her arms. They walked her over to my desk and sat her down.

The Sheriff immediately said, "Detective McNair, Woody, I'm so sorry for your loss and I'm here to say that whatever you need, I'll personally see to it that you get it. If you need personal time, it's yours. Jake has briefed me on the murder. I promise you that the investigation will be full bore from this minute on. Every member of the department will focus every spare minute to assist on the case."

Woody looked at the assembled team and took a deep breath. "Guys, I'm devastated that Cameron's been killed. I'm also enough of a professional to know that you have lots of questions for me. I'm going to try to maintain a professional demeanor and answer your questions calmly. To begin with, Cameron was a dear friend. That's it. He was just a friend. We weren't romantically involved. We jogged, occasionally ate, flew his hawk, and took in a few movies together. Other than that we had no deeper relationship. The last time I saw Cameron was about one week ago. We flew Titiana at the same place where we first met Gunter and Rebecca in Post Falls. I think that's the basics, ask what you want. I'll try to maintain my composure."

"Woody you're doing fine. You **do know** the drill! You're right those were the basics. We haven't had a chance to run Cameron in the data system. Do you know if he has any relatives here in Coeur d'Alene or close by? I'm sure you know his home address. We've got to run by his house to see if the killer or killers wanted something from his house. We can get a telephonic warrant from a judge quickly. I'll be the Affiant for the warrant. We can send a marked unit to secure the residence until we get there."

"Jake, let's call in the Watch Commander to get this operation rolling. Apparently you're a couple of steps ahead of me in analyzing the steps we need to make this investigation successful. I guess becoming the sheriff has removed me from the street too much."

The Detective Division became a beehive of activity as Woody provided Cameron's home address in Hayden Lake. The Watch commander dispatched a marked unit to that address. Woody gave Morgan Cameron's parent's name and address in Rathdrum. She also added that Cameron had one brother, Michael, who lives in Spokane. She didn't know his exact address. Cameron worked at the marina at the Coeur d'Alene Resort. Woody remained calm and very professional during the entire ordeal. Morgan left her side only momentarily to make computer entries. Rebecca sat beside her the entire time.

I was on the phone to the weekend on-duty Deputy District Attorney to provide the critical information for the search warrant. Once the D.A. was satisfied, they did a conference call with a Superior Court Judge. The judge asked why we were requesting a telephonic search warrant. I explained that time was of the essence. It was possible that the killer or killers may have killed Cameron in his home or abducted him, and are, even now attempting to burglarize the residence. Based upon Cameron being deceased, the judge felt that there was no one with 'standing' to object to the warrant being issued. The judge gave the verbal approval. David, Gunter, and I left the office immediately.

The drive to Hayden Lake was accomplished quickly. We discussed our strategy for searching Cameron's house. Gunter would cover the rear entrance. David and I would knock at the front door and make a forcible entry if there was no response.

We drove around the block to see if there were any vehicles parked that looked out of place. There was no car in Cameron's driveway. We parked four houses down from Cameron's address. Gunter got out and strolled down the street casually, as he passed Cameron's house he stopped to tie his shoe. He gave the house a thorough examination and flashed a four finger 'Code Four' all clear sign to David and I. Hiding the sign behind his leg on the street side so any observer inside the house would not detect the signal. He walked down the neighbor's driveway and quickly scooted behind the house.

David and I then took a stroll and approached the front door. We rang the bell and then knocked loudly. Hearing no response, I used the tried and true burglar trick of holding a jacket in front of the window beside the door latch and striking it with the butt of my pistol. Burglars normally use a rock or tire iron. I improvised.

I reached inside the small window turned the inside latch and opened the door. We both drew our weapons and I made the 'Announcement:' "Police officers! We have a search warrant. If there is anyone inside the house, come out with your hands in the air."

We heard no response and cleared the living room and moved room by room to make sure there was no one present. Once we cleared the house, we had Gunter come in through the back door. The house looked untouched and there were no blood stains visible.

"O.K. guys, it doesn't look like Cameron was abducted from here. Everything looks normal. We'll have to wait for his folks to come in here and see if they notice anything out of place or gone. Maybe we can get his parents and brother here at the same time. I'll call our evidence techs to come repair the broken window. Once we've completed the autopsy, we may have house keys to make our second entry easier."

David went to the closet in the kitchen and got a broom and dustpan and cleaned up the broken glass.

I radioed the uniformed deputy that had been parked across the street that we were 'Code Four' and he could resume normal patrol. We continued to look around the house for signs of anything out of the ordinary. The Evidence Team arrived and did a highly technical sweep of the house for evidence of blood or other body fluids.

Ron said, "Jake it's clean. We see nothing out of order. Sherry has finished replacing the window and we're ready to leave. We checked the garage for blood stains and trace body fluids and it was clean also. No car in the garage."

David, Gunter, and I left with the evidence team and returned to the office. The sheriff had insisted that Woody take a few personal days off. Morgan said that she protested but the sheriff prevailed. Rebecca had taken Woody home. Morgan had time to do a complete data work-up on Cameron and had printouts lying on our desks when we arrived at the department. The printouts revealed information fundamental to any work-up. The basics of name, age, date of birth, social security number, home address, driving history, and criminal history. Cameron had no criminal record and one citation for speeding five years ago. Morgan had also done a complete financial work-up that was slightly hindered by it being the first day of the weekend. Cameron Jeremy Haynes had two credit cards that he paid the full balance monthly. He had $8,000.00 in a savings account, a checking account with a balance of $3,400.00 at the U.S. Bank on Sherman Avenue in Coeur d'Alene. He was an employee at the Coeur d'Alene Resort. He worked as a valet in the winter and as a marina courtesy employee in the summer. His base salary was $ 9.50 an hour and he had full medical coverage from the Resort. Morgan had a close friend who also worked at the Resort who advised that valets and marina courtesy employees received ample tips associated with their jobs. Cameron paid his taxes on time and did declare his tips as a supplement to his base salary. He owned outright a nineteen ninety-nine Dodge pickup. Was buying the house he occupied and had equity of $50,000. The house is valued at $ 140,000.00.

The financial work-up didn't disclose any unusual information that might provide a motivation for murder. Cameron seemed to be the proverbial 'Straight Arrow.' Morgan's work-up didn't disclose any indication of his hobby of falconry either. While we were at his house, we didn't see his bird or any sign of a coop or aviary. This fact would require us to disturb Woody to ask if she knew where he kept his bird or birds. The county assessor's files didn't disclose any additional property in his name. I had Gunter call Rebecca to see if she was still with Woody.

"Rebecca, honey, are you still with Woody? You are? Good! We have a quick question for her can you put her on the phone?"

"Woody, Gunter here. Jake asked me to call. We've searched Cameron's house and it's clean. No blood. It doesn't appear that anyone has been inside. Were you ever at his house? You were? Good! When we contact his folks, could you possibly go to the house with them to verify that nothing is missing? Morgan did a financial and basic data work-up. There's one thing missing. There was no bird coop or aviary at his house or in his garage. Where did Cameron keep Titiana?"

"He rents a coop jointly with the rest of his club. It's located just outside of Rathdrum. I say a coop, but it's a really big shop. Each falconer has a cage inside the shop where they keep their birds. Titiana and his other hawk, Bismarck, are kept in Cameron's cage. His cage is actually divided to keep the two birds apart. Each club member takes turns doing the cleanup. Each member has a rigid schedule of feeding. There's a huge refrigerator-freezer in the shop where they store their bird's food. If you're ready to release his name to the public, maybe you should call the club to make sure that someone feeds his birds. Cameron's brother, Michael is also a falconer. Once you contact him maybe he'll come over and check on the birds."

"Woody, that's a huge help. You've solved a big puzzle for us. We're sorry to bother you but we really want to get rolling on all aspects of this investigation. The sheriff said that when you come back from the personal days, he wants you and me to assist Jake and David on the case. I'll do my best to cover all bases until you're back. No matter what happens, the three of us will keep you up to speed. Get some rest and clear your mind. The three musketeers are on the case. We'll be a better team with the fourth musketeer or mouseketeer joins us. I'll let you go if you'll let me speak to Rebecca before we hang up.

Honey, the sheriff has assigned me to the case. That means I'll probably be coming home at odd hours. I want you to keep all doors and windows locked and keep that pistol beside you at all times. I'm not trying to freak you out or instill fear. I just want you safe. We'll use the same security word when I come home. When are you starting for home? O.K. Spend as much time as you want with Woody. You're super. Bye!"

"All right team mates, here's the skinny. Woody says that Cameron rents a shop just outside Rathdrum with the other falconers in his club. That's where his birds are. His brother Michael is also a falconer and once we get the family notified, he may jump into the gap and assume responsibility for the birds. Rebecca said that if we get too pushed, she'll step in and do the tending until we can contact both the club and Michael. You know that she has the skill and motivation so we can relax on that subject. So where do we go from here?"

"I think we have to do a 'Sit-Down' right now. David and I have been chatting while you were on the phone. I'm calling Morgan into the conference room and we'll do a quick 'Sit-Down' to discuss what each of us has to do to get a handle on this very complicated case."

The Evidence Team, Watch Commander, Morgan, David, Gunter, and I assembled in the conference room. I took the lead and asked for input and open discussion on the following ideas.

#1. We need to determine when and by what method Dr. Matile returned to Coeur d'Alene. I've received the names and phone numbers of the contact persons at Spokane International Airport from Neal Sealock, the Airport

Director. With this information we can see if Dr. Matile was on any flight coming into Spokane Airport.

#2. We need to notify Cameron's parents and brother.

#3. Once we notify Cameron's relatives, we need to get them to Cameron's house to ascertain if anything was stolen.

#4. We need someone to contact local hardware and tool supply stores to see if they have sold identical awls recently.

#5. David, you've done the initial liaison with Ammo. I think we need to really get him and Onions to step up their U.K. inquiries.

#6. I've had one long telephone conversation with Inspector Forbes. He's on-board with making formal, official inquiries for us in Northumbria. I think we need to bring in the sheriff to make that same request to the RCMP in Kamloops.

#7. If possible, we need a liaison with the U.S. and Canadian State Departments to see if we have any recent immigrants from the U.K. or Canada that have settled in the area.

#8. We need quick service on all of our laboratory submissions. Our DNA evidence may answer important questions.

#9. We need to assign someone to attend Cameron's autopsy. This is the second most pressing issue we face right now.

#10. We need a formal definitive translation of Fahn Quai. We've been operating on the "White Devil" and "White Ghost" translation. That has to be confirmed.

#11. Once we get a formal translation, we need to check local and national data bases to see if we get a hit as a 'street name or 'nickname.'

"I've laid out what David and I've discussed informally, please give us your input. We need your training, experience, and expertise on this case."

Jay Bass spoke first, "I guess the obvious response from me and my team is that we'll handle the forensics portion of the case. I'll personally attend Cameron's autopsy not only out of respect for Woody, but to collect all items of evidentiary value. I'm assigning Sherry to liaison with the ISP laboratory for all chemical and fluid evidence. Ron will accompany the team that goes to Cameron's house with his parents. He'll do the photo documentation of the walk through."

Captain Nearing, the Watch Commander, spoke next, "I'll have marked units available to transport Cameron's parents. I'll also have marked units make inquiries in the hardware and tool supply stores to see of they've had a run on awl sales. Jay, will you make photos of the awls used available to patrol? I'm afraid that marked units can only function here in Kootenai County and the immediate surrounding area. If you expand your inquiries we'll have to leave that up to the Detective Division."

Morgan was the next to speak, "I can make the calls to the airline companies that Mr. Sealock provided. I'll ask they make passenger lists available for review. I'm sure we don't want to rely on having one of their employees do the search for us. I can contact three registered translation agencies and get their official translation of the 'Fahn Quai' signature. I can also contact the State Departments and request immigration data. Those sorts of things I'm skilled at. This'll allow you boys and Woody when she returns, to do the 'Leg Work' which detectives are famous for, if not in real life, at least in novels and on TV. I won't be able to do anything until Monday. If I make any calls today or tomorrow, I'll just get a weekend duty person with no clout to do what we want done."

"It seems like we've got most of the numbered things I've laid out covered. That leaves the notification of Cameron's parents and brother and one of the three of us to attend the autopsy. Any volunteers?"

"Gunter said, "I'll do the autopsy. It'll be difficult! I've never viewed an autopsy on someone I knew personally. This'll leave the 'Advisement' up to you and David. I don't want to challenge your record of so many in such a short time."

"Gunter you're too kind! O.K. I think we've a handle on this. Let's go do it! David, let's notify the parents right now. Once we've done that, we can drive into Spokane and notify Michael."

CHAPTER TEN

Ira and Debbie Haynes lived in the Twin Lakes area around Rathdrum. Twin Lakes boasts a great golf course community where you encounter as many golf carts on the streets as normal vehicles. Ira was a lank wiry man. Debbie was petite and gracious. David and I knocking at their door didn't alarm them, but they immediately sensed that we were law enforcement officers.

Ira asked, "What's the problem officers? Both our vehicles are properly registered and insured. I'm sure that I haven't run any red lights and been caught on one of the traffic cameras. Debbie have you been speeding again? Sometimes you drive that golf cart like it's a race car."

I reluctantly interrupted Ira's conversation by identifying David and myself.

"Mr. and Mrs. Haynes, I'm Detective Jake Lowry. This is my partner Detective Bruce David. We're members of the Kootenai County Sheriff's Department. It's my very unpleasant duty to inform you that your son Cameron Jeremy Haynes was murdered last night in Coeur d'Alene. Detective David and I've been assigned to investigate that crime. We know this is a shock to you and there's no easier way to make this notification. Is there a clergyman or neighbor we can call to provide you some assistance during this difficult time?"

Ira said, "Our pastor lives just three doors down maybe you could walk down there and speak with Pastor Jacobs. See if he's home and could come down to sit with us. After a shock like this we're going to need some pastoral counseling. Debbie, you better sit down. I think I'll take a seat also."

David volunteered to go to seek Pastor Jacobs.

Debbie Haynes had been silent during our brief conversation. She was now seated in an overstuffed chair. She had pulled a handkerchief from her sleeve and dabbed at her eyes. Now she blanched and seemed to collapse against the chair back. Ira rushed to her side and took both her hands in his.

"Momma. Are you all right? I know this is a blow. We need to ask these officers how Cam was killed and find out what we need to do. Did you say your name was Lowry?"

"Yes Sir, but please call me Jake."

"O.K. Jake. I guess I'll ask. How was Cam killed? Was he involved in a fight or accidentally shot in a drive-by shooting?"

"No Sir. Cameron, Cam, as you call him, was stabbed in the heart by an awl. This is the second such murder we've had in the past few days. We've no idea who the killer or killers are. The only link we have is that Cam was a friend of one of our Detectives."

"Oh! You mean Woody McNair. We've met her once. She and Cam met us at Michael D's restaurant on the edge of Lake Coeur d'Alene. Michael D's is a breakfast and lunch spot that serves great food. We had lunch there to celebrate Cam's promotion at the Resort. He'd been promoted to senior courtesy agent at the marina."

"Yes Sir that's right. Woody's been extremely helpful in the initial stages of this investigation. The sheriff ordered her to take a few days off to get over the shock of Cam's death. Detective Gunter Lenca, her partner is keeping her continually briefed on the progress. Detectives David, Gunter and I went to Cam's house to see if the killer or killers possibly wanted something from Cam's house. By all appearances everything seemed normal. We'd like to ask you and Mrs. Haynes as soon as you feel like it to meet David and me at Cam's house to do a walk-through to verify that everything is in place and nothing missing. As soon as David comes back with Pastor Jacobs, he and I are driving to Spokane to meet with Michael to tell him of this horrible tragedy. We have his home address, but don't know where he works."

Mrs. Haynes said, oh, he works at Tomato Street on North Division. He's the assistant chef there. He should be at work now. He normally goes in early. He works five days a week, but his week runs from Friday until Tuesday. Should I call him and tell him you're on the way?"

"No Ma am, we'd prefer that you don't. This kind of news, albeit difficult to hear and equally difficult to report, is best done face-to-face. We'll just drive over and meet with him. Woody told us that Michael is also a falconer. We want to make sure that Cam's birds are cared for. Detective Lenca's wife, Rebecca, is also a falconer. She and Cam flew their birds together. She has volunteered to step in until Michael can make arrangements to assume those duties."

"You boys thought of everything haven't you? Are you always this thorough on every case or are you just being nice to two old folks?"

"No Ma am. We try to be this thorough on every case. I'll admit that everyone in the Detective Division has a personal interest in identifying Cam's killer and bringing that killer or killers to justice. So we may be a little extra diligent in dotting the 'i's' and crossing the 't's'."

David and Pastor Jacobs knocked at the door and Ira Haynes let them in. David has obviously briefed Pastor Jacobs. He went immediately to Debbie Haynes and spoke to her in a low voice. Although she appeared to have handled the news stoically as she talked with me, the moment Pastor Jacobs spoke to her she lost her composure. Ira was at her side and also muttering soft words of comfort. David and I verified that Pastor Jacobs had everything under control, gave each of them our cards and asked them to call when they were ready to go to Cameron's house and left to drive to Spokane.

I asked the manager of Tomato Street if Michael Haynes was on duty and got an affirmative answer. Michael emerged from the kitchen wearing the traditional white chef's jacket and black and white checkered trousers. I was a little disappointed that he wasn't wearing the huge white chef's hat. Instead he was wearing a black hat with a sort of muffin top. I introduced David and myself. I and asked if there was a quiet place we could talk?

Michael said, "Am I in trouble? It must be something big if they sent two cops."

"Michael you're not in trouble. Detective David and I are here as bearers of bad news. I've been a law enforcement officer for twenty plus years. In that time this job hasn't gotten any easier or more pleasant to perform. Michael, your brother Cameron was murdered last night in Coeur d'Alene. We've just come from your folk's house in Twin Lakes. Pastor Jacobs was with them when we left. We're sure you have a ton of questions and we're here to answer whatever we can. I'm speaking for both of us when I say that we're sorry for your loss. Cameron was a friend of one of our colleagues. The entire department is focused on solving this case. Not only for that reason, but that is a real motivator."

"I'm sure you're referring to Woody McNair. I met her with Cam when he was flying Titiana. Woody seems like a nice person. Cam thought a lot of her. How's she taking the news?"

"The sheriff ordered her to take a few personal days off to process Cameron's murder. She's taking it pretty hard! She'll join the investigative team when she returns. Her partner Gunter Lenca is on the team and is keeping her informed of any developments. Michael we know you're probably in the initial stages of shock, but we do have some questions to ask and some additional information to share with you. Before we start, do you have any questions?"

"I'm not good with names. You said your name's are? ~~ I'm sorry. Did you say Jake and David? I can't recall your last names."

David spoke, you've got the important names correct and that's what counts. My last name is David but I go by my last name. I'm Bruce David and my partner is Jake Lowry. But please, just call us Jake and David."

"O.K. Here goes, you say Cam was murdered. How? When exactly and how did your department get involved? You said he was killed in Coeur d'Alene. I know Coeur d'Alene lies in Kootenai County, but shouldn't Coeur d'Alene, P.D. be here?"

I said, "Those are a couple of questions. We'll try to answer them in the order asked. First of all Cam was murdered by having an awl plunged into his heart. We can only say that the murder occurred last night. We can't give an exact time. The autopsy is being conducted right now. That will give us a pretty close approximation. The Sheriff's Department is involved because Cam's body was discovered in the county area. Kootenai County and the City of Coeur d'Alene are a patchwork of little areas. This is a result of uncontrolled growth. We're working with Coeur d'Alene, P.D. and other agencies. I can tell you that Cam was the second person killed in this fashion. The first body was found in the same location where Cam's body was found. This is why we have multiple agencies working on the case."

"O.K. that answers my questions for the time being. Now you ask yours."

David jumped in, "Michael, Woody told us that you're also a falconer. Would it be possible for you to take over the care of Cam's birds? Secondly, we've asked your parents to go to Cam's house for an inspection. Jake & I were there and everything looked in order, but if you are familiar with Cam's house, we need your eyes and memory to see if there is something missing or out of place. Once we hear from your folks, we can set up a time. We also need to know when was the last time you saw Cam?"

"I stacked questions together, so I guess you doing it back to me is fair. I'll do you the same respect. Yes I'll go to the club shop and care for Cam's birds. A second yes, I'm familiar with Cam's house. I lived with him for a while when I was between jobs. I'll go to my folk's house as soon as we're finished here. If they're in any shape, we can go to Cam's today if that'll help. Thirdly, I saw Cam three days ago. We were flying our birds in an informal club competition up in Sagle, Idaho. Cam's Titiana was declared the winner for speed of target acquisition and capture. That's sure a wonderful bird. It'll be a real pleasure to care for her."

I said, "Michael you're handling this very well. You have taken a huge load off our minds. David and I'll speak to your manager if that will help you to get some time off."

"That won't be necessary. She and I have a great working relationship and once she hears that Cam is dead, time off won't be a problem. I'll go tell her now unless you have something more for me."

"Nope that's it. David and I'll be heading back to the office. Thanks again Michael. We'll see you when you come to Cam's house with your folks."

CHAPTER ELEVEN

Morgan and Gunter were at the office when we returned. Gunter was slightly ashen faced and was sitting down. Morgan had compiled more data printouts that were lying on David's and my desk.

Morgan said, "I did get some additional data on Cameron and I've gotten the airline schedules and passenger manifests from Air Alaska/Horizon Air. Although they appear to be two separate airlines, they operate as the principal airline that flies from Spokane to Boise. I called Heidi Matile. She said she dropped off Dr. Matile at five A.M. for a six fifteen flight from Spokane to Salt Lake City to Boise. He preferred that route rather than fly from Spokane to Seattle to Boise or Spokane to Portland to Boise. There are no direct flights from Spokane to Boise. It's almost like the old adage 'You can't get there from here.' More surprisingly, one of the most popular connections goes from Spokane to Sacramento to Boise. Apparently, because you can fly from Spokane at seven thirty five and still be in Boise by one fifteen."

"I did find Dr. Matile's name on the passenger manifest just as Heidi said. I haven't had time to search for his name on a return flight yet."

I said to Gunter, "You don't look too well. Is there something wrong?"

"Jake, I just finished Cameron's autopsy. I've done a couple previously, but this one was particularly hard. This isn't my ideal way to spend Saturday afternoon. There were no startling revelations. As we suspected, the awl through the heart was the cause of death. Dr. Hardcastle took fluid and tissue samples for laboratory testing. Jay took possession of the samples for hand carrying to the ISP laboratory for rush processing. Time of death is put at twelve midnight. I did recover Cameron's house and vehicle keys. He had the usual assortment of business cards in his wallet and forty-eight dollars in cash. I've started my report in the main frame with all the specific details. Dr. Hardcastle says that his report will be in the mainframe before Monday morning."

"Listen guys, it's late and it is Saturday. Let's call it a day and resume on Monday morning bright and early. We all need some time away from this case and I can't personally see any profit in wearing ourselves out by trying to obtain additional information on a Sunday. Are we in agreement?"

The chorus of yes was immediate. We each took our personal copies of Morgan's printouts. Gunter assured us that he'd personally brief Woody prior to going home. We turned off our computers and walked as a group to the employee's parking lot. I called Liz to see if she needed anything before I started the drive to Kingston. No grocery orders were forthcoming so I started my drive home.

CHAPTER TWELVE

Sunday was bright and cheery. Liz and I decided to get in our UTV and drive up the Old River Road along the North Fork of the Coeur d'Alene River. We grabbed some water bottles and a camera, donned light jackets, and took off just before noon. The river was still entertaining a moderate number of 'floaters.' Sometimes whole families tied their inner tubes together and simply floated along with the river's current. Entrepreneurs along the main river road offer tubes for sale and also had sign boards offering to take folks up the river to a put-in point so they would arrive back at their vehicles after the float. Camping spots along the river were full with tents, travel, and fifth wheel trailers. Some folks would park their camp gear on Memorial Day and leave it in place until Labor Day. Camping spots along the riverbank were sold and leased at premium prices.

We were about ten miles up Old River Road when Liz shouted for me to stop.

"I think I saw a bear there on the edge of the clearing."

Admittedly skeptical, I turned the UTV around and slowly drove back to the spot Liz was indicating. Sure enough a medium sized black bear was eating elderberries. When we stopped to get the camera out of the case he "Huffed" and stood to his full height of about six feet I grabbed the camera and passed it to Liz. She got off two shots before he decided to amble further back into the foliage. I kept the UTV running in case his first "Huff" was a preamble to a charge. We had a fifty-foot safety zone so I was sure the UTV could outrun him, but I was taking no chances. Liz was bummed. She wanted more pictures. I drove further up the road and doubled back on the off chance he might have resumed his elderberry meal but he was nowhere to be seen.

We resumed our drive and did get one picture of a beautiful doe. The doe's fur was almost a brilliant red. The deer we feed on our place have a sort of neutral tan color. Wildlife adapts to the terrain where they live and perhaps this color was more adaptable to that area. I've noticed that elk we see further up the river have a reddish tinge to their fur also.

We stopped at the "Y" for an ice cream cone and to stretch. We decided to drive home on the main river road, less dust and a much smoother ride. Traffic was light as many campers were stretching Sunday to the limit and would leave for their week-day residence just prior to dusk.

We did the almost mandatory stop at the "Snake Pit." More politely called the 'Enaville Resort' by the state sign painters. Although they do put 'Snake Pit' below the Enaville Resort lettering. Joe Peak, the owner, was in fine form and was going to celebrate his twentieth year in business the following week. Liz and I wished both him and his beautiful wife Rose Mary well and enjoyed a great steak and baked potato meal.

We live only about two miles from the "Snake Pit." So we were home prior to dark. I fed the horses and replenished the bird feeders which would be empty tomorrow morning. Not so much from hungry birds, but from the nightly onslaught of deer coming down to eat the cracked corn in the deer feeders and then emptying my tubular bird feeders by sticking their tongues in the small holes and virtually emptying all of the feeders.

The expense was well worth it to Liz and me to be able to look out various windows in our home and see clusters of wild birds, small groups of wild turkeys (groups too small to be labeled a flock) and deer of all ages at the feeders. This year we had a new buck with an unusual rack. His left side was fully formed with five points in a normal configuration. His right side was also five points but only about one third the size of his left. I had put out my scouting camera to get some feeding pictures of him to verify what I had only glanced once out the window.

Bedtime came early as Liz had another Susan G. Komen breakfast meeting on Monday. I know that the start of the week would require me to do a lot of 'road' and 'leg' work.

CHAPTER THIRTEEN

"Jake, this is Lori Larson. I'm probably being paranoid, but I think I'm being followed. I can't say that it's anyone specific, but on the way to work Friday and again this morning, two different cars were behind me from my house all the way to the office. When I was jogging this morning, two people, I'm not even sure if they were male or female, were about one hundred yards behind me all the way. I ran my usual three-mile circuit from my house out a mile and a half and back and they stayed behind me the whole way. I run in a nice neighborhood and there are many joggers out at six A.M. but I recognize most of the regulars and my two followers just seemed out of place. I hate to bother you at home first thing Monday morning, but I'm scared"

"Lori, you did the right thing. I'm glad you called. What does your day look like? Could you break away for maybe an hour and meet David and me for lunch? If lunch isn't possible, if you'll choose a time, we'll meet you anyplace you choose and let's talk this thing over. Paranoia is not necessarily a bad thing. It might be a coincidence, or maybe you have a new or some new admirers and they are trying to work-up nerve to speak to you. Let's hope that the latter case is true."

"I'm going to be on the east end of Coeur d'Alene around noon. Could we meet at a restaurant on the east end?"

"Actually, David and I can kill two birds with one stone if you'll meet us at Michael D's at the edge of the lake. It's a quaint breakfast and lunch place and we need to ask some of the employees there some questions on a case we're working on. Let's say twelve o'clock sharp. We won't keep you long. I've heard that the food is excellent there."

"See you there at twelve. Bye"

Well Jake it looks like Monday is going to be busier than you had planned. I don't like it that another of the people involved in the Ken Kunkle murder is now possibly being followed. This isn't a coincidence. O.K. Boy you better collect yourself and get into the office.

I finished dressing and made the drive to the office without incident. David and Gunter were already there when I arrived.

"David, Gunter, we may have a new wrinkle in this case. I got a call from Lori Larson this morning. She thinks one, or possibly two people, are following her. She isn't sure and can't say whether they're male or female. She saw them about one hundred yards behind her when she was jogging this morning. She thinks she was followed to work on Friday and again this morning. She had an early appointment this morning so she called me from her work as soon as she got in the office. As we three well know, Lori was one of Ken's steady girl friends. This would be the third person involved with Ken with something hinky happening. I arranged to meet her at Michael D's for lunch at noon. This throws a monkey wrench in any plans you may have made over the weekend. I think this may be important and we'll just have to flex our schedule and minds."

"Jake, I'm flexed. Over the weekend I've been thinking that it might be a smart thing to call together all of the people connected with Ken's murder and do an informal briefing to alert them to be on their toes. Dr. Matile, we might check off as a coincidence, but the death of Cameron coupled with the note is for sure no coincidence. There is someone or a couple of people out there in our area of responsibility that is stalking anyone even loosely connected to Ken Kunkle. I've gone over security procedures with Rebecca. She is on her toes and asked if we shouldn't brief Clyde, Roberto, Consuelo, Maria and Husam. Maybe my wife has a good handle on the threat and we should consider even bringing in Michelle, Lori, and Kim."

David jumped in the conversation. "Guys, Gunter has a point. This development with Lori is troubling. Even though Woody is on personal days off, I think we should bring her in for the briefing. That would require some coordination with the sheriff and maybe the patrol commander. But my vote is for a briefing and we should do it soonest!"

"O.K. let me be the voice of constraint here. What are we going to tell them? We have two dead bodies and a note from an unknown entity. We have an extremely attractive female who may be, and I repeat maybe, is being followed. WE KNOW Nora is dead! What we don't know is if she had siblings or close friends who may have moved to our area and for some reason are bent on revenging her death. I think what we DON'T know far outweighs what we DO know. That having been said, I suggest that we three walk down to the sheriff's office right now and tell him what we DO KNOW and what we SUSPECT! After we've shown our poker hand, we should beg him to let us do a briefing. I think he'll concur so we'll err on the side of safety."

I called Patti Nelson to ask if the Boss was in and got an affirmative. Patti said to come on down. The three of us grabbed our case files and discussed what we would say as we walked to the sheriff's office. The sheriff was standing beside Patti's desk when we entered the outer office.

"I see that we now have three against one on an early Monday morning. I'm sure that's not fair so I'll do the French thing and surrender right now and we can call off the fight. O.K. boys with those serious faces, I guess we better go in my office for a little talk. Who is going first?"

"Sheriff, I can say that the three of us have come to a conclusion that might not set well with you. This morning about seven thirty, I got a call at home from Lori Larson. She suspects one or two persons are following her. She's pretty convinced that they followed her to work Friday and again this morning. She also feels that two people were following her when she jogged this morning. They stayed about one hundred yards behind her but she didn't recognize them. She runs the same three-mile route daily so she's in a routine and recognizes the regulars on her route. Just to jog your memory, Lori Larson was one of Ken's four female companions/girlfriends. Based on this being the third person loosely associated with Ken, we feel that we should, for safety's sake, bring in all of the folks associated with Ken's case and brief them of the possible danger. Up front we also admit that we don't know much and may be accused of fear mongering. I personally couldn't live with myself if we had a third person hurt."

"Jake you've laid out a well thought out case. I must say the import is an emotional one, but there are few solid facts to back-up your request. Cold hard reason tells me to deny your request. David's and your track record tells me to grant the request. Gunter you and David haven't said anything. But Jake did say he was speaking for the three of you. So I'll assume you concur. I'm mulling this over and am sure you're many steps ahead of me on this matter, but as I see it, we're gonna need some outside help on this case other than the help we've requested from the RCMP and the U.K. We're gonna need some local help. We also need to bring in our own resources. I propose we schedule the briefing for Wednesday to give folks time to clear their calendar. Let's do this briefing off-site to lessen the chances of the media catching wind of our plans. I'm thinking a nice quiet conference room over in Spokane Valley in one of the up-market hotels could be reserved for a meeting of like-minded business people. Jake you create a good innocuous name for the company and I'll have Patti make the reservations. We'll do this after normal business hours so we won't interfere with folks work schedules. Let's say around seven P.M. How's that sound to you boys? I'll have the Patrol Commander, ISP local Commander, Coeur d'Alene P.D., Post Falls P.D., and the D.A. Investigators attend so we'll have complete investigative coverage if this is as big as we suspect."

I said, "O.K. Sir I think we're all on the same page in our thinking. I'll have Patti make reservations for Blyth Consulting Inc. for Wednesday evening in a conference room that will seat thirty folks. We'll ask for a set up that will include a screen to show visuals and a sound system. This way it will sound legitimate to the hotel. We won't use either. If we keep our comments at normal speaking voice level we won't have eavesdroppers to worry about. Boss, if you'll ask everyone to come in business casual clothes and no uniforms we can pull this off and not draw attention to our mission. This Wednesday meeting will give the three of us and Morgan time to do leg work and additional computer searches. Hopefully, we may have some input from Ammo or Forbes by then to add to our briefing. Otherwise, we're going to look silly."

"Right boys, I'm sure you'll have enough stuff for a good briefing. Let's get cracking!"

The three of us went back to the bullpen and took a few moments to boot up our computers. Once that was done, we could begin to do some planning and rethinking of where we needed to go with this case. Morgan saw us at our desks and walked into our area.

"I've some good and some puzzling news for all of us. The puzzling news, Dr. Matile wasn't on any flight leaving Boise enroute to a final stop in Spokane on the day of his death or the day preceding. So he didn't fly back up here. You've already determined that he didn't fly into Coeur d'Alene Airport. So my next task was to try to determine how he came back. Now the good news, apparently, according to the conference organizers, Dr. Matile met and became friends with a husband and wife veterinarian couple from Deary, Idaho. They offered to give him a ride to Coeur d'Alene. Apparently they were going to Canada for a few days. The early cancellation of the conference gave them some extra days to spend in Canada. The organizer is trying to determine the names of the couple as I'm telling you this."

"I've contacted the U.S. State Department. They are searching files for recent immigrants that selected the Pacific Northwest as a final destination. The Canadian Foreign Ministry has asked that we deal with them through the U.S. State Department for protocol purposes that is in the mill also."

"Morgan you're wonderful as usual. It seems like our new hot investigative lead is to talk to the two Deary Vets."

"Jake, I'll call you the minute I get the names."

"Super! We're going to have a special conference at a hotel in Spokane Valley Wednesday evening at Seven P.M. to discuss an interesting development in the case. I got a call at home early this morning from Lori Larson saying that she believes she is being followed. The Boss is calling in additional outside investigative support to assist us. David how are we coming with Ammo and Onions?"

"I'm calling Ammo right now."

"Good it's still early enough in England that I can catch Robbie Forbes. Gunter, would you call Patti and give her the name of Blyth Consulting for her to make the conference reservations. Then call Woody and ask her to plan for Wednesday's conference. I just had a flash of brilliance. When you're talking to Patti would you ask her to suggest to the Boss to ask everyone attending the conference to attend in personal, not unmarked, vehicles. This'll further conceal our true purpose in holding the meeting off-site."

"Done! Good idea. I'll pick-up Woody in my personal car to make sure that she's O.K."

David, Gunter and I grabbed a telephone and began dialing. David reached Ammo first.

"Ammo, David here. How's it going? Good! Do you have any news for us? O.K. give me a minute to connect the tape recorder to the phone so I won't lose any information. The other guys are on the phone doing other business otherwise I'd put you on speakerphone. You don't mind if I record the conversation do you? Thanks! Here goes."

Gunter connected with Patti and completed his business with her. He then called Woody. She was anxious to come back to work and readily agreed to attend the conference. She felt that this was the perfect entrée for her to return to full duty.

I caught Robbie Forbes just as he was heading out the door for home. Sadly, he had no news for us. I explained our increased need for current intelligence and how we planned to step up our investigative efforts. Robbie assured me that he'd re-focus his efforts on our behalf and would positively have some results for us before Wednesday's meeting.

Morgan came back into our area. "The mystery has seriously deepened, the conference organizer, Doctor Mark Line, President of the Northwest Veterinarian's Association, has carefully checked the registration roster for the conference attendees and there is no husband and wife veterinarian team from Deary Idaho registered. Dr. Line is certain that he met them and is also positive that they had the proper name tags for the conference hanging around their necks. He remembers meeting them with Dr. Matile at a cocktail party the first night of the conference. I have now contacted our ISP Commander who has the source in the Boise Embassy Suites to check the roster for a couple from Deary, Idaho. I've also asked Dr. Line to conduct a records check of the Northwest Veterinarian's Association for any vets living or practicing in Deary, Idaho. As soon as I'm finished here, I'll do that same computer check myself."

"I've also received Dr. Matile's credit card bills. He was staying in the Boise Embassy Suites. He checked out the day prior to our discovering his body. There are no unusual charges on his credit card. The usual room charges for a single occupancy room, meals, and one charge for dry cleaning. I'll try to track down what he had cleaned with the hotel manager personally. This may allow me to develop an additional source of information."

The phone rang just as Morgan finished. Patti told us that we were booked into the Hampton Inn in Spokane Valley. She was making the calls for the sheriff to all of the local law enforcement agencies and wanted to know if she should also call others that were associated with the Kunkle murder. Gunter, David, Morgan and I had a quick discussion and decided that it would be better if we made the calls to those folks.

We listed whom we should call. First off, Gunter would call Rebecca and Clyde. He would ask Clyde to notify

Maria, Roberto and Husam. He would ask Rebecca to notify Consuelo. David would call Heidi, Emilee, Michelle and Kim. I would call Lori. I would notify Jay, Sherry and Ron on the Evidence Team and Dr. Hardcastle and invite them to the conference.

Now we had to deal with the mystery vets allegedly from Deary, Idaho. At the moment with no name we were stuck. We couldn't even call Canadian Customs to see if the couple had actually crossed into Canada. You didn't have to list your occupation when crossing the border.

We all got busy on the phones. Clyde would bring Maria, Roberto and Husam. Michelle and Lori would car pool. I would do a discreet tail on them to see if Lori was being followed. Rebecca was bringing Consuelo and would also pick up Kim. David would tail them to see if they were being followed. The three evidence techs would carpool. Dr. Hardcastle would drive himself. All attendees were cautioned not to discuss the meeting with anyone.

The noon hour was upon us. David, Gunter, and I just had time to drive to Michael D's to meet Lori. Michael D's is wood paneled and very cozy. The décor is that of a casual rustic cabin. The menu offered many tempting choices. Lori walked in just as David, Gunter, and I were being seated. Having a low-key meeting with Lori Larson is impossible! Every red-blooded male in the restaurant stopped eating, gulped and immediately envied the three of us. Lori was dressed in a casual beige business suit that emphasized her curves without appearing to notice she had any. It has been a while since we had seen her and the pleasant shock of her innate beauty was apparent on our faces. She causally kissed each of us on the cheek and took her seat.

"I can't thank you enough for meeting me today. I've been a nervous wreck since Friday. My weekend was spent hovering inside my house peeking out my windows with the curtains drawn to see if there was anyone lurking in my neighborhood. I didn't see anyone and thought that maybe I was just nuts. But this morning when I went for my jog, all the fear and paranoia came flooding back. I just don't feel safe. The papers telling about Dr. Matile's death didn't scare me, but when Cameron Haynes was killed I totally freaked! The two people I thought followed me on the jog were just far enough back so I couldn't get a good look at them, but they were there for the whole three miles. Both of them here wearing 'Hoodies.' It's cool in the early morning but no one wears 'Hoodies' at this time of the year. Some women wear headbands over their ears and some guys wear stocking caps all year. But 'Hoodies' never! They were also wearing gloves. It's not the dead of winter and you've got to have delicate hands to wear gloves this time of year. If I wear gloves now, my hands sweat like crazy. They had on running tights and black 'Hoodies' but lots of people run in tights all year long. So that wasn't unusual. I did notice they had a nice stride. It appeared to me they were runners. Not someone who was pretending to be joggers. That's about all I can tell you. I didn't notice them at first but after about half a mile they didn't pass me. I'm not a fast jogger. Usually the only people that don't pass me are old people. Most everyone else just leaves me in their dust."

"Lori, your observations are pretty accurate. How tall would you say they were? I'm six feet, David is five eleven, and Gunter is five ten. Think about our height and try to measure your followers against our height."

"I'd say one was about your height Jake, but the other was smaller and maybe slightly taller than I am. I'm five seven."

"Is that what gave you the impression that one of the followers might be a female?"

"I can't be sure, but I just got that impression. Their jogging stride was almost identical, almost as if they were moving to music. You know what I mean, when you see army guys jogging, they all seem to be in step and take the same sized stride. That's what these two looked like. I couldn't see if they had on ear buds or had a Walkman strapped to their arms like some joggers do, but they did jog like they had done it together for years."

"Were they wearing running shoes?"

"I didn't specifically check, but I assume they were. You know if someone had boots or some other type of footgear it would draw attention. I didn't notice anything unusual about their feet."

"Great! Lets order and we can continue our discussion."

The waitress arrived with a pot of steaming coffee. Lori ordered French toast, Gunter ordered Bacon and eggs, David ordered a cheeseburger and I ordered a bowl of chili.

David asked, "Lori, you felt you were followed to work. What gave you that impression?"

"Well initially I thought that a dark blue SUV was following too close when I left my house. Then it was gone. But as I pulled on to I-90, a small Toyota the same dark blue, was right beside me in the left lane and then slowed down and pulled in behind me. It wasn't as if they didn't want me to know they were there. It was almost as if they wanted me to see the vehicles. Both drivers were wearing wraparound sunglasses and ball caps. About half way to work the SUV pulled in close behind me again. Not enough to make me call 911, but enough to make me uncomfortable. When I pulled off I-90, the blue Toyota was there behind me again. Friday I thought it might be juveniles pulling a prank. But they did the same thing this morning. After the jogging incident, I figured I'd better call Jake."

I asked, "Did you get a license plate?"

"Neither car had a front plate. They stayed behind me so I never saw the rear of either vehicle. Again, Friday I wasn't paranoid, but today I was trying to do the 'Good Citizen' thing and get physical descriptions and license plate numbers. Today both vehicles had tinted windows. They were the same dark blue. A SUV and a small Toyota. There are so many SUV's on the road, I can't tell one make from the other. I recognize Jeeps and Cadillac Escalades, after that they all look the same to me. I'm sorry! Both drivers were wearing wraparound sunglasses and ball caps but that is all the description I can give you."

"By you saying 'wraparound sunglasses' do you mean something like Oakley's or Gargoyles?"

"Yes. Cops wear those types of glasses. Sometimes they are mirrored other times they're just dark lenses."

Gunter reached into his jacket pocket and extracted a pair of Oakley wraparound sunglasses, happily, not with mirrored lenses. "Is this what you mean Lori?"

"Exactly!"

"Those types of sunglasses do provide good facial covering. Here's my plan. We're going to ask you leave after we do. Give us about five minutes. We'll set-up in a place where we can watch you and lookout for any dark blue vehicles. We'll be close enough so if anything happens, we're on top of it. We'll provide a very loose tail until you are safely in your building. Call us about thirty minutes before you leave for home and we'll have some cars tail you home. Travel your normal route and if you need to stop in a store do that. It might not be David, Gunter or me, but we'll have trained officers very close to you. Go for your run at six. We'll have both male and female officers jogging on your route. If they see the people you suspect are following you we'll at least detain and identify, if not arrest them. At the moment, we don't have a valid charge but we might dream up something to assure that we do identify them. If you'll excuse me, I'm going to talk to the manager discreetly about some other matters and then we'll be ready to go."

"David, you and Gunter get any additional info you can while I talk to the manager."

My conversation with the manager was brief. He did remember Cameron, Woody and Cameron's folks being in the restaurant. He remembered Cameron because he occasionally docks his boat at the Resort Marina and had chatted with Cameron there. He had personally invited Cameron to Michael D's to sample the fare. To the best of his memory, Cameron had only been there the one time. He'd seen and chatted with David at Capone's some months ago but hadn't seen him recently. He didn't recognize Gunter at all. I knew I was reaching for straws, but on the off chance that there might have been some incident in the restaurant that might have given us another investigative lead. I gave David the 'Code Four' sign and he and Gunter rose to leave. We met at the car and drove out as if we were leaving the area. Gunter drove a few blocks and then wove our way back using small side streets to a spot so we could see Lori's car.

Lori got in without incident and drove down Sherman Avenue heading west toward the center of the city. We sat still for a few minutes observing the restaurant parking lot. No one dashed out of the restaurant to follow her. We established a loose tail staying about five cars behind her. No dark blue SUV's or Toyotas in sight. We couldn't determine if she was being followed at all by the traffic patterns. No cars dropped out and then returned and no one vehicle was behind or in front of her the entire route to her office. Traffic consisted of the usual mix of sedans, SUV's, Mini-vans, and pick-ups. Wraparound sunglasses and tinted windows were scattered throughout the drivers observed. We all agreed that we couldn't detect a pattern of anyone following her. Once she was safely inside her office, we discontinued the surveillance and returned to the office.

CHAPTER FOURTEEN

Morgan was waiting for us when we returned, "I've done some more computer searches while you were frolicking with the beautiful Lori Larson. Don't look at me like that! Remember, I had lunch with her and Michelle at the Kunkle Compound. You boys were probably hard pressed to concentrate on your meals. Quick, tell me what you ate. Ah! Hah! I didn't think you could. Anyway, back to business. I got a password from Dr. Line and searched the Northwest Veterinarian's Membership Roster. No husband and wife licensed in or around Deary, Idaho for a fifty-mile radius. I ran husband and wife vet teams and the closest one is in Boise proper. There are some in Washington, Oregon, Montana, and British Columbia. After the search, I called Dr. Line back. He is positive that when he met them they said Deary, Idaho. He said he's been racking his brain to remember a name but can't. I'm wondering if it would be a viable idea to send our sketch artist to Boise or ask Boise P.D. or ISP interview Dr. Line and see if he can give them enough physical descriptions to produce a sketch?"

"Morgan, what a great idea! I think using a Boise or ISP sketch artist makes more sense. It'd be faster and much cheaper."

"O.K. Jake." Gunter said, "I'll make the call to see which agency has an artist available and ask them to make the appointment with Dr. Line."

"Additionally, I went to the Oxford University Registrar's web site and ran a student roster for the Veterinary School during the period that the real Rori Atkins was a student there. You'll be surprised to know that the only name we are familiar with is that of Emilee Tish Lukin. There are over fifty names that were either entering, enrolled to study, or graduating during the period that Rori was there. So we'd have a broad search to initiate. Our only saving grace is that we can compare those names against names provided to us by the U.S. and Canadian State Departments to see if we get any matches."

"You'll have to forgive me, but this line of inquiry is assuming that Rori and Nora associated closely only with veterinary students. If they had close or even intimate friends outside the veterinary school, then we have a huge problem."

I said, "Morgan you've hit gold again! Great work! With this additional information we've some definitive steps we can take that might produce faster results. I guess the only hold up now is the information from the State

Departments. Once we have that we can ask Robbie Forbes to interview Rori Atkins parents and ask them if any names we've matched were close friends with Rori and Nora. The real issue is Nora's propensity to glom on to a male and fantasize about them being 'Star Crossed Lovers' or 'Soul Mates.' If she did that, possibly Rori's parents wouldn't have known or noticed. One of the things we've never asked about is if Rori kept a diary. If the Atkins still have that book that might give us some additional insight."

David asked, "Am I correct in assuming the next thing we can do locally is a more thorough work-up on Emilee Lukin? I've had a bad feeling about her ever since the first meeting. She was too hostile initially, then too smooth and cooperative"

"Partner, you're becoming a very suspicious guy. I personally didn't think butter would melt in Emilee's mouth and now you're bad mouthing her? What kind of a person have you become? I too, have been cautious of removing Emilee from the persons of interest file for the same reasons you mentioned. Morgan, can you do a thorough work-up on Emilee? We did a good initial run at her and her surroundings. Maybe a really in-depth look at her might reveal something we missed at the outset."

"Yes Boss, I'll get right on it."

"Gunter, perhaps you might make a nice informal visit to Dr. Matile's Veterinary Office and do a 'Non-Interview Style Interview' with Miss Lukin's co-workers. I'm afraid I might have burned David's and my bridges with the staff there. Speaking of staff, I didn't see any males at Dr. Matile's office. I find that unusual. Usually they have some big farm boy to do the heavy lifting. Matile wasn't that big. Maybe there's a reason for the lack of males. You might explore that area of questioning."

"O.K. I'll run over there now."

Jay Bass came in from the evidence lab. "Folks I have the initial lab report on Cameron's evidence. The ISP lab outdid themselves in doing this rapidly. Just like Dr. Matile's, the DNA on the awl was Cameron's only. The shoe impressions we got matched the Zats footprints at Dr. Matile's crime scene. Cameron's blood did contain a trace amount of 'Roofies' just like Dr. Matile. No other chemicals or drugs were detected. The ISP lab is going to go to Gunter's house with a pair of Zats and load them with weight to try to approximate how much weight it took to make that deep an impression in Gunter's grass. They have a new instrument that can impose a load on a specific object and determine how much weight or force is required to produce a specific action. Based upon other tests they have conducted, they are estimating the person who made the impressions weighed close to three hundred pounds. They then opine that a person weighing that much can't possibly fit into that small a shoe. So their premise is the person was carrying a weight externally on their body. We naturally are assuming that they were carrying Cameron's body."

I asked, "So once we get their results, we can deduct Cameron's known weight and come up with a close approximation of the weight of at least one of the suspects. I'm not sure what benefit we would derive from that, but it would give us one more piece of data."

My phone ringing interrupted any further conversation. "Jake Lowry here. How may I help you? Mr. Haynes, so nice to hear from you. We really didn't expect to have you call so soon. Michael is there and you're all ready to go to Cam's, house. We don't want to rush you but if you're sure, we'll meet you there in twenty minutes. Thanks! Goodbye."

"Well you heard my end. The Haynes are ready to go to Cameron's house. They want to do this as soon as possible to make sure his property is safe. After they check the house, the three of them are going to check on Cameron's birds. Gunter can you call Woody, go pick her up and meet David and me at Cameron's house?"

CHAPTER FIFTEEN

David, Ron, and I arrived at Cameron's house just one minute prior to the arrival of the Haynes. Gunter called on my cell to say they were five minutes out. I had made another mistake and not gotten the keys to the house from Gunter. I got out of my car and asked the Haynes to wait until Gunter and Woody arrived. Apologizing for my inept behavior.

Gunter pulled up and when Woody got out of the car Mrs. Haynes and she embraced and shared a few tears. Both saying how sorry they were. Ira was standing directly behind them and also muttering soft words, patting both of them on the back, and wiping his eyes. Michael stood to one side and was rather stoic. He did give Woody a sort of wave and head bob, but little else.

Gunter said, "I have the keys for the front door so we can go in when you're ready."

He opened the front door and stood to one side to allow Ron to do the video documentation of the walk-through. Ron entered and stared the video. Ira Haynes was second through the door followed by Debbie and Woody. Michael hung back and let David enter next. I followed Michael in and Gunter brought up the rear.

Ron said, "I've done the living room so if you'd look around now and see if you notice anything missing or out-of-place. If you do, please tell me what you see so I can do a close-up first. Then we'll discuss what you've seen and why it's unusual. I'll be taking a video record of your comments, so look directly into the camera when you make your comments. Michael, Jake tells me that you lived with Cameron for a while. Perhaps you should be the first observer/commentator."

Michael nodded and started walking around the perimeter of the living room from left to right. As he walked he muttered softly, "This is o.k., this is o.k., this is right, and yeah this is right."

Michael said, "I don't see anything missing or out of place. I've been gone for two months, so if Cam moved anything I don't see it out of place. I don't see anything missing either. Woody you have been here since I was. What do you think?"

Woody had been standing to one side. Silently observing the entire room. As Michael moved, she was nodding her head in conjunction to Michael's muttered comments.

"I agree with Michael. I don't see anything disturbed at all. The rocker has been moved slightly, but I'd expect that to be done if you were vacuuming. You can see a slight depression in the carpet where it was previously. I'd be glad to check to see if there's something wrong with it if you like Jake."

"That's alright. David, if you would put on the protective gloves that we use for checking junkies to prevent needle punctures, and check the cushions for anything out of the ordinary."

"I've got to run to the car and get them out of my 'War Bag.' Give me a minute."

Debbie Haynes asked, "What is a 'War Bag?' Were you boys expecting the burglars to be here? You don't think there will be any gunfire do you? Ira, I think we should leave if there is going to be shooting. Michael you should leave too."

"Mrs. Haynes, there isn't going to be any shooting. David and almost every law enforcement officer calls the bag in which they carry forms, evidence tags, nitrile gloves, spare batteries for their flashlights, tape measures, and other assorted junk that we use on the job, a 'War Bag.' I guess it's one of those 'Cop Speak' things that we fall into. No self- respecting cop can carry all the stuff he needs in a normal briefcase. So we get a special carrier bag with lots of pockets and dividers. Our terminology for that carrier over the years has become 'War Bag. I guess as a result of us fighting the war against crime. We didn't mean to alarm you."

"To answer your other questions, no we didn't expect the burglars to be here. The reason I asked David to put on the puncture proof gloves is to protect him from an accidental puncture. On the off chance that the killer or killers had made entry into Cam's house and set booby traps for us, we take every precaution we can to prevent injury. A simple needle stick contaminated with HIV can end an officer's career and seriously threaten his life. The few minutes it takes to don protective gloves are well worth the wait to see if there's a problem with the rocker. The person who killed Cam and the other victim are very wise. We're proceeding as rapidly as is safely possible, but the key word is safely.

David reentered the house carrying a large black nylon bag. He placed the bag on the floor beside the rocker and held up his hands showing that he had on gloves. He nodded to me and dropped to his knees beside the rocker. From his knees he went flat on the floor on his stomach and shone his flashlight under the rocker. Sweeping it left to right.

"I don't see any wires or anything hanging down from the rocker. There aren't any dust bunnies under the rocker either. So maybe Woody was right it might have been moved to vacuum. I'm going to slip my hand carefully down the sides of the cushion to see if I can feel anything. Here goes."

David slowly slipped his gloved hand down each side of the cushion. As he slid his hand down the left side he stopped suddenly.

"I've made contact with something that feels solid. Ron can you shine your video light directly down this left side for me? Maybe with a little extra illumination I can see what it is."

Ron moved over to shine his light down the cushion side.

"Ah ha! It's the spine of a magazine. Ron hand me a set of those long forceps in the right inside side pocket of my

'War Bag' please. I'll slowly start to extract the magazine. If I feel any resistance, I'll stop and have you all leave the house and call the bomb squad. If there's no resistance, I'll continue to remove it from the rocker."

The room was extremely tense as David slowly grabbed the spine of the magazine and began to lift it from the space between the cushion and side of the rocker. His movements were slow and very deliberate. With a huge sigh, he lifted the magazine clear and then let out a huge guffaw!

"I know this isn't a time for hilarity Mr. and Mrs. Haynes, but apparently Cameron was a 'Playboy' reader. As we all say when someone observes us doing that, 'I only read it for the stories.' I'm sure that's true in Cameron's case.

David placed the magazine on the coffee table and continued his search of the rocker. Again asking Ron to provide additional illumination as he gently probed the space on both sides of the cushion. He did bring out one piece of popcorn and one blue M&M.

"I think we have to go with Woody's observation. The rocker was moved for vacuuming. I guess we had this small bit of drama for nothing, but like Jake, I'd rather be overly cautious rather than sorry."

I said, "Let's go into Cam's bedroom if we can now. Ron, lead the way. It's kind of small so Ron you do the video first and then we'll let Mrs. Haynes in first, then Ira, and them Michael. If you see something out of place call Ron and he'll squeeze in to video your observations."

We repeated these procedures for the second bedroom, kitchen, and garage. Nothing seemed to be missing or out of place. In a locked metal locker in the garage, we did find a starter pistol that fired .22 caliber blanks and a 12 gauge shotgun. We ran the registration in the national computer to verify they were registered to Cameron. Michael took custody of the two guns.

We concluded the search and thanked the Haynes family for their quick and caring response. We secured the house and gave the key to Ira.

Gunter, Woody, David and I held a short de-briefing of what had transpired and all came to the conclusion that Cameron's house had not been entered illegally. Woody was a little shaken and said that she was surprised that entering the house had affected her that much.

"Maybe the sheriff was right. I do need a little personal time to deal with this. I'll be ready tomorrow night at the meeting. I want you three guys to tell him that I'm ready to return to full duty. If you don't I'm going to throw myself on the floor of the meeting room and have a 'Hissy Fit.' You know I'm kidding about the 'Fit' but I'm really serious about being ready."

Gunter said, "Don't throw that fit in my car, but I'm ready to take you home partner. You can count on me to speak favorably to the boss about you, but only if you promise not to throw a fit in my car."

"O.K. I guess I'm going to have to live with that 'Hissy Fit' comment for the rest of my life."

I said, "Oh no! We wouldn't do anything like that. We're too caring and sensitive of your feelings to kid you or create a continual jibe to a coworker."

"If I believe that, I'm also sure you have ocean front property to sell me located in Downtown Coeur d'Alene.

Gunter let's go! These guys need to head back to work and I need a little quiet time."

Gunter and Woody left. David and I followed. We arrived back at the office with just enough time to make our entries in the main frame computer, have a brief chat with Morgan and head out the door for home.

CHAPTER SIXTEEN

Tuesday, started exactly like every other day this week. I had just gotten in the office when the front desk called to say I had a package. I walked up to the front desk and there was a tan 8" X 10" envelope with my name on it. No return address. I asked where this had come from. The clerk said a young man about twenty came into the front desk at seven forty-five and asked for me. They said I wasn't available and he handed them the envelope and asked that I get it first thing. The envelope was flat but did have what felt like papers in it. There were no oily stains and my name was spelled correctly. Those are usually indicators of a letter bomb. I decided to take it to the evidence lab to see if they could x-ray it or at least scan it for presence of explosives.

No joy! The collective minds of the evidence techs said to call the bomb squad from Fairchild AFB to come and x-ray the package and also to use their explosives sniffer to see if it contained any trace elements of an explosive.

This was not on my schedule for today! Jay Bass call Fairchild and they said their ETA was an hour and a half. At least I didn't have to sit with the envelope on my lap for that period. I could go back to the bullpen and do some work. Jay secured the envelope in a fireproof safe. I went back to work.

This exercise had consumed over twenty minutes so my colleagues were already hard at work when I waltzed in.

"Good afternoon Jake, nice of you to join us. Did we miss the memo that we were to start today at eight not our usual two A.M.?" This remark came from my partner David.

"Sorry folks, I had a mystery package delivered to the front desk this morning. A flat envelope with what appeared to have papers in it, but no return address. It was hand delivered at seven forty-five. To be safe we've called the Fairchild, Bomb Squad and they're enroute, ETA about an hour and a half. Meanwhile, I thought I'd grace you with my presence. Anything happen in my absence?"

Gunter said, "Captain Nearing came in with a preliminary report on patrol's efforts to see if there has been a run on awls in our local hardware and tool supply stores. Sad to say no clerk on duty yesterday could remember selling an awl lately. They've asked the managers to query all cashiers to see if any of them remember selling an awl or group of awls recently. The managers will also check the computer print-outs of the registers to see if there were any awl sales."

Morgan added, "Well we're in luck! I have the written results from three separate translation services. They all say that there're many ways to say both "White Ghost" and "White Devil", but the way the note was signed is the more popular colloquial way of doing it." They lean toward "White Devil"

David jumped in, "Well we're all fountains of news this morning. I got a call from Coeur d'Alene P.D. they've found Cameron's truck. This is not good news. It was found, torched, outside Sagle. The possibility of evidence collection is just about nil. I've got an evidence tech assigned to accompany our contract tow company up to Sagle to collect it and bring it back here."

"If it didn't rain information it pours. Well that wraps up our investigative tasks for today. We might as well all go home. It seems that info pours in when we aren't here to receive it. I briefed the sheriff on the envelope and he briefed me on the sketch artist in Boise. Apparently Dr. Line's memory was pretty sketchy, no pun intended. The sketch artist has produced a likeness of both persons, but cautions us not to rely too heavily on his results. We should be getting a jpg attached to an email this morning. They will follow-up with a fax to make sure we get the best picture possible."

The phone rang. It was the front desk. Apparently the EOD (Explosive Ordnance Disposal) Squad made good time and were at the front desk. I walked to the front to escort them back to the evidence lab.

Senior Master Sergeant G. J. Hiwans, the leader of the team started asking me questions a few seconds after we met.

"Detective Lowry, do you have any known enemies? Did you shake the envelope? Did you smell any unusual odors emanating from the envelope? Do you want us to try to preserve the original envelope for fingerprints? Were you expecting any packages? How heavy was the envelope? Did you notice any oily spots on the envelope?"

"Hold on Sarge. You're firing them faster than I can answer them. Let me try to answer the questions in the order asked:

#1. I've locked up tons of people in my career. I'm sure that none of them love me. I don't get birthday or Christmas cards from any of them.

#2. I didn't vigorously shake the envelope. I did rustle it to see if I could feel any stiffness in it. I didn't feel anything other than what I would consider paper inside. I should have been more careful. I'm as little out of practice in being overly suspicious.

#3. I didn't detect any odor from the envelope.

#4. Depending on the procedures you need to perform and the contents of the envelope, preserving it might add to any subsequent investigation we might need to do.

#5. No. I wasn't expecting any packages. The front desk telling me I had one was a surprise.

#6. I would estimate the envelope at less than eight ounces. I'd say the normal weight for an envelope of that size containing papers.

#7. No oily spots. If I'd seen that in conjunction with no return address, I wouldn't have moved it from the spot I first saw it and you guys would have been called sooner than we did. That would have rekindled my suspicious gene and probably my paranoia gene right away."

"I think I got them all if not ask away."

"Nope you got them all. Where's the envelope now?"

"Here in the safe in the evidence lab."

We walked into the lab, as I said that and were greeted by Jay Bass. I introduced Sergeant Hiwans.

Jay asked, "Sarge how do you want to handle this? I've got the envelope locked in our portable, fireproof safe. Jake handled it in a pretty cavalier manner bringing it in here so I don't think we have to worry about mercury switches. We can put the safe on a hand truck and roll it outside if you like. We're at your disposal."

Sergeant Hiwans said, "I'll have one of my team suit-up in one of our protective suits. He'll take it outside to a safe place where we can begin our examination I would like for all of your personnel to evacuate the building until we get the safe to a pre-determined distance from the building. Even though Detective Lowry was lucky, unstable explosives have a mind of their own. I'd rather err on the side of safety."

I said, "That's going to be a problem. Although they are two separate entities, the Sheriff's Department and the jail are physically connected. There's no way, without much prior preparation, we can evacuate the jail. We have two saving graces. First and foremost is the evidence lab is on the opposite side of the building from the jail. Second, I defer to your superior knowledge of explosives; I've been involved with a few items that go boom in both my military and law enforcement careers. I've breached some doors, evaporated walls and other structural things using a wide variety of explosive materials. Based on my handling of the envelope, admittedly a bit cavalierly, there's no way that

that envelope can contain enough explosives to endanger people housed or working in the jail. As a precaution, we'll evacuate all personnel in this end of the building. I'll run my decision by the sheriff and get his concurrence, but I'm willing to assume the responsibility for the safety of all inmates and jail personnel."

"Detective Lowry, that's a big assumption. My team and I are fully briefed on the very latest explosive devices. Once you call us we assume all responsibility for identifying and safe handling of the device in question. I'll admit that I've never had someone tell me that they know a little bit about explosives while we were at a scene. I'm going to have to ponder this a bit. You call the sheriff. If he concurs with your estimate, I'm inclined to go along with you. I probably should call our regional commander to get his approval, but we'll just roll with the blow this time and proceed."

I called the sheriff and brought him up to speed. He concurred. He notified dispatch to make a public address announcement that we were having a fire drill to evacuate the building going out the front entrance and assembling in division groups for a proper headcount.

Sergeant Hiwans team member arrived in his huge olive drab bombproof suit complete with thick, shatterproof glass face shield helmet. Jay had rolled a hand truck in beside the safe. Sgt. Hiwans spoke to his man using a portable radio to the headset built into the helmet. We left the building. The bomb disposal guy also had a closed circuit television camera built into the helmet. He broadcast live pictures of his loading the safe onto the hand truck and wheeling it out the rear door of the department.

We were inside the bomb disposal truck with a panel of television monitors to watch every motion made. Hiwans explained that they taped all of these actions as training devices to show what to do properly and if something went wrong what not to do.

Hiwans asked Jay for the combination to the safe and repeated it to the disposal guy. We watched him gingerly open the safe. We could hear his breathing rate increase as the door swung open. The disposal team had driven their huge disposal trailer behind the building. It looked like a huge water tank lying on its side. The disposal specialist then took what appeared to be a microphone and waved it all around the envelope. Sgt. Hiwans said this was an explosive sniffer. It would detect even microscopic traces of all currently known explosives.

Once he'd used the sniffer, he reported to Sgt. Hiwans over the radio that the envelope was negative for explosives. He even more gingerly slid the envelope out of the safe, keeping it lying flat onto a flat square ceramic looking plate.

Hiwans said this was the carrier for the x-ray. He called for the portable x-ray machine. A second specialist in an identical bomb suit rolled the x-ray machine into view broadcasting from a second CCTV camera to the bomb disposal truck where we were seated with Sgt. Hiwans monitoring the action.

The specialists set-up the x-ray and passed it over the envelope. In just a few seconds Hiwans was looking at a picture of the contents on another television screen.

"Well folks it looks like there're just papers in the envelope. We see no dust or powder packet in the envelope or any type of trigger to propel any contents out of the envelope once it's opened. I'll have my men slit open the envelope at the bottom so as not to interfere with any possible DNA on the flap. The suits they're wearing have an internal re-breather system so if they have coated the paper with any type of substance it won't affect their breathing. We don't have the capability to test for contaminants and would caution you to put on breather devices and wear protective clothing prior to handing the papers if they're in any way suspicious."

"O.K. Boys slit the bottom open and extract the contents. What have you got?"

"Sarge this looks like a report of calls to 911 from the phone company. It lists the time, date, caller I.D. and length of time the caller was on the line. There's a 'Post It' that says. "Jake here's your list;" it has two initials 'T.T.' it looks legitimate."

"Detective Lowry were you expecting this?"

"I guess the correct answer is: Yes and No! I have a source in the phone company. In order to get this information it requires a search warrant. That takes time. We don't have time. We're trying to trace a 911 call that told us the location of a murder victim. I asked my source to do me a favor and get this on the 'Q.T.' so, yes. I was expecting it. No. I didn't think it would come this soon or in this manner. This usually costs me a lunch. I get the info in a manila folder at that lunch. This is the first time it's come in a plain brown envelope. You'd almost think I'd ordered porn or Viagra. The description the front desk gave of the delivery person could have been anyone. Now that I think back, it was probably my source's son."

"Guys, I can't apologize enough for this entire fiasco. I feel like a perfect fool."

Sergeant Hiwans said, "Detective, no one's perfect but this came pretty close. I'll have my men wrap-up this exercise and bring you in the envelope. Those suits are pretty hot and they'll be glad to get out of them. I will tell you, we'll be chuckling about this tomorrow, but today we'll still be shaking our heads all the way back to Fairchild."

"David, please call the sheriff and tell him that the 'fire drill' is over and we're all 'code four.' I'll wait here for the envelope. I want to personally thank the disposal guys for risking their lives for this phone data. As soon as I can, I'm calling 'T.T.' to extend our collective thanks for the prompt service."

I was truly grateful to the disposal specialists. They had willingly risked their lives or at least maiming to examine the envelope. Even though it turned out not to be harmful they didn't know that. How do you express gratitude to someone who will do that for a stranger? Not once in their entire life but sometimes multiple times daily. I was deeply humbled to be in the presence of these men.

I now had to focus on the phone logs that 'T.T.' had furnished. We knew the time and date so the examination didn't take much time. The anonymous call had come into dispatch on a "Pay as you Go" cell phone. It was virtually untraceable. In the investigation's business we term these phones, 'Throw Aways.' Every smart crook uses them for conducting their business and then literally throws them away. Reliable, untraceable, inexpensive, and considered the 'cost of doing business.'

We were at a dead-end on tracing. Our only hope now was to be able to match the voice recording that is automatically made of every 911 call with a possible suspect once we had identified either him or her.

Tuesday was turning into a lousy day!

Morgan came into the bullpen holding two pieces of paper over her head.

"I have both the fax and email from Boise P.D. the two sketches are very similar. I printed the jpg picture from the email. The fax transmitted pretty clearly also. I personally like the jpg from the email more. I think it'll reproduce better on our copy machines. The edges of the sketch are sharper. You boys take a look and see which you like."

We all took a look and concurred with Morgan that the jpg was the better source for making copies.

Our next issue was to find someone who resembled the persons drawn by the sketch artist. Close examination by all four of us didn't bring any startling revelations. We all agreed that Dr. Line's memory was indeed sketchy. Our likenesses could be any Jack or Jill from Any Street in Anyplace U.S.A.

Tuesday was really turning into a lousy day.

We all agreed on one item. It was definitely time for lunch. I being the 'dunce of the day' felt obligated to spring for the meal. Morgan suggested Michael D's. David suggested Pho Thanh. Gunter wanted to go back to Famous Willies in Post Falls. I was feeling slightly Oriental and suggested Takara on Lakeside Drive downtown for a Bento Box. Morgan was the only one of the group who knew what a Bento Box was and seconded my suggestion.

Enroute to Takara, with Gunter driving, Morgan and I conducted a very brief session on Bento Boxes, Miso soup and the joy of healthy eating. I had time prior to departure to call Liz to join us. She'd walk over and be there when we arrived. Takara was only two blocks from the art collective. When Liz walked in she asked our waitress for her name. She said her name was Emma. Liz asked where she had gotten her very attractive necklace. Emma said she had purchased it at the art collective on Sherman Avenue.

Liz said, "I thought I recognized it. It was made by one of our local artists. She collects the stones and casts them in silver. It's beautiful."

All five of us were seated in one of the small semi-private rooms on the left side of the restaurant. The room was created so you could sit on cushions with your feet in a depression under the table and still have the table at normal height. This simulated the traditional Japanese style of kneeling to eat your meal. Shoe removal was required prior to stepping into the room. Colorful cotton curtains with Japanese lettering and figures decorated the curtains, lending an air of authenticity to the setting. Hot green tea in jade colored stoneware mugs was brought to the table immediately. The day's special was Pork Tonkatsu, Tempura, Rice, Cabbage salad, and Teriyaki Beef. We all ordered the Bento Box. The Miso soup with small squares of tofu and small bits of green onion was steaming and delicious.

Lunch was over much too soon. I reluctantly said goodbye to Liz and got into the car for the return trip back to the office. After that great lunch, maybe Tuesday won't continue to be a bad day.

My opinion changed upon our arrival at the office.

Our contract tow operator had a new employee working on the tow truck. After they loaded Cameron's truck on the flatbed, he forgot to properly secure the winch. As they were traveling down route 95 at fifty miles an hour, the winch brake disengaged and Cameron's truck rolled off the flatbed. Luckily, it didn't hit any other vehicles. It did roll five times and is now a total loss. The extensive body and frame damage would preclude any additional efforts to inspect the interior for any items of evidence. Even though the truck had been burned and was essentially only good for a few salvageable parts, dropping it off the tow truck increased its worth to almost full value. The tow operator's insurance would reimburse the Haynes family for Cameron's truck. The accident may have been a blessing in disguise. They can use the money for other purposes and not have to look at Cameron's truck every day.

Hooray for Tuesday!

I called Ira to tell him the news. Ira was understanding and assured me that he would cooperate with the tow operator's insurance company. He wasn't out to make a killing due to their misfortune. That took a load off my mind.

David was at his desk when his phone rang.

"Detective David here. How may I help you? Ammo! How nice to hear from you. I sure hope you've got good news. Today hasn't been one of the best for our team. O.K. I'll put you on speakerphone. Hey guys listen up. Ammo has some news for us. O.K. Ammo you're on the speaker."

Sergeant Amadeus Vecchio, 'Ammo,' of the Kamloops Detachment, Royal Canadian Mounted Police has been a good friend and excellent source of investigative assistance. Ammo and his team, particularly Detective Onions, were instrumental in solving Ken Kunkle's murder. Ammo and his team accompanied us to Newcastle, England in pursuit of Nora Wallace. David had called him to ask Detective Onions to again exploit his U.K. sources for additional assistance in this case. I was hoping that Onions' sources had come through with information on Nora's friends or close relatives who may have recently immigrated to the U.S. If they hadn't immigrated, perhaps they were here on an extended vacation.

"Hello everyone. David said I was on the speaker so I'll continue with the small bits of information that I presently have. Detective Onions' contacts in the Oxford University area have emailed us some interesting tidbits. After we discuss what we have, I'll forward you copies of their emails.

#1. Nora Wallace had no siblings. We already knew this but this is confirmed for a second time.

#2. Nora had three cousins who were very close. Neighbors confirm that they initially thought the four were sisters and brothers. Two of the cousins were female, one, obviously was a male. Their names were Loni, the oldest; Ronnie, the male second in line; and finally; Amie. Loni and Ronnie could pass for twins. Their last names are Scudder.

#3. Amie resides in Manchester and was seen last weekend at the Wallace house. Loni and Ronnie allegedly immigrated to the U.S. or Canada over one year ago. They supposedly left on an 'Exceptional Skills Visa.' Onions' sources don't have any idea what the alleged 'Exceptional Skills' were.

#4. Thames Valley Police, they service the Oxford University area, are checking with the British Home Office

Consular Affairs Bureau to see exactly when they left the U.K. and what their final destination was.

#5. No member of the immediate Wallace family has been known to visit the columbarium where Nora's ashes are entombed. Nora's former neighborhood is a very close-knit community. People know when you buy facial tissue or a six-pack. They shop at Morrison's and Safeway. They drive an older Vauxhall.

#6. Mr. and Mrs. Wallace attend the local Church of England in their neighborhood and also attend any flower shows that occur in the immediate area. Other than that they are not very social. Not unfriendly, just not very social.

We've requested photos of the Scudder children. They should be forthcoming very soon. I wish I had more but that taps us out on information at the moment."

David spoke first, "Ammo we're indebted to you and Detective Onions again. Do you guys want to transfer down here to Kootenai County? If they offered raises for solving cases, you guys would be in line for a big one. We're anxiously awaiting the emails. My guess is you gave us all the info in the emails and that will just be paper confirmation. When you say that we can expect the photos of the Scudder kids soon, do you have an estimate?"

I jumped in next, "Ammo, I'm sure you have it, but you didn't mention the DOB's for the Scudders. Were they close to Nora's age?"

"Sorry Jake. Yes, we do have DOB's in the emails. Loni was two years older than Nora, Ronnie the same age and Amie one year younger. I've contacted our Federal Office for Consular Affairs to see if the Scudders are in Canada.

It'll take a couple of days for an answer to get back to me. You'll have the answer two minutes after we get it."

"We won't hold our breath, but we'll be anxiously awaiting that info. Anything else you haven't mentioned?

"Jake are you a mind reader, or has Onions given you a 'Heads-up Call' behind my back?"

"I haven't spoken with Detective Onions since we landed back here in Coeur d'Alene from Newcastle. So I'm in the dark still."

"O.K. I was saving the very best for last. Nora, Loni, and Ronnie attended a number of parties with Rori Atkins when she was attending Oxford. Onion's source commented that the parties were usually at the lodgings of the American students. The source, I'm sure you've realized it by now, was also a student at Oxford Veterinary College, particularly remembers a tall willowy redhead by the name of Emilee. She was the life of the party and seemed to have an attraction to Ronnie. The source can't remember them dating, but they were very close at the parties. I think the coincidence is, how shall I say it, remarkable! Has your Dr. Matile's sister-in-law mentioned any contact with the Scudders?"

"O.K. Ammo, You got us! No. Miss Emilee Tish Lukin has not mentioned any contact with Nora or the Scudders. You've just put the icing on the 'Proverbial Cake' for us here in Idaho. This is a lead we'll jump on with the full team and both feet. Thanks, is a too small and overused word for what you just gave us. Stay in touch! You'll get our results two minutes after we create some."

"Will do. I'm signing off now. Stay Safe!"

I looked around the room at the team. Each of us sat slightly thunderstruck. We still had Emilee Lukin on our 'Persons of Interest List' but she hadn't been at the top of the list. This news shot her to the top. I lifted my shoulders in the universal, 'What's up?' shrug and slowly looked into everyone's eyes.

Morgan folded first. "I never liked the stuff we were getting on Emilee. It was too pat and almost seemed like she was a too perfect 'Goody Two-Shoes.' Maybe we should think about Heidi's safety since we willingly sent her to Emilee's house."

"If we rush over there and jerk her out of the house, we'll alert Emilee to our suspicions. David, maybe you and I should drop by Emilee's house and assure Heidi that we've determined it's safe for her to return home. We could even offer to give her a ride. Once we get her in our vehicle, we'll squirrel her away in a safe place. Then we can bring in Emilee for some serious questioning. It's getting toward the end of the day. We could do that short rescue mission on the way home and plan on bringing in Emilee first thing in the morning. How's that set with you?"

"Good plan! With one exception, you have to go down the hall and get the sheriff's approval for a 'Safe House' expenditure. That means a secure motel, meals, and an officer inside the motel or in the room next door. Gunter and I'll put Heidi in my car while you do the paperwork and begging. Once you get approval, call me on my cell and give us the name of the motel. I'm sure that Heidi will want to go by her house to pick up some other clothes. What do you think? Is that going to be safe?"

Woody spoke up, "I have a better idea. Why don't David and I go to Emilee's? Heidi and I sort of bonded on our initial meeting. Once she's in our car, she can tell me what clothes she wants. I'll go to her house and get the clothes. Gunter can park about two blocks from Emilee's and I'll take his car and he can jump in with David and Heidi. That way we have two officers with Heidi and I can meet the three of you at the 'Safe House.'"

"Woody you're a genius. I'm off to see the boss and do my begging. You folks get rolling. David, you're the point of contact. I'll call you the minute I get approval for the 'Safe House.' We'll meet at the motel and I'll brief Heidi. This is going to be rough. Larry dead and now we suspect her sister of possible collusion with potential suspects."

They entered their assigned cars and departed for Post Falls. I walked down the hall to brief the sheriff and beg for money to establish a 'Safe house' for Heidi.

A 'Safe House' is a term that is used rather loosely on TV. If you have a threatened witness of victim you need to establish lodging that is secure and not readily visible to the potential stalker or persons wishing to do them harm. Contrary to popular belief high-end hotels are not used, too visible and too much traffic. The ideal 'Safe House' would be a quiet country cottage filled with nice Craftsman style furniture, miles from well traveled roads, surrounded by an eight-foot electrified wire fence, and patrolled by vicious dogs.

In addition to being impracticable and very expensive, those properties only exist on film and TV. The reality is that you look for a three star hotel or motel in a nearby town that has adjoining rooms. A well lit parking facility and discrete desk clerks that can't be bought or intimidated by the bad guys.

The second issue is the staffing it requires to assure that your witness or victim is kept safe. You need five officers to staff a 'Safe House' for one week. This allows for days-off, possible illness and other unforeseen emergencies. If you work the officers on a twelve hour-on and twelve hour-off schedule, you can get by with four officers. After two seven-day periods even this schedule wears on morale and physical readiness.

My hope is that we wouldn't have to keep Heidi in a 'Safe House' that long.

The sheriff assured me that we would have the necessary money and personnel to facilitate Heidi's safety. Spokane Valley and Liberty Lake, Washington are west of Coeur d'Alene and meet the necessary criteria. The City of Spokane was only ten miles further west than Spokane Valley and had more choices and would still be a reasonable drive. It was large enough to allow Heidi to leave the motel and not become a victim to 'Cabin Fever.'

I called David on his cell and told him to head for the east end of Spokane. I would meet him at I90 and Division in Spokane to select a suitable destination. Woody called to say that Heidi has asked for additional clothing. She was enroute to her house to get the desired items. I asked her to wait until I could meet her on Sherman Avenue and we'd go in together as a safety precaution. I had a niggling feeling at the back of my neck that caused me to be overly cautious. Maybe Sergeant Hiwans had awakened my paranoia genes.

Woody and I rendezvoused, collected Heidi's clothing without incident. She'd volunteered to take the first watch at the 'Safe House' and followed me to Spokane. We were sure burning a lot of gas and overtime but safety wasn't cheap.

I selected a chain motel just below Sacred Heart Hospital. They catered to families that had patients in either Sacred Heart or Providence Hospitals. There were near-by restaurants and convenient parking. Our undercover vehicles would not stand out in a long line of vehicles and it had quick and easy freeway access.

The rooms were clean, spacious, and furnished in typical modern motel style. They had an indoor pool, cable television, and fitness room. A big plus is that it would not drive the sheriff's department into bankruptcy. We checked Heidi and Woody in under a suitable alias. Woody took Heidi to dinner and we started the drive home.

CHAPTER SEVENTEEN

Due to serious scheduling difficulties, our evening meeting had to be moved up to a morning meeting. We'd decided that a ten o'clock meeting would look more casual than trying to get everyone in the conference room at eight. This would allow commanders to put out any early morning fires before leaving for the joint agency meeting. Everyone had followed the sheriff's request and arrived in business casual clothing. No holsters or badges in sight. When law enforcement agencies really apply themselves, they can produce real undercover vehicles. Usually they have a close connection with a vehicle rental agency or used car dealer.

I was working undercover in Oakland and needed a clean car for a major buy. We had a good relationship with a small used car dealer and he provided an older Mustang.

It was shiny and looked like a good dope dealer's ride. Unfortunately there was an electrical short in the steering system so if you turned left it would short out the engine and the car would stop. I had to plot my trip to the meet site and then with the seller to the buy site by making only right turns. My cover officers had a good laugh once we finished the deal and returned the car to the dealer. He wasn't aware of the electrical problem and thanked us for making him aware of it before he sold the car.

Patti Nelson had arranged for coffee, juice, and finger sandwiches to be provided. Everyone took seats and we closed the doors to the conference room. After the manager personally checked to make sure we had everything we needed for our meeting.

Everyone was on time except Dr. Hardcastle, the coroner. The sheriff asked Patti to call his office to see if he was delayed.

He decided to start the meeting and said that Hardcastle could catch-up when he arrived.

"Good morning Ladies and Gentlemen. Thank you for arranging your schedules to make this meeting. As I'm sure you are aware, we've had two murders in Kootenai County that have all the indications of a serial killing. Late last evening we had additional information that caused us to place the wife of the first victim in protective custody for her safety. Before we start I'd ask you to place your cell phones on vibrate so we can begin the briefing. All of you personally, or members of your agency or department contributed to the Ken Kunkle murder investigation. We're convinced that our two recent murders are directly connected to Nora Wallace, the murderess in that case. I'll turn the remainder of the briefing over to Detective Jake Lowry and his team. Jake take it away!"

"Good morning! Thank you for coming. I'll give a quick recap to bring everyone up to date. Our first victim, Dr. Lawrence Matile, was Nora Wallace's former employer. He led us to his office where we discovered leather straps identical to the strap that confined Ken Kunkle in the tanning bed. Dr. Matile was killed by having an awl plunged into his heart. His body was positioned against the rock wall of the house formerly owned by Ken Kunkle. Our second victim Cameron Haynes is a close friend of Detective Woody McNair who was part of the protective detail for the Kunkle family. Cameron was also killed by having an awl plunged into his heart. The unusual twist to that murder is that there was a note affixed to his body by the awl. It said: *Nora Gone? That's a Folie A Deux.* It was signed with the name *Fahn Quai*. We've had that translated. If you'll look at the screen you'll see that 'Folie A Deux' translates to 'A Shared Delusion.' and 'Fahn Quai' translated to 'White Devil' or 'White Ghost'."

"We've checked the moniker, alias, and nickname files locally, with ISP, and the FBI. They have no matching name. We're at a dead end with Fahn Quai. Our sources in the U.K. can't find any Chinese associates of Nora Wallace nor can they discern she had any unusual interest in things Oriental. When we searched her residence after we returned from England, there was no indication of any Oriental connections in her possessions. We shipped her property to her parents so we can't go back and do a re-examination for something we might have missed."

"Last night Sergeant Amadeus Vecchio of the Kamloops Detachment, Royal Canadian Mounted Police called, Sgt. Vecchio goes by the nickname "Ammo." Ammo was also instrumental in pursuing Nora. Just to jog your memory, Nora murdered Ken Kunkle and Stuart Lynne here in Kootenai County and attempted to kill Darlene McDonagh. She also murdered Nigel Patrick in Kamloops, B.C., Canada. We're sure you're aware that Nora committed suicide and killed Angus Wickley incidental to her driving the Jaguar off the dock into Seaton Sluice."

"Every member of the team was present when we brought the Jaguar out of the North Sea and we all verified that the female inside was Nora Wallace. I personally attended the autopsy conducted in the presence of Inspector Robbie Forbes. There's no doubt in our minds that Nora is dead."

"Ammo has learned that Nora had three close cousins. Ronnie, Loni and Amie Scudder. Ronnie and Loni could pass for twins; Amie is currently in Manchester, England. Ronnie and Loni received visas to enter the U.S. and Canada. We're at present unsure of their physical location. Interestingly enough, Dr. Matile's wife's sister, Emilee Tish Lukin, attended Oxford University Veterinary College at the same time that Nora's friend, Rori Atkins, did. Nora, Ronnie, and Loni attended parties at the dormitory used by American students at the college. Ammo's sources said that there appeared to be a close attachment between Nora and Ronnie and Ronnie and Emilee"

Gunter was fidgeting at the back of the room and finally raised his hand to interrupt.

"I apologize for the interruption, but I got a text message from my wife marked '911'

That's a signal there's a dire emergency at my house. I sent a text back and have distressing news. A jogger was running on the beach by our house and saw a man slumped against our wall. He checked on him to see if he was O.K. the man was dead. The jogger knocked on our door and Rebecca called the sheriff's office. A deputy has responded and the victim is Dr. Hardcastle. He's been killed by having what appears to be an ice pick stabbed into his heart. They've frozen the scene. I'm sure all of us will be getting calls immediately."

As Gunter finished the sentence most of the members of the sheriff's department were reaching for their cell phones. Some had text messages, some voice mail.

The sheriff rose and apologized while we tended to business. It was decided after a short conference that we'd leave Woody to finish the briefing. She had gotten some sleep at the motel and been relieved by another deputy at eight this morning. Woody knew all the details as well as any of us did and could handle anything thrown at her by the other agencies. David, Gunter, Jay Bass, Sherry Lee, and I would roll toward the office and trade our clean cars for our assigned vehicles and go directly to the crime scene.

CHAPTER EIGHTEEN

Dr. Hardcastle was posed exactly like Lawrence Matile and Cameron Haynes. There was an identical awl not an ice pick plunged into his heart and there was a note attached to his chest by the awl. The note read: "***NORA LIVES! YOU WILL NOT!***" It was signed again by ***"FAHN QUAI"*** but this time, there were Chinese characters stamped after the name.

We didn't have a clue what they meant.

Jay and Sherry began processing the scene. We had little chance of collecting any meaningful shoe impressions. The jogger and responding deputy had wiped out any chance of an uncontaminated crime scene. Jay taped a large sheet of brown paper over the note and then covered the brown paper with an even larger sheet of plastic. This would protect the note form any additional contamination when we moved the body to the morgue. The issue facing us now was who would conduct the autopsy. Gunter excused himself and went to his house to check on Rebecca. Rebecca had texted Gunter to say that she had asked the jogger to wait for the sheriff's department. The responding deputy had placed him in his marked unit. The jogger would be David's and my next source of inquiry. I called dispatch on my cell and asked for a body transport to roll code one so we didn't attract undue attention. They advised it would be fifteen minutes. The ambulance crews were working a traffic collision on State Route 95 at the east end of the lake. Route 95 wasn't called 'Blood Alley' for nothing. The politicians had been promising widening on that road for years. Some of it had been widened, but it still was two lanes over rolling hills for miles. Impatient drivers would try to pass. Fatal collisions were all too frequent. While we were waiting for the body transport David and I brought the jogger out of the marked unit and seated him in my car.

"Hello, I'm Detective Jake Lowry with the Kootenai County Sheriff's Department. This gentleman is my partner Detective Bruce David. We appreciate your sticking around to talk to us. This probably messed up your run didn't it?"

"You might say that. I've never seen a dead person before. I think I'm still in shock. Would you mind if I borrowed your cell phone to call my wife to tell her why I'm so slow coming home. I usually run for an hour, sometimes maybe an hour and a half. It's been over two hours since I left home in Fernan."

"Of course, if you'll give me the number, I'll dial it for you. I'll even talk to your wife to explain if that will help. Before we do that I'll have to ask your name and basic information. Would you state your name and spell your last name please?"

"My name is Brian Fox. Fox F.- O. -.X. I live at 334 French Gulch Rd. in Fernan. My phone number is 208 664 6456. My wife's name is Annalee. I'd appreciate it if you'd call her. She might believe that I stopped off at a bar instead of doing my jog."

David pulled out his cell and dialed the number. He put the phone on speaker. A strong female voice answered

"Good afternoon. This is Annalee who is calling please?"

Mrs. Fox, I'm Detective Bruce David. Your husband Brian is O.K. but we've asked him to stay here with us for a few minutes. He was a witness to a crime. We interrupted his jog so he could answer some pertinent questions. Brian asked me to call you so you wouldn't worry. I'll put him on the phone if you want to speak with him. You're on speaker."

David handed the phone to Brian and he went along with the witness story. He handed the phone back to David. David assured Annalee that Brian would be driven home in about thirty minutes.

"Brian, would you please tell Detective David and me what you saw and how you happened to be jogging on the beach?"

"Sure, I'm training for the Coeur d'Alene Marathon. Running on the beach tightens my legs and allows me to get in condensed training. I know I'm not supposed to run on this part of the beach because it's private but I've been doing it for about two weeks and no one has said anything yet. By running on this private part, I can do about six full miles of sand running by going out and back. I alternate with running one day and biking on alternate days. I swim at the community pool every evening after work. I don't anticipate winning, but I would like to finish in a respectable time."

"Brian that's great, but we need to hear what you saw."

"Oh! Sorry! I left the house about nine thirty. Today is my late day I go in to work at one and work until nine tonight when the store closes. I work at Best Buy in the Valley. I was making good time when I see this guy slumped against the rock wall. His head was sort of slumped to the right and his posture didn't look normal. I know that a dead guy was found here not too long ago so I was suspicious. I stopped jogging and walked over to him and asked if he was O.K.? I didn't get a response and shook him by the shoulder. He just fell over and I saw the ice pick sticking out of his chest with the note. I jumped back and ran to the house. I knocked on the door and some woman's voice asked who I was through the closed door. I told her that there was a dead guy out here and she said she would call 911. I didn't know what to do. In a few minutes the lady hollered through the door for me to wait here for the sheriff's officer to arrive. A deputy drove up in a sheriff's car and asked me to sit in the back seat. I've been there until you guys opened the door and brought me over to this car. That's about it."

"Brian that was great. We'll need to verify your employment and would like for you not to discuss this information with anyone else. We'll drive you home now. If you'll tell us the proper turns to make we'll have you home in less than ten minutes."

I was at the wheel and David was in the back seat. Brian gave us the directions and we walked him to his front door. His wife answered our knock. We identified ourselves and assured her that Brian wasn't in trouble. We shook hands and left them to chat. As we were driving away, David asked if I thought that Annalee and Brian looked very much alike. I agreed and said that the old adage that dogs and owners tend to resemble each other after a while may apply to young marrieds too. We returned to the crime scene so David could pick-up his car and make sure that either Jay or Sherry rode to the morgue with Dr. Hardcastle's body. Gunter would do a loose surveillance on Brian Fox to make sure he left for work at Best Buy. Brian hadn't seen Gunter so a loose surveillance would work. Although Brian had a pat story, it just seemed too pat. Neither Gunter nor Rebecca has reported seeing any tracks on their beach in the past two weeks.

The ambulance had just arrived as we drove up. Sherry volunteered to ride with the body. Jay would drive the evidence van. David would follow the ambulance to the morgue and I'd return to the office.

What David had said was replaying over and over in my head. Brian and Annalee could have passed for twins. Why did twins keep ringing in my head? I couldn't shake the odd feeling.

When I got to the office none of the departmental members had arrived from the meeting. The bullpen was quiet. I thought that the meeting would've ended by now and called Woody's cell. She answered on the second ring.

"Hi Jake, what can I do for you? Morgan and I are about ten minutes from the office. Were you worried about me handling the briefing? It went like a breeze. The Boss stepped up and got commitments from the other agency chiefs to lend us personnel and equipment as we need it. I'll fill you in when I get there."

"Right! I also have some news for you but it'll keep until you arrive."

As promised, Woody and Morgan walked into the detective division in ten minutes.

Woody went first. "The Boss really went to bat for us and put the squeeze on the other agencies. The Coeur d'Alene Chief has detailed three detectives to report here tomorrow at eight. ISP has again promised full access to their lab for any forensics we need to run. We have standing offers for clean cars from Liberty Lake and Spokane. Spokane Valley has received a grant from the Feds. They have all of the latest digital video and still camera gear plus top of the line CCTV equipment. I have a list of contact numbers and the sheriff says for any of us to make direct contact without going through him. I think we did pretty well. Now tell us your news."

While Woody was relaying her information, Morgan had gone to her desk to check incoming email and to the fax machine for any new transmissions. She came jogging back to the bullpen waving a sheaf of papers.

"We've received Ammo's email and fax with the photos of the Scudders. With this new hard data we can distribute copies of their pictures to patrol and to all of the other agencies. We could get lucky and someone might spot them."

Morgan handed a copy of the papers to Woody and me and then walked over to David and Gunter's desk. I was thumbing through the emails and came to the fax copies of the photos.

"Guys, we don't have to get lucky. I just had Ronnie Scudder in my car. I met Loni at their home. Gunter is waiting to do a loose surveillance on Brian Fox or as we now know him, Ronnie Scudder as we speak. I'm calling Gunter right now to give him a heads–up."

"Gunter, Jake here. Has Fox left his house yet?"

"Actually both Fox and his wife just left. I'm running their plates as we speak. She's driving. They just got on I-90 heading west. They're running at the speed limit and driving normally. Why do you ask? Wait a minute! Dispatch is calling me with the DMV info. Hold on. The plates come back to Nicole Logan at 334 French Gulch Rd in Fernan. The vehicle matches a 2007 Dodge Durango. That's what they're driving. Did Fox mention they had a roommate?"

"Gunter, where are you right now? Woody, David, and I are heading for your position right now. Please don't lose Fox. Just a warning, Fox isn't Fox! He and his wife are Loni and Ronnie Scudder. We just got the fax from Ammo. I had a weird feeling in the back of my head when I met them. I said to David that they looked like twins. Remember what Ammo told us? Stay loose but keep them in sight. We're rolling right now! P.S. I'm convinced that Brian Fox killed Dr. Hardcastle. I think his intention was to also kill Rebecca, but her caution in not opening the door may have saved her life."

"Jake, I'll keep you advised as we roll. I may tighten up the surveillance to make sure I keep them in sight. We're passing the Fourth Street Overpass now. Speed at seventy. Traffic's light. They're in the left hand lane. I don't think they've spotted me. I'm five cars behind them."

As we dashed out the door, I yelled at Morgan to notify dispatch that we were going to Tactical Channel Two. Tac Two is a scrambled channel. This will prevent any civilians with police scanners from monitoring our discussions. It will also prevent the media from monitoring this surveillance and trying to video it as it developed.

Once I was in the car and switched over to Tac Two, I asked dispatch to alert Post Falls, Liberty Lake and Spokane Valley that we had an active surveillance of two possible murder suspects and could be entering their jurisdictions. All three of us rolled down Government Way code three, lights and sirens going full blast. I hate traveling in the city code three but we couldn't afford to lose the Scudders. Gunter had about ten minutes start on us. Code three was our only possible way to catch him on I-90.

"Jake, passing Highway 41. Speed at seventy. Still in the left lane. Ronnie has crawled over the front seat and seems to be changing clothes as Loni drives. He left the house wearing a Best Buy shirt but it looks like he is putting on sweats. I'm too far back to be certain. You guys better hurry, I don't want to get burned."

"Gunter we're on I-90, rolling code three. Just passing Northwest Boulevard. We'll shut down as we get closer. I've alerted Post Falls, Liberty Lake and Spokane Valley. They'll have marked units sitting on the off-ramps if we need them. Stay loose until we're closer. We don't want to heat them up and force them to do something stupid."

"Got it! I'm loose! You guys keep coming. I can't hear your sirens so code three is still cool."

"All units, a quick reminder, at present, the Scudders are only suspects. We have no proof they have committed any crime. I'm having dispatch send two marked units to the Fernan address. We need to see if the registered owner of the Durango the Scudders are driving is O.K. We have no probable cause for a traffic stop unless they commit a traffic violation. The only thing we can do is follow them. I'm going to ask for additional unmarked units to join in the surveillance from Liberty Lake, Spokane Valley, and ISP. It might take them a while to scramble their detectives so it's up to us four to keep them in sight."

"Jake, passing Spokane Street. Speed up to seventy-five, Left lane. Ronnie is back in the front seat."

"We're just passing Seltice. We're going to shut down our sirens. Gunter can you hear them yet?"

"No you're still cool. Traffic seems to be running at seventy-five. Even though the limit is seventy. They're still in the left lane. They're getting all the breaks with the traffic. I haven't seen Loni flash her lights to make anyone move over. They're just lucky. I'm trying not to weave in and out of the lanes so I won't attract any undue attention. I'm six cars back."

"We're running code two with all lights active. Passing Cabelas. Liberty Lake has an unmarked at the on-ramp to assist you. Re-broadcast the plate number and vehicle description so they can join in."

"Here goes! Vehicle is a grey 2007 Dodge Durango with Idaho license: Kilo, niner, niner, six, two, Adam Bravo. We're currently passing the Liberty Lake Off-Ramp in the left lane at seventy-four miles an hour. Liberty Lake please provide your vehicle description so I can ease back."

"Kootenai County, Liberty Lake Delta Three here. I'm driving a Green Hyundai Sonata. Washington Plate: John, Paul, Mary, one, niner, three. I've got you in sight. I'll do a 'header surveillance.' Passing the subject vehicle as I speak. I've got a remote mike switch on the floor and mike in the headliner. I'm wearing a blue tooth so it looks like I'm on my cell phone. Kootenai you can ease off. Delta Three is on the job."

"Welcome aboard Delta Three! I'm Detective Jake Lowry, Kootenai County, Call sign: Delta six. We appreciate the help. At this point, our targets are merely suspects. We have no probable cause for a traffic stop. If and this is a hopeful IF, they commit a moving violation, we can stop them using a marked unit. We have two marked units enroute to the registered vehicle owner's residence to verify her well-being. We'll keep you advised."

The three of us caught up with Gunter and the Liberty Lake detective just as they crossed the Spokane Valley Line. We now had five cars for the surveillance. The suspects did not take the Sullivan Road/Spokane Valley Mall off-ramp. The speed limit dropped to sixty MPH just before the Valley marker. The suspects had reduced their speed. There was a second option to drive to Best Buy. They could take the next off-ramp and approach Best Buy on the outer circle road. If they didn't take that off –ramp then Best Buy wasn't their actual destination and we had a problem.

"Kootenai County, This is Spokane Valley Detective Rick Elm, Delta 12 on Tac Two. I've been detailed to assist in the surveillance of your suspects. I've been monitoring

Tac Two. I'm at the I-90 and Pine off-ramp. If they continue on I-90, I can pick them up. I'm in a Cobalt Blue Chevy Monte Carlo, Washington License Oscar Mike Bravo Six Two Eight. I've got your Durango in sight. Liberty Delta Three I'll slide in behind the target and you can ease off."

"Delta Three easing off. Welcome aboard Valley Delta 12. You've got the point."

"Kootenai Delta Six, Valley Delta Twelve I'm behind you in a green Mercury. Idaho license Kilo Fiver, Four, Two, Niner, Six One. You can pull back a bit. Gunter Fall in behind me. Woody, you're clean take the 'header' in the left lane and hold at sixty so no one can pop in between us and the target. They're obviously not going to Best Buy. I'm calling dispatch on my cell to see if they've heard from the two uniforms sent to Nicole Logan's house. Most marked units don't have Tac Two so we're going to have to rely on dispatch for a relay of info."

I made the call that temporarily distracted me from the surveillance.

Delta twelve came on the air screaming, "They have made a "U" turn on the shoulder. They're going the wrong way on the Argonne On-Ramp. Any units approaching Argonne take the off-ramp and pick them up. I can't follow. I'm too far past the on-ramp."

Woody answered, "I'm stuck in the left lane and can't change lanes fast enough. Gunter, David can you pick them up?"

David said, "I just passed the off-ramp. I'll try to back-up on the shoulder, but I'll be way behind unless they crash going up the on-ramp. Gunter can you make the off-ramp?"

Gunter said, "I'm on the off-ramp with about six cars ahead of me. I'm going code three to see if I can pick them up. At least we have a traffic violation to make a car stop."

"All surveillance units. This is Kootenai Delta Six. Hold your traffic. Gunter do you have them?"

"Jake they have stopped all the traffic on the on-ramp. They're on the far side of the on-ramp I can't see the Durango. I'm slowly making my way across Argonne but traffic is heavy. Going is slow. I got the Durango in sight! People are getting out of their vehicles. Something is going on! I need some help. Anyone who can get here come quick! The Durango is empty!"

"Jake they've car-jacked a red Mustang. They're headed south on Argonne. I can't get to them. We need Spokane Sheriff and Spokane Valley marked units here now. This is a mess. I'm trying to get the plate on the Mustang. They took the car at gunpoint. No one injured, but the owner is rattled. The license plate is Washington Personalized: Two Cute. That's Tango, Whiskey, Oscar, Charlie, Uniform, Tango, Echo. Come on guys I really need some help! This is a real mess."

David had been able to back up on the shoulder and turned on his lights and siren. The Argonne intersection with I-90 is a veritable "Spaghetti Bowl" at the best of times. A car driving up the on-ramp the wrong way and then abandoning their vehicle on the shoulder and car-jacking another vehicle made a bad situation even worse. David had to crawl across the six lanes of Argonne traffic to get to Gunter on the on-ramp. His emergency lights and siren were of little use. Woody, Liberty Delta Three, and Valley Delta Twelve went to the next intersection and doubled back. They were now trying to muscle through the traffic jam stretching across the overpass on the south side of I-90 caused by the activity on the north side of Argonne. I took the same route the suspects had taken and drove up the on-ramp in the wrong direction. Traffic had come to a complete standstill so my highly illegal maneuver didn't put any innocent citizens in danger.

David, Gunter and I were trying to sort out the traffic, identify any viable witnesses, and calm down the car-jacking victim. We really needed assistance from marked units to clear up the ever-increasing traffic jam stretching north and south on Argonne.

I grabbed my cell and called an old friend, John Preston. John was the coordinator for the Spokane County Sheriff's Helicopter Support Unit. If the Sheriff's chopper was up they would have a better chance of spotting the Mustang than we would trying to play 'catch-up' on the many surface streets running east and west off Argonne.

"John Preston here how may I help you?"

"John, its Jake Lowry. I need some helicopter assistance. We're on Argonne and our suspects just car jacked a Mustang. Is your bird in the air?"

"Yes it's on the southwest side of the county. They had a multiple vehicle crash and they were on-scene to provide med-evac if needed. I can scramble them now. They just cleared the scene. Give me the make model and plate on the vehicle."

"It's a red Mustang. Washington Personalized: Two Cute. That's Tango, Whiskey, Oscar, Charlie, Uniform, Tango Echo. My partner is talking to the victim as we speak. Once you get the bird enroute, I'll fill you in."

A few seconds went by and my cell was quiet except for John's voice talking to the chopper. He came back on the line.

"Birds on the way. Give me some details. I'll have to brief my sheriff. Normally we wouldn't scramble on that little bit of info, but since we go way back I trust your judgment Jake."

"Thanks for the vote of confidence. I need some morale boosting right now. We had a six-car surveillance of a possible serial killer couple that we followed from Coeur d'Alene. They were only suspects. We had no probable cause for a stop. We've had three identical murders in our jurisdiction and the male allegedly found the third victim while jogging. We now think he was using a ruse to enter the house and commit the fourth murder. Liberty Lake and Spokane Valley loaned us two detectives to supplement our rolling surveillance. The male suspect allegedly worked at Best Buy in the Valley and was enroute to work. They passed the Sullivan and Evergreen off-ramps and made an illegal "U" turn and went up the Argonne on-ramp. That created a massive traffic jam and we had only one car that could make the off-ramp. Everyone else was out of position. They capitalized on the confusion and car jacked the Mustang at gunpoint. Thus far this is the only crime to provide probable cause for a stop and arrest. The vehicle they were driving came back registered to a Nicole Logan at the address the male suspect provided. I have two marked units enroute to that address to check on Logan's well being. My partner and I are trying to sort out the viable witnesses and calm the victim. I've sent three of my team and the two Detectives from Liberty Lake and the

Valley south on Argonne to begin the search, but you know that area it is full of side streets and will be like looking for the proverbial 'needle.'"

"Got it. That's enough to brief the boss. What frequency are you working and what's your call sign? I'll have the chopper notify you when they are two minutes out."

"We're working on Tac Two and my call sign is Kootenai Delta Six. Thanks John! I owe you big time"

"If my bird spots your Mustang, I'll expect a big steak at your house with Liz doing the cooking. I've seen how you operate the grill."

"That's a deal even if your bird isn't successful."

Gunter had identified two good witnesses. He had them pull their cars to the far right shoulder of the Argonne on-ramp so traffic could begin to flow. He had placed the victim in his car to allow her to calm down. I'd driven up the right hand shoulder so my vehicle was facing Gunter's. I got in Gunter's car to talk to the victim.

"Good afternoon Ma am. I'm Detective Jake Lowry from the Kootenai County Sheriff's Department in Coeur d'Alene, Idaho. I'm so sorry for what happened to you. It must have been terrifying! My partner and I are so happy that you weren't physically hurt. I've had a few guns pointed at me in my professional career and I can vividly recall each instance. I know this is a difficult time, but we need some information from you to provide that data to the Spokane County Sheriff's' helicopter. They're joining the search for your car. I can say that with rare exception car jacked vehicles are usually recovered intact. So there's hope."

"First of all we do have your license plate. Can you tell us the year of the Mustang?"

"Yes it's a nineteen sixty seven Mustang. It belonged to my Dad. He bought it brand new from Wendle Ford in Spokane. He loved that car and took such good care of it. I love that car and have also taken good care of it. It only has six thousand original miles on it. It's sort of like the old story about the 'Little Old Lady from Pasadena' Dad only drove it on weekends. I usually do the same. I was on the way to the dealer on Sprague for an oil change."

"Wow! That makes it an extremely valuable vehicle. May I have your name please?"

"I told the other officer. My name is 'Reta' Duggan. It's actually Lareta but I go by 'Reta'.

"Do you want to see my driver's license? Luckily, when they stole my car they let me keep my purse. The woman made the man give me my purse off the back seat. He was the mean one of the two. She was scary too don't get me wrong. He had the gun and kept waving it in my face screaming for me to, "Get out! Get out!" I was terrified. I'm still shaking! The woman jerked open the passenger's door and was pushing me against the driver's door while he was trying to open it. I usually keep both doors locked but I had just left a friend's house and they had been in the passenger's seat. The driver's door was locked but I had the window rolled down a little. I thought he was going to shoot me through the open window."

"There is assistance available for victims of a crime. I'm sure that we can arrange some counseling. As I said earlier, you'll remember this day for a long time. I know that counseling helped me. We are going to arrange for you to be transported to your home. My partner, Gunter Lenca, is getting details from the other witnesses and I've called for another member of our department to come and take you home. We'll keep you advised on the status of your car. Excuse me, please, I just got a notice that the helicopter is two minutes away from here and will start the air search for your car. We have also broadcast a BOL to all local agencies for your car."

"What is a BOL?"

"I'm sorry cops get in the habit of speaking jargon. A BOL is a BE On the Lookout. All local agencies have the license plate and vehicle description of your car and will stop it if they spot it. The helicopter greatly increases our chance of spotting it. They can fly faster than we can drive and cover more territory. I'll be frank. The suspects have a good lead on us so it may take a while. If they're desperate, they may try to car jack another vehicle."

"Oh I hope not. I don't want anyone else to have to go through that. It's a horrible experience."

"Reta, I agree with you. I'm betting on good luck that we'll spot the Mustang and can arrest them without any problem. A helicopter hovering overhead tends to discourage irresponsible behavior. If you'll excuse me I'm expecting a call from dispatch. While I'm in my car, I'll check on the ETA of our officer."

"I know ETA that stands for Estimated Time of Arrival. I guess some jargon does cross career paths."

"You're correct. I'll be back in a flash."

"Dispatch Delta Six here. What's the ETA on a unit to transport our carjacking victim?

"Delta Six ETA five minutes. The sheriff told us to dispatch a female unit to hopefully commiserate with the victim. It'll be Lima Thirty. How's the Vic holding up?"

"She's shaken, but I think she'll be O.K. Of course, everything depends on the recovery of her vehicle. Her Dad bought it brand new and she loves that car. I hope our suspects don't rabbit and cause a crash. Then she won't be so hot. By the way, what have you heard from the marked units you sent to French Gulch Rd?"

"They're at the front door now. No answer. Shall we do a forced entry? The house appears secure. One deputy went around back and all doors are locked, curtains drawn, no one screaming for help. It's your call."

"Dispatch, let me get back to you. Ask the two deputies to hold fast at the scene. I'm going to call the sheriff for his consent."

I hit the sheriff's number on my sped dial and brought him up to speed. It was my opinion that if Nicole Logan was in the house, her safety was in jeopardy. The Durango had been registered to her since 2007. This was prior to Ken Kunkle's murder so I could assume that Nicole Logan wasn't an alias created by the Scudders. We had no idea what Logan looked like, but her imminent danger gave us probable cause to make a forced entry into the home. These opinions were relayed to the sheriff and he concurred. He advised that he would personally call dispatch and tell them to order the deputies to make the forcible entry.

Gunter came over to my car to tell me that Lima Thirty, Shayla James, had arrived to transport Duggan. I walked over to Gunter's car to say goodbye. I also relayed that thus far the chopper hadn't spotted her Mustang.

"Miss Duggan be assured the moment we've found your car, you'll be notified. We're anxious to get your car back. I realize you're even more anxious but we want you to get your car back without damage. Those kinds of endings are best for everyone involved. Deputy James will be monitoring the radio and I have your cell phone number.

My fondest wish is to be able to call you before you arrive home."

James drove off with Reta and I went back to my car. Sky One was calling.

"Kootenai Delta Six this is Sky One we have the Mustang. It's in the Target parking lot on East Sprague. Unoccupied. If you'll give us the physical descriptions we may be able to spot them around the store."

"Sky One I'll have Delta Ten come up on this channel and relay the descriptions. He interviewed the witnesses. The victim was too shaken to provide a reliable description."

"Delta Ten would you give Sky One the physical descriptions for the suspects?"

Gunter came on the air and provided the descriptions to Sky One. The descriptions were of little value. They would fit anyone on the street. Brian was wearing a blue golf shirt and Levis. Annalee was wearing black slacks and a white blouse. Both had brunette hair and neither had unique hairstyles. That description would fit every third person on the street. Not a lot to go on. If this wasn't enough of a problem, Most of us were out of position to head for the Target parking lot. It would take us at least ten minutes to reposition ourselves. Sky One advised that they hadn't seen anyone matching the suspect's description. They ordered a Spokane County marked unit to proceed to the Target lot to secure the Mustang. The marked unit was also ten minutes out.

Dispatch called to say that the deputies had made entry into the house and were doing a search. Thus far they had not located anyone. No one had responded to their shouts identifying themselves as law enforcement officers.

That was a good thing. At least Nicole Logan wasn't lying in the living room bound and gagged or worse yet, dead.

I asked all Delta units to head for the Target parking lot but asked them to drive as slow as possible as they drove down East Sprague toward the lot. If luck was with us we might spot Brian and Annalee. East Sprague is a major east-west thoroughfare and carries a lot of traffic. This is also a key public bus route from the valley in to Spokane. At the west end of East Sprague, there are numerous car dealerships and rental agencies. The Scudder twins picked the perfect place to avoid capture. This was no fluke. They were organized and obviously skilled at eluding authorities.

"Delta Six, Dispatch. Morgan advises that Inspector Forbes from the U.K. has called you on Skype. He has some information about Amie Scudder. Nothing pressing, he'll call again tomorrow. Morgan talked with him briefly and assured us it does not pertain to the incident you are currently working."

"Thanks dispatch, we don't need any more on our plate right now. As present we're doing a surface street search for the suspects. Sky One has located the car jacked Mustang. Spokane S.O has a marked unit enroute to secure the vehicle. Would you advise Lima Thirty on channel one, that until we verify the condition of the Mustang and process it for forensics, we won't be able to release it to the owner. We'll expedite that process."

"Copy Delta Six. Lima Thirty is advised on channel one. Stay Safe!"

We had no luck spotting the Scudders on East Sprague. The Mustang was parked properly and the keys were lying on the driver's seat. No visible body damage. The Spokane S.O. unit was on scene and had called for their evidence unit to process the car. I would rather have used our evidence team. But since the crime was committed in their jurisdiction, they assumed responsibility. The deputy on the scene assured me that they would provide us with their report. Spokane S.O. would release the vehicle to Reta Duggan as soon as it was processed. My concern is when they process for fingerprints they really throw the powder around. It can stain upholstery and carpets and is hard to clean off the steering wheel unless you use a special cleaner. I didn't want Reta Duggan to come pick up her car and find it essentially trashed by law enforcement when it wasn't damaged by the thieves.

It took fifteen minutes for the evidence van to arrive. Four techs stepped out of the unit. Their procedure was almost identical to ours. One tech was doing a video one was taking digital stills. The other two techs were unloading evidence collection equipment boxes. I identified myself to ask that they use fingerprint powder sparingly. Explaining that the owner really treasured the Mustang. They assured me that they would be extra careful. Once that assurance was given they set to work. They started on the outer door handles and then the inner door handles, steering wheel, rear view mirror and gear shift, seat adjustment handle, and turn signal lever. It took them less than fifteen minutes to process the car. They did a cursory search of the trunk nothing seemed out of place. They took over thirty minutes to clean the car and asked me to notify Miss Duggan that she could take possession of the car.

"Dispatch, Delta Six, has Lima Thirty delivered the victim to her residence?"

"Negative Delta Six, she's apparently still enroute. She hasn't cleared the call."

"Would you ask her to return with the victim to the Target store on East Sprague? Her vehicle appears to be undamaged and is ready for release."

"We're turning her around right now. At least you have one happy person in Spokane Valley?

"I really need happy right now dispatch."

I called all of the surveillance team to meet in the Target parking lot. We had a very serious discussion about where we were on this detail. Sky One was still doing aerial search, but wasn't having any luck. I asked Gunter and Woody to go into the Target store on the off chance they might have gone in there to try to avoid being seen. We fully realized that the chances of seeing them in the store were slim to none. I asked Gunter to go into the men's dressing rooms and Woody into the women's. I asked the Liberty Lake and Valley Detectives to take each end of the lot and keep their eyes open. David and I went into the store and did a diminishing concentric circle search of the entire Target store with no success. Gunter and Woody also struck out.

We rendezvoused back at the Mustang. Spokane S.O.'s marked unit would release the Mustang to Miss Duggan. I felt good that she would recover her vehicle. We all agreed that we should call off Sky one, return to our respective areas of responsibility, and log this failed surveillance up to experience. We could learn a lot of lessons from this event and hopefully never make the same mistakes again.

We advised dispatch that we were 10-8 enroute back to the Department and would operate on channel one. The drive back to Coeur d'Alene was not going to be a pleasant one. I dreaded having to brief the sheriff on our failed surveillance. The trip was interrupted by a call from dispatch.

"Delta Six you and your team are to proceed code two to 334 French Gulch Road, Fernan. The marked units have made an interesting discovery that will require your attention."

"Ten-four dispatch, we're enroute from Sullivan and I-90 code two."

"Delta Five, Ten, and Eleven do you copy?"

David, Gunter, and Woody replied in the affirmative. The four of us activated our P.R. lights on our rear deck and activated our behind the grill emergency lights and flashing headlights. Code Two does not allow excessive speed, but will clear traffic ahead of you. This allowed us to get in the fast lane and drive at the speed limit. There are always drivers who get what we call 'Black and White Fever' and pull into the median or slow down to twenty miles an hour afraid that they are the ones that are subject to the emergency lights.

CHAPTER NINETEEN

We made it to Fernan in twenty-five minutes. Not a speed record, but good time in late afternoon traffic. There were four marked units outside the Logan house and the Watch Sergeant and Commander were among the uniformed officers standing outside the house. As we pulled up, the evidence van pulled in behind us. This did not bode well for Nicole Logan.

"Captain Nearing, Sergeant Corker, this must be something big. Both of you here and it looks like you have established a perimeter. What's going on?"

"Jake you all aren't going to like this. Our uniforms found, what we believe is Nicole Logan, in the chest freezer in the garage. She's also been stabbed in the heart with an awl. This makes four dead bodies killed in an identical manner. I understand that you boys may have almost had the killers. Sergeant Corker and I were monitoring the surveillance on Tac Two. Those Scudder kids are pretty smart. I don't think this was their first rodeo. That was a smart maneuver on Argonne. You'd have to know what you're doing to pull that off. I think the Scudder boy had you figured from the jump. There's no note that our uniforms saw on Miss Logan. The moment they saw the body, they froze the scene and called for backup. I see that Jay and his team have arrived, so we'll let you go do your magic."

"Thanks Captain. Your comment about the Scudders and this not being their first rodeo is really on point. I've been kicking myself since they made the "U" turn. I should've called for aerial coverage the minute the surveillance started. I was only mildly suspicious of Mr. Brian Fox. I'd asked Morgan to do a work-up on him, but things happened too fast for us to get the results. Morgan called me on my cell while we were enroute to this scene and told me that she could find no record of a Brian or Annalee Fox. They don't have Idaho driver's licenses or a social security number in the national system."

"O.K. folks. Captain Nearing has advised that we have a fourth victim in the freezer. If you haven't been following our surveillance, I'll give you a quick update. The suspects we were following allegedly live at this address. The vehicle they were driving is registered to a Nicole Logan also at this address. Miss Logan's 2007 Durango has been registered in her name since 2007. Based on what we now know, I suspect that the victim may be Logan. I'm having Morgan do a work-up on Logan while we process the scene. If we're lucky, we may be able to collect some DNA from what we believe are the Scudder twins. They were the suspects we were following. I'll tell you right now they escaped using very skillful avoidance techniques. This crime scene may give us the hard forensic evidence we need to tie them in to the other three murders. I want us to take our time and go over this house with a proverbial fine-toothed comb. Let's go slow and collect anything that draws your attention."

Jay Bass asked, "Are we going to follow our previous protocol? Sherry on video, Ron on digital stills, David the recorder, me marking what we identify, you being the 'Finder of Record'? We've now got Woody and Gunter to assist. What do you want them to do?"

"Good point Jay! Yes we'll follow that protocol. Gunter and Woody, I'd like you to each take a room and shout out the minute you find anything. We'll all start in the garage. Work out from there. Our first issue is who is the Acting Coroner? We need someone in an official capacity to 'Pronounce' on the body in the freezer. I'll ask Sergeant Corker if they've been advised who to call by the D.A."

I asked Sergeant Corker if Patrol Division had been advised who had been selected to become the Acting Coroner.

Sergeant Corker said, "We've been advised to call a Doctor Roman Landon. He's a local M.D. One of my uniforms said he was his family's doctor. I've got his twenty-four hour number. I'll give him a call and get an ETA."

"Thanks Sarge. We'll start processing up to the body until he arrives to make the Pronouncement."

"O.K. gang. Sgt Corker is calling the new Acting Coroner. We can start at the roll-up door and move toward the freezer. We won't touch the freezer until Dr. Landon arrives."

Woody said, "Dr. Landon? He's my doctor. He's a real cool dude. I'll be, Dr. Landon the new Acting Coroner. It's going to be interesting to watch him work with all of us around. He's cool, but awfully quiet. Jake he's seen me naked. So you make the first contact with him. I'm afraid I'll be too embarrassed."

"Too much information Woody!" David joked.

We began the crime scene processing. It was slow going even though the garage was spotless. It contained the usual stuff you find in any garage. Gardening tools, a gas lawn mower, shovels, rakes, cans of paint, insecticides, plastic storage boxes, gardening gloves, and other miscellaneous junk you would find in every garage.

Since we didn't know for sure who was in the freezer, collecting elimination prints from the handles of the tools, storage boxes, and paint cans was tedious. As we examined the items in the storage boxes we found nothing unusual. Winter clothing, older pots and pans, Tupperware, and old date books from previous years. Sgt. Corker came to the door to say that Dr. Landon was enroute. ETA fifteen. We used the time to continue processing. Nothing of evidentiary value other than the latent prints on the tool handles was collected.

A tall, well dressed, man in a three-piece pin striped suit with well-shined black shoes walked through the open roll-up door.

"Dr. Roman Landon. I'm the new Acting Coroner. I'm afraid I don't know who you all are. I must assume you're members of the Sheriff's Department from all the marked units outside, but I'd like to know your names for my report."

"I'm Detective Jake Lowry. That's L-O-W-R-Y. This is my partner, Detective Bruce David. David common spelling. He goes by his last name only. The tall fellow is Detective Gunter Lenca. L-E-N-C-A. The lovely lady in plain clothes is Detective Wodehouse McNair. M-small C-N-A-I-R. The Black haired Gentleman in the white bunny suit is Jay Bass. Bass common spelling, Lead Evidence Technician. The Oriental Gentleman is Ron Wong, Wong common spelling, Evidence Technician. The Lady with the Video Camera is Sherry Lee. Lee common spelling, also an evidence technician. Glad to meet you Doctor. May we assume that you'll be doing the autopsy on our friend Dr. Hardcastle?"

"As a matter of fact, I will. Why do you ask?"

"The entire team worked closely with Dr. Hardcastle on a number of cases. We'd become close colleagues. Doctor if you'll make the 'Pronouncement', we'll get on with our work. If you could give us a date and time for Dr. Hardcastle's autopsy, we'll make sure that someone from the team is present. If you're unaware, we believe that this is the fourth victim of the same murderer, or team of murderers. We believe that Dr. Hardcastle was the third victim."

"I'll examine the body for you now."

Dr. Landon was slow and deliberate as he approached the body. A casual observer would assume he was almost afraid to touch her. There were ice crystals on her clothing. The awl protruding from her chest also had ice crystals on the handle. Landon had gloved up and gingerly leaned over the freezer chest, placing his ear near the awl and then the victim's mouth. He then took her wrist feeling for a pulse. He straightened and said, "This woman is dead. Is that what you need?"

"Yes Doctor. That's all we need. I'll arrange for the victim to be transferred to the morgue. Detective David and Ron Wong will accompany the body to the morgue to assure we maintain the chain of custody. We look forward to working with you in the future."

"Thanks Detective. I'll be a little slow to start, but once I get my sea legs, I think we'll have a good working relationship. I interned in Washoe County, Nevada. I did a rotation in their Coroner's Office. These won't be my first autopsies."

"Washoe County. That's interesting. Did you by any chance work with Gordy Johnson in Reno?"

"How do you know Gordy? I sure did. He's a great detective. He and I worked on three cases together. What a small world."

"Gordy and I attended a training class together. He was instrumental in providing some valuable intelligence that helped us solve case. As a matter of fact, these four murders are connected to the case Gordy helped solve."

"I still have a lot of friends back in Reno. I'll make sure that they say. "Hi!" to Gordy for you."

"Thanks Doc. I'd appreciate that."

I called for a body transport for our victim. Jay covered the awl with a brown paper sheet and covered the paper with a plastic sheet to seal it from any possible outside damage or contamination. Now that we had the 'Pronouncement', we could continue our evidence gathering. Jay stayed with the victim. Sherry and Ron entered the house doing the photography. David, Gunter, Woody, and I followed. Once Sherry and David had completed their video and stills, I assigned each detective to individual rooms to begin the detailed search. Woody got the living room; Gunter the dining room and kitchen; David the two guest bedrooms. I saved the master bedroom for myself. Sherry and Ron would stand by to document any evidentiary items.

Woody was the first to call out.

"I think you need to come see this."

Woody was standing at the antique oak desk sitting just inside the front door. The finish literally gleamed. I don't know a lot about antiques, but would guess that this piece was crafted around the mid seventeen hundreds. It had a bow front with original brasses on the drawer pulls. The intricately carved delicate legs showed excellent craftsmanship. The original brass casters had been polished which probably reduced the desk's value if it were appraised on the Antiques Road Show. I tried to ignore the desk's beauty as Woody was pointing inside the opened drawer.

Sherry, Ron and I drew close to peer into the opened drawer. What we saw was an opened wallet lying open to an Idaho Driver's License with the name Nicole Logan and bearing a picture of the body in the freezer. My worst fears were realized. Nicole Logan was the body in the freezer. We yelled out the garage door to Jay that we had a positive I.D. on the victim. He shouted back, "Is it Logan?"

"Yes it is," I replied.

Sherry did the video, Ron the stills. Woody with her blue nitrile gloves slowly opened the plastic photo holders as Sherry and Ron documented what we were seeing:

#1. A Bank Card from the Idaho Independent Bank.

#2. A United Airlines Mileage Plus Visa Card.

#3. A Citi-Bank American Airlines Visa Card.

#4. A Color photo of a Chow dog with the name 'Bear' on it.

#5. A Color photo of a group of people. The victim was in the photo.

#6. Two dollars in One-dollar bills.

The wallet was a fine, smooth, black, leather. Not worn in any manner. Apparently Nicole had recently acquired this wallet. It appeared brand new. It hadn't been bumped around in a purse or pocket. Woody gingerly picked up the wallet by the edge and placed it on top of the desk. Immediately under the wallet was a travel brochure for Vancouver, British Columbia. There were notes on the brochure. It almost looked like notes written to remind the owner. "Met the nicest couple. Ronnie and Loni Scudder. Make plans to see them when they visit here." There was a date on the brochure, Jun 2009. The brochure also contained other notations on the beauty of Busch Gardens and the elegance of the Canadian Legislature buildings. As far as we could discern, no other notes pertinent to our case.

June 2009 was a broad period to be concerned with but it did give us a time period.

If Nicole had only known, she may have been just the person the Scudders were looking for. Was their meeting an accident or had the Scudders stalked her? This mystery was growing exponentially!

I grabbed my cell phone and called Morgan.

"Morgan, Jake here. I've got some credit card numbers for you to run in conjunction with the work-up you're doing on Nicole Logan. Are you ready to copy? Put in a quick call to Ammo and ask him to contact Canadian Customs. Have them look in 2009 for the Scudders living in Vancouver, B.C. Also have him check for border crossings of the Scudders in that area. While I have you doing all our work, would you call U.S. Customs and Immigration to see if they have the Scudders crossing into the U.S. from Vancouver? We haven't located any passports, but we're in the very early stages of the house search,"

I gave Morgan the card numbers and asked her to call the companies immediately to see if Nicole had duplicate cards issued recently. If so, the Scudders may be using her credit cards to aid in their escape. I wanted a block put on all accounts to prevent that from happening.

Woody carefully handed the brochure and wallet to Ron. He placed them in appropriate evidence bags, initialed and dated the bags. I also added my initials. I made the appropriate entries in my evidence log. Woody then slid some loose papers on the bottom of the drawer apart. They were blank pieces of bond paper and one empty envelope. There were: three yellow #2 pencils and two Bic ballpoint pens. Ron placed those in an evidence bag for latent print processing. Woody closed the middle drawer and opened the right hand drawer: more pens, a two-hole punch, stapler, staple puller, and ruler. We might be able to get a palm print from the two-hole punch. That would be an added bonus. My log was growing and the evidence bags were increasing at the same pace. Forensics would have a long, tedious, job to scour for latent prints on the off chance that the Scudders had used any of the items.

The left hand drawer held the real treasure. An identical type of paper to the notes affixed to the victim's chests. There was an opened cellophane package of this paper. It had a Staples store label on the cellophane wrapper. We wouldn't be able to positively state that this was identical unless we had a full forensics work-up done on the paper left in the package. The drawer also contained a box of paper clips, staples for the stapler in the right hand drawer, and a box of thumbtacks.

If the rest of the house was as productive as the desk, we were on a roll!

We returned to our assigned rooms, each, all the while hoping that we would be the next to shout out with a found treasure.

I got lucky in the bedside table closest to the bedroom door. A pistol magazine for a .380 caliber pistol, fully loaded, was lying at the front edge of the drawer. I gave out a shout. We repeated the procedure. Sherry videoed then Ron took stills. I bagged and 'tagged' (initialed and dated) the magazine and handed it to Ron. I made the log entries and an extra notation to see if the lab could get latents off each round. You really have to handle bullets to load them in a magazine. Hopefully we could get enough latents for a positive match. Also in the drawer were the usual scattered items that you collect in a bedside table: One notepad, one pen, three barrettes, assorted hair pins, a small pocket knife, a TV channel listing, two emery boards, and a nail clipper. We bagged and tagged the pistol magazine. I made the log entries.

The team again returned to their assigned rooms. Very little time passed until I was again lucky in the walk-in closet. I gave a shout and we reassembled in the master bedroom. In the walk-in closet were three expensive suitcases. Two of them had baggage tags with the name Nicole Logan on them. The Logan bags had airline luggage tags on them showing Spokane as a Destination and Vancouver as the departing airport. The third had the name Loni Scudder on a leather tag. It was a carry-on type case with the extending handle and two wheels. I gingerly moved the case. It felt very light. We were all naturally concerned about a Booby Trap. After my last experience with the Fairchild EOD Team, I was hesitant to call them for assistance. We could see no visible wires extending from the bag. It was the first bag of the three. As if it had been placed in the closet last. Gunter had not been close enough when he had the house under surveillance to see if the Scudders had loaded bags in the Mustang. Since Ronnie had changed clothes while the car was moving, apparently they had some spare clothing in the car or had actually loaded suitcases. I had everyone leave the bedroom. I grabbed a wire hanger and untwisted the hook and made a long semi-straight wire. I fashioned a tight hook in the end of the wire and used that as an extension tool. I very carefully started to unzip the bag. It moved effortlessly. Once I had the zipper fully opened I pulled the flap open. Clothing tumbled out. Luckily, no big boom, no noxious gas hissed. I decided that we actually just had a suitcase. Again, I used the extended hanger to pick up each piece of clothing individually. Nothing was concealed in the jumble of clothing. I asked the team to reassemble at the closet. I discarded my wire hanger and looked closely at each piece of clothing.

The clothing bore exclusive labels, size zero and two. Woody and Sherry said that just because of the labels and the clothing sizes they hated Loni Scudder. Even considering the four murders, no real woman wore size zero or two clothing. This gave us all a chuckle. The zipper pocket on the outside of the case was empty. A close examination of the clothing gave us no additional clues. We placed each item in individual paper bags. We would process them for DNA. Ron and I bagged and tagged them.

Everyone returned to their assigned rooms. My shout had not been very productive. DNA, if we could extract it from the clothing, might be helpful if we could also extract matching DNA from Nicole's body or other items.

There was no men's clothing hanging in the walk-in closet. Either Ronnie had taken all his clothing with them or he and Loni had not shared a bed. I was anxious for David to turn up something in one of the guest bedrooms. All of the shoes in the walk-in were lined up perfectly and seemed to be the same size. I called Jay on my portable and asked him if it were possible for him to remove one of Nicole's shoes for a size comparison. He had a little difficulty, but said she was wearing size seven shoes. All the shoes in the closet were size seven Woody and Sherry had monitored my transmission. Both shouted in unison that they also hated Nicole. I had checked the clothing hanging in the closet and it was all size four.

Sherry came into the bedroom and said, "I'm not going to operate the camera anymore. It just isn't fair. I work a fifty or sixty-hour week, go to the gym, watch what I eat, and still can't fit into a size four dress or size seven shoes."

"Sherry, you look fine to both me and the guys. We admire your initiative and the fact that you also take care of your Mom. I admit there aren't many women who wear size zero, two, or four. Liz wears an eight. She always complains when she sees some of these tiny women in the stores being able to buy the sample shoes that are top of the line but don't come in a size eight. I guess it's a cross that average women have to bear. I also admit that men don't pay enough attention to those little details. The only reason I'm commenting now is we're trying to get a more definitive description on Loni Scudder. One thing is obvious from the clothes in the carry-on suitcase is she dresses well and knows fashion. That gives us a small window into her psychological make-up"

"Jake you know I'm kidding, but it's frustrating. We don't know anything about the Scudders. They must have surely killed Nicole and Dr. Hardcastle. We can assume they killed Dr. Matile and Cameron Haynes. At the moment, we only have one thing connecting the four murders: The awl through the heart. But if they are from the U.K. how did they learn about the Coeur d'Alene myth? From the travel brochure we can again assume they met Nicole in Vancouver last summer. Now we're left with a big time gap. How they got here, why they want to revenge Nora's death and how did they learn the detailed names of people connected to Ken Kunkle's murder investigation?"

"Sherry you're absolutely on point. Those are the primary questions we're facing. That's why I want the team to go slow on this search. We have to Nit Pick any possible item that can positively tie the Scudder twins to all four murders. We may never know what their psychological make-up is, but if we can get them with hard physical evidence that'll satisfy me and the courts."

The other two bags with Nicole's name on them were empty. The only items of interest were the white airline luggage tags with the bar code and the Vancouver point of origin and Spokane as the destination. This validated the notes on the travel brochure. Nothing else in the room drew my interest except the bedding. Ron and I carefully folded the blanket, sheets and pillowcases into individual paper bags for DNA testing.

I finished the remainder of the master bedroom search without finding anything of evidentiary value. Woody finished the living room without any new discoveries. Gunter struck out in both the kitchen and dining room. The onus was now on David to produce some remarkable evidence from the two guest bedrooms. We all walked to the door of the first bedroom and gave him the 'Stinkeye.'

"What are you all looking at? I'm being methodical. Thus far this guest bedroom appears unused. There's a portable sewing machine and some sewing materials in the closet, but nothing at all in the bedside tables. My guess is that Nicole did some sewing in this room and kept it in reserve for guests. I'll be finished in one minute."

We all looked at each other and smiled.

"O.K. partner, we'll just stand here and let you move on to the other bedroom. By the way, we've found nothing putting Ronnie Scudder in this house. So you'd better come up with something outstanding and you better do it quick."

"I can't fabricate stuff belonging to Ronnie Scudder. If it isn't here, it isn't here. So go away and don't bother a master at work. I'll call for you three when I find something. Now go away and leave me alone"

The team moved out to the garage. The ambulance had arrived and Jay was assisting the two medics to load Nicole on the Gurney. She was stiff and very cold so they had to handle her with extreme care. Once she was in the ambulance, I walked in the house to tell David that I had substituted Woody for him to accompany the body to the morgue. Sherry said if David found anything, she could do both the video and digital stills. Woody and Ron entered the ambulance and it took off for the morgue. No need for lights and siren. Low profile was the order of the day.

Jay had started a detailed search of the freezer chest. There were a few boxes of frozen peas and some mixed vegetables that had been under Nicole's body. Jay sprayed luminal on the boxes and shined the detector light to look for blood. No blood was detected. We had assumed she was stabbed somewhere else, but had no idea where. Obviously the body had been placed in the freezer after she was killed. Thus far we had not located the crime scene for any of the four murders.

David shouted that he needed Sherry, Ron, and I. We all rushed toward the remaining bedroom.

"What have you found partner? I hope it is something that will tie the Scudders to all four of our murders."

"Jake, I have found men's clothes in the closet and a small wooden box containing eight awls. I think they're identical to the four we've found so far in our victims. They must have bought a dozen from somewhere. The wooden box is large enough to hold the additional four awls. We need to process the box for latents. I haven't touched the clothes yet. You guys pressured me so much I started at the closet. When I swung the door open, I saw the box there on the floor. Is Jay available to process for latents? Where's Ron? Did he go with Woody and the victim?"

"Good job Partner! Yes, Ron and Woody went with the body. Sherry will do both the video and the stills. I'll call Jay. He just sprayed luminal inside the freezer and didn't find any blood. I don't think there's much more he can do inside the freezer. Stand by."

Sherry did the photography and stepped back. Jay carefully dusted the exterior of the box and developed a number of latents. The underside of the box appeared to have thumb prints. The topside had a clear four-finger impression. The little finger, even though it is used, is seldom visible when someone grasps an object unless they are swinging it like a hammer or a baseball bat. I was busy making entries in the evidence log. That process took at least ten minutes. While Jay and I were busy, David started examining the men's clothing. If these clothes belong to Ronnie Scudder, he also had excellent taste in expensive clothing. After examining the clothing we now know that the owner wore a size forty two jacket, a sixteen inch collared shirt with a thirty four inch sleeve, trousers with a thirty four inch waist and thirty inch inseam. His shoe size was nine 'D'. Although expensive, all of the clothes seemed to be off the rack. No custom tailoring was visible.

Gunter had taken the responsibility of examining the bedside tables. The drawer in the table furtherest from the door was totally empty. The table drawer closest to the door had some very interesting items. Gunter called for Jay,

Sherry, and I to come to his location when we were through with the closet.

"O.K. Gunter what have you got? We finished with the closet. We've a good physical description of Ronnie from his clothing. We can add this data to the B.O.L. broadcast. We have their picture from Ammo and now we can give specifics on height and a good estimate on weight. Now we need some good forensics. Show us your treasure."

"Let's get Sherry to do the video and stills first."

Gunter pulled the bedside table drawer fully open. He stepped back so he wouldn't be in any picture that might later be introduced as evidence in a court of law. Sherry did the video first and then took close-up digitals of the drawer's contents.

We all leaned in toward the drawer and saw a passport from the United Kingdom. The U.K. Passport bears a distinctive crown. This one looked authentic to the casual observer. Gunter in light blue, nitrile gloves gingerly picked it up and opened it to the owner's name. Eureka! The name Ronnie Reed Scudder was there. The passport was valid until November 8, 2012.

Why had Ronnie left his passport in the bedside table? The only answer I could come up with was: He had another passport or phony identification. We hadn't located a passport for Nicole Logan. She and Loni were of similar size and appearance. Possibly Loni was posing as Nicole.

Suddenly my mind clicked into overdrive. Cameron Haynes ~ Lawrence Matile! We hadn't located a passport for Cameron or Lawrence Matile. At the time we had no need to look for one. Could Ronnie possibly be posing as one of our two previous victims? Once we identified someone, usually from a driver's license, no officer routinely seeks a passport from a suspect, victim, or witness unless the crime involves international violations. This is one of the advantages of living in America. You can travel thousands of miles and not have to show a passport or identity document to cross the border into a neighboring state. When I was operating in Europe, and the Balkans, you could drive sixty miles in any direction and be in another country with border guards and customs checks. Of course, Ronnie may have taken advantage of that freedom.

"Guys I think we've all we can extract from this house. I don't know about you, but I'm famished. Let's go out of service and I'll treat the team to dinner at the new Texas Roadhouse on Highway 95. I hear they do a great steak and a pretty good baked potato. I'll call Woody and Ron on the cell they must have secured Nicole in the morgue by now and they can meet us. Gunter why don't you call Rebecca and I'll call Liz, we'll make a party of the dinner. We all need some free time after this long and frustrating day. Any Takers?"

The team universally agreed to my proposition. I informed dispatch that we were 10-10.

CHAPTER TWENTY

We caravanned onto I-9. West to 95 a short right on the off-ramp and a few blocks north to the Texas Roadhouse. We were greeted at the door by a bouncy waitress and whisked to a very large table. There were small, galvanized buckets containing peanuts in the shell. The custom here was to eat the peanuts and throw the shells on the floor. For the tidier of mind, there were empty galvanized buckets to place your shells. We had just begun to order when Lori Larson and Michelle Keller were seated at the table just opposite ours. We all waved and they came over to chat.

Michelle said, "We just heard on the radio about poor Nicole Logan. What a shame. Jake are you and David working her murder?"

I asked, "What did you hear?"

"We heard that she's the fourth in a series of identical murders, that we have a serial murderer here in Coeur d'Alene. The radio said the Sheriff's office has a team of detectives working with other agencies to solve the case. We assumed that this meant you two guys. If you're working the case how are Brian and Annalee handling this? They must be in shock."

David asked somewhat incredulously, "How do you know Brian and Annalee?"

"Nicole works out at the same health club we do. She brought Brian and Annalee so they could workout also. We only met them twice. They seemed like a nice couple. We made arrangements to have lunch later this week. I hope they can make it. It'll be a very sad lunch meeting."

I jumped in, "Michelle, Lori I need you to listen to me very carefully. I don't want to scare you unnecessarily, but your lives are in serious danger. Brian and Annalee aren't Brian and Annalee. They aren't a couple. They're brother and sister. They were apparently very close friends with Nora Wallace. Their real names are Ronnie and Loni Scudder. At this time we believe that they're our murder team. They're apparently avenging Nora's death. Everyone they've killed so far has some connection to Ken's murder. If they've met you two, we must believe that you may also be targets. You don't have to do anything right now. Stay here and have dinner. But when you finish, we'll all go directly to the Sheriff's Department and make arrangements to have you placed in protective custody. Earlier today, we had them under surveillance. They escaped. At the moment, we don't know where they are, but they're loose and we can't guess their next move.

All of us are ramping up our personal security procedures. I hate to break this horrible news to you so blatantly, but there is no gentle way to make sure that you are aware of the very serious nature of this threat."

"Gee Jake; you sure know how to put a damper on a birthday celebration. It is bad enough that I'm turning twenty-seven, but now you tell me that both my life and Lori's life are in danger."

Lori was visibly shaken. She said, "Jake I know you're not kidding, but this seems too bizarre to be real. We played 'Wally ball' at the health club with Nicole, Brian and Annalee or what did you call them? Ronnie and Loni? That's too weird. They said they met Nicole in Vancouver and were moving to Coeur d'Alene to start a veterinary practice. They had such a cute British accent. Now you say they're murderers. What do you mean about protective custody? Will we be still be able to go to work and live in our homes?"

Gunter answered, "Lori, Michelle, I know this sounds harsh, but we think they tried to trick Rebecca into opening the door to our house. Because the dead bodies were all positioned against the rock wall of Ken's former house where Rebecca and I now live, we had increased our security procedures. That one step may have saved Rebecca's life. To not put too fine a point on this procedure, no! You won't be able to go to work and you won't be permitted to live in your normal dwellings. That is until we apprehend the Scudders. They're very elusive and seem to know about every person that was in any way connected to Ken. We see no reason for some of the victims chosen, but they all had some link to Ken's investigation.

The waitress arrived and took our drink and dinner orders. I told her to put Lori and Michelle's check on mine. It was the least I could do after the scare we had just given them. The remainder of our dinner was slightly subdued. Our celebration was tempered by the thought that we should now have to warn every person who was even tangentially involved with Ken Kunkle's murder investigation. I excused myself and walked outside the restaurant to call the sheriff on my cell.

"Boss, Detective Lowry here. We just got a new twist in our Coeur d'Alene murder case. The team accidentally ran into Lori Larson and Michelle Keller at dinner. They met the Scudders with Nicole Logan, our latest victim. They were still using the Brian and Annalee Fox alias. They have an arrangement to meet for lunch this week. On the surface, this seems innocent enough, but this may have been a ruse to acquire two more victims."

"Jake, I'm a little foggy on who Larson and Keller are. How are they connected to Ken's case?"

"Both Lori Larson and Michelle were two of Ken's frequent companions. Michelle is now the office manager in Ken's former business. She replaced Morgan Lenca there. Lori is still working for Doctor Johnson. The entire team believes that they, and everyone else in any way connected to Ken or his murder investigation may be in danger. The most obvious threat is to Clyde and his close associates. I'm asking that a security detail be sent immediately to Clyde's compound and remain there until we locate and apprehend the Scudders. Boss, to tell you the truth, I'm having cold chills even discussing this. The Scudders have had almost five hours of freedom since they shook the surveillance.

Hopefully they left the area, but if not, they've had ample time to initiate some drastic revenge plans. I hope you agree."

"O.K. Jake, I see where you're going. Consider it done, I'll call the Watch Commander and get him to call in some off-duty personnel. We'll get a security detail over to Clyde's immediately. I'll personally call him to tell him what's happening. I ran into him at the supermarket a couple of days ago. He told me that Husam's family is due in this week. They were looking for a nice house close by the compound. Do you think we should include them in our protection scheme?"

"Most assuredly, If Husam is going to move out of the compound and the Scudders have as good an intelligence base as we fear, his life and his family's life are in danger too. That'll be a tough advisement. Newly arrived in the U.S. and suddenly they are possible targets for serial killers."

"Jake, I'll handle my end. You and the team handle your end. We're going to catch the Scudders. Good night"

"Good night Boss. Thanks for the support."

I returned to the restaurant and joined the team.

"Folks, I've called the Boss. He's onboard for the protection teams. He's going to personally call Clyde and will have the Watch Commander dispatch a team there immediately. I do have some good news. Husam's family is due to arrive here this week. I guess that's both good and bad news. Apparently Husam is looking for a house for his family. That means he's leaving the compound. So we'll need an extra team for his family. Gunter we'd appreciate it if you'd have Consuelo remain in the house with Rebecca. I think allowing her to return to her apartment would be terribly dangerous. Rebecca is keyed in for extra security. We'll also have a team outside your house until we apprehend the Scudders.

"We've got to contact all our sources and see if they have any news from the jungle telegraph. We assume that the Scudders have at least one gun. The .380 is not a powerful pistol, but apparently they might use that. We don't know if they have a spare supply of awls. It looked like the box held a dozen and those are accounted for. Let's go home and sleep with one eye open. Tomorrow is a new day and we've got to hit it hard."

CHAPTER TWENTY ONE

I asked Liz to call in sick today. I asked her to go to Gunter and Rebecca's house for the day. We had a long and serious discussion last night. I didn't want her in the public eye today. Calling in sick was a small lie, but telling her co-workers that her life may be in danger was a little too dramatic. Gunter and Rebecca had created a very secure system. Both Liz and Rebecca were skilled with firearms. She and I drove in together and I dropped her off. Gunter followed me to David's house and then the three of us caravanned to the office. To the casual observer this might seem a little paranoid, but of all the targets, David and I were probably the prime targets for the Scudders.

When we arrived Morgan was in the office.

"Morgan, good morning. Thank you for volunteering to be the second female at the 'Safe House' for Heidi. I'm sure you know that asking you to go there was not our only concern. We wanted an armed deputy in the next room to provide both protection for you and Heidi."

"We have Lori, Michelle and Kim stashed in another motel in Liberty Lake. David volunteered to be the armed deputy in the adjoining room, but I burst his balloon and told him we needed him here all day. He was one sad fellow."

"Jake, I'm not an idiot. You calling me at home and asking me to go to the 'Safe House' was just the cherry on top of the sundae. I monitored a lot of traffic on Tac Two and then the chatter on our primary channel gave me a good idea of the flow of this case. If my life may be in danger, I don't mind taking precautions. Thanks for thinking about me."

David smiled and Gunter chuckled.

David asked, "Where's Woody? Your cell call to me didn't mention her at all."

Gunter said, "Woody was the other Deputy at the 'Safe House.' She was catching some sleep while we have another deputy watching Heidi."

"O.K. Guys, I've been mulling over our next steps in this convoluted investigation. The only available link we have to the Scudders is Emilee Lukin. Let's go pick her up and bring her into the department. I'm not sure we'll get anything out of her. She seemed like a rather cold and calculating person on our previous meetings, but if we charge her with being an accomplice to four murders that might drive a wedge into her cool exterior. We got enough info from Ammo to give us what might appear to her as enough to charge her and bring her to trial. If, as Ammo's sources say, she had a close relationship with Ronnie Scudder, that relationship may not be worth facing four murder charges. What do you think?"

David said, "Jake you and I are on the same track. My only concern is that the Scudders are pretty smart. They may have fled to Emilee's condo. She may be an expendable 'friend.' I think the first place we should check, and I recommend that we do it surreptitiously, is her place of employment. If she's at work we can bring her from there. Going to her condo, may be tricky. She may be a hostage in her own home or if we consider the worst case scenario, she may be our fifth victim."

Gunter chimed in, "I think you're both on point. Why don't we send one of our female detectives to the Vet's Office where Emilee works to see if she's there? We've got some time. They probably open at eight hundred hours, but if we hold off until around ten hundred we'll have time to get organized.

Morgan said, "Jake, I'm in civilian clothes and don't look like a cop. Plus, Emilee hasn't seen me. I can go into the office and inquire about neutering my dog. If she's there, I can come back here and say so. If she's not, I can ask for her, professing that she was ordering a special item for me. That way we can learn if she is on a normal day-off or called in sick. If you guys are worried, you can park close by. You don't anticipate any trouble with someone just going into the Vet's office do you?"

"Morgan you're right. We'll do some of our Mainframe entries and then we'll drive you to the office at 10:00. If

Emilee is in the office, we can go in and get her. If not, we can go to Plan 'B'."

David asked, "What is Plan 'B'?"

"We don't have a Plan 'B' yet. Maybe instead of making Mainframe entries, we should formulate a Plan 'B'. Let's discuss the possible options that we're faced with.

#1. Emilee is at work:

A. We bring her in. Charge her with being an accomplice in four Homicides.

B. She denies knowing where the Scudders are.

C. We ask for permission to search her condo.

D. She gives us permission and we don't find the Scudders.

#2. Emilee isn't at work:

A. She's on a normal day off.

B. She called in sick.

#3. Emilee is on a normal day off:

A. We make a extremely cautious approach to Emilee's condo and determine if she's safe. That could be done by one of our female detectives utilizing a ruse. If Emilee answers the door, we try to gain entry. If one of the Scudders answers the door we retreat and go to Option #4.

#4. Emilee called in sick:

A. We assume she's being held hostage by the Scudders, or is in cahoots with them

B. We make a tactical entry

C. We capture the Scudders

D. We capture Emilee assuming she has harbored the Scudders.

E. CASE Solved

Anyone have anything to add?"

Gunter said, "Jake, sending a detective to Emilee's door is a very dangerous maneuver. I'd opt for a deep cover detective. Maybe we need to fall back on an 'Avista power outage or gas leak ruse'. This would require some coordination with Post Falls, Coeur d'Alene P.D., and additional personnel. We'd also have to evacuate neighbors close by to make the ruse appear on the up and up if Emilee or the Scudders were conducting surveillance from inside the condo."

David added, "Jake I'm going to have to agree with Gunter. If the Scudders are inside, they'll be paranoid. Anyone coming to the door will be suspect. Unless our contact ruse is perfect they may take the detective hostage. I'm not sure we want to risk that. The Scudders made a fool of us once. We don't want to give them a second chance. Plus we don't want to place one of our officers in harm's way in the process."

"You're a bunch of Woosies. I'm all for kicking in the door, kicking butt and taking names. You have to come up with sensible safe alternatives. Thanks guys! I'm afraid I got target fixation and didn't think this through. Seriously, your ideas are much better than mine. I think it's time to go to the Boss and have him call some of the other chiefs for personnel and possibly equipment. Who wants to go with me?"

David volunteered. We walked down the hall to the sheriff's office. Patti Nelson was her usual cheerful self and gave us a big smile.

"I'm sure this isn't a good omen. Every time you come without calling it's an emergency. One of these times I'm not going to be able to grease you in. He's free. I'll buzz him, but I'm sure you can go in."-

"Come on in boys. What do you have for me? I hope it's something good."

I spoke first, "Sheriff, the team has discussed our next steps in this case. We think we have to bring in Emilee Lukin. Our information from Ammo is that she was a close associate with the Scudders in the U.K. It's our belief that we can charge her with being an accomplice to the Scudders in the four homicides. If we can convince her she's facing a long time in prison, she might roll over on the Scudders. The other possibility is that she's truly an accomplice and the Scudders may have holed up in her condo. At present we're thinking that our first step will be to go to Dr. Matile's veterinary office where Emilee works. If she's there, we'll bring her in for questioning. The issue gets cloudy if she's not there. Morgan has volunteered to go to the office. We think that's an activity without risk. If we find that Emilee is on a normal day off, we thought about going to her condo on a ruse. Our operator would try to gain access to the condo. If on the other hand, Emilee has called in sick, the issue clouds. Is she sick? Or is she shielding the Scudders or worse yet have the Scudders taken her hostage?

We think that if Emilee isn't at work, we have a safety problem. David and Gunter have suggested that we fall back on the 'Avista gas leak or power outage ruse.' I concur. We know that'll require additional personnel and equipment. Your clout can get those things from other agencies. David and I'd appreciate your thoughts on the tentative plan."

"Well you're hitting me with some big issues early in the morning. You've obviously given this some serious thought. Give me a minute to absorb what you just told me.

I'll say quickly, that I see no problem with sending Morgan to the vet's office. We'll hope that works. Realistically, hoping doesn't accomplish much. Am I being too philosophical? Action accomplishes things. I'm not ready to put any officer in danger. Let's get Captain Nearing and his Sergeants in here and hash this out with more eyes and brains to focus on the problem."

"Patti, would you call Captain Nearing and ask him to bring in the Shift Sergeants with him?"

"Sheriff, Captain Nearing is on the street. His ETA is fifteen minutes."

"O.K. thanks. When does the vet's office open Jake?"

"Probably at eight hundred hours. We've figured if we shoot for ten hundred, we have about an hour. We want to provide cover for Morgan so we're not planning on sending her in alone. We'll park down the street and in the adjacent parking lot. Morgan is slick. She can bring it off. Shall David and I come back in fifteen?"

"Why don't you get Gunter, Woody, and Morgan and we'll meet in the conference room."

"Sir, Woody has been doing the night shift for Heidi Matile. She's at the 'Safe House' right now. We can call her and fill her in once we come up with a hard plan if that's O.K. with you?"

"That'll work. Maybe we should bring in Jay Bass on this brainstorming session. He has an analytical mind and might give us insight us 'Road Dogs' might miss."

"We'll stop by the lab on the way back to the bullpen to get Gunter."

Fifteen minutes seemed to fly by. We almost had to run to make the conference room on time. Jay was already there.

The sheriff started the meeting by outlining our plans and possible obstacles. I was amazed at his grasp of both the problem and possible solutions. No one on the team could have done it better.

Gunter called Woody to bring her up to date. She advised she was enroute.

The collective discussion from the assembled supervisors was at times heated. Cooler heads prevailed. After about half an hour a tentative plan evolved.

As we were prepared to reduce the plan to writing on the whiteboard, Woody arrived.

She apologized for being late. The sheriff explained that she had been on duty all night and was doing double duty at a 'Safe House.'

Due to operational security he didn't elaborate. "Safe House' operations are discussed on a 'Need to Know' basis. No one, other than our team and the sheriff knew why it was in operation and who was being protected.

Gunter was at the whiteboard to write out the agreed upon plan. As he wrote the words, 'Avista Gas Leak/Power Outage', Woody tentatively raised her hand. The sheriff recognized her and asked for her comment.

"I apologize for having been late, I'm also aware that there are a lot of people in the room with a lot more law enforcement experience than I have. But I think the 'Gas Leak/Power Outage Ruse' has been used in every cop show on TV. If the Scudders are as sharp as they have led us to believe, they won't fall for it. They'll stay in the house and we won't be any wiser. May I suggest that we modify that ruse? Terrorism is on everyone's mind. Why don't we do a 'Bomb Scare?' That way we can dress our officers in protective gear and get people out of their houses. If there is no explosion, they'll be grateful and no harm done. I hate to hog the floor, but we had a good experience with Fairchild EOD. Perhaps they can roll their truck here to make it look more realistic. I'll shut up now."

Woody sat down. The room was dead quiet. Woody blushed a bright red. Gunter stood at the whiteboard looking very perplexed. The sheriff was standing, but also looking slightly befuddled. He gathered himself and gave a slight cough.

"Well, I guess we all learned a lesson from Woody. Do we all concur that her plan was better than ours?"

There was general agreement. Everyone pitched in and fine-tuned the details of the plan. The sheriff had Patti Nelson call EOD. She said that Sergeant Hiwans would roll his team at eleven hundred hours unless he received an actual emergency call. I called John Preston to see if he could scramble Sky One for air cover. The plan was coming together.

Ten hundred hours was fast approaching. The sheriff dismissed the meeting and we returned to the bullpen to get ready to send Morgan into the vet's office.

Morgan would drive her personal car to the office. Woody taped the body transmitter on her. We checked the transmitter for sound quality. All four of us would provide cover, each in their individual vehicle. Woody would be the closest car. We left the office and drove to the edge of Post Falls and the vet's office.

Morgan went into the office. We sat in our car totally focused on our receivers. Emilee wasn't in the office. Morgan asked if she'd be in later? The receptionist replied that she had called in ill. She wasn't expected until tomorrow. I called the sheriff to say that we were going with 'Plan A.' He said he and Patti would make the activation calls.

Writing out plans on a whiteboard and tear sheets is pretty simple. Mobilizing the logistics to implement the plan is difficult. In my personal and professional experience, the best laid plans always have a failsafe clause. Our fail safe clause was Sky One. This was to provide cover if, when people in Emilee's neighborhood evacuated their homes, the Scudders got into a vehicle and tried to leave the area. We'd contacted Post Falls P.D. and arranged for wooden barricades to surround the immediate neighborhood. This would support our alleged search for the bomber and bomb itself. Post Falls has a relatively small P.D. We had asked Coeur d'Alene P.D. to supplement both their P.D. and our department. We'd done the basics. Now we had to 'Put Boots on the Ground.' And implement the plan.

CHAPTER TWENTY TWO

Our plan required a Post Falls officer to actually knock on Emilee's door. The Post Falls patch on the officer's shirt would reinforce the ruse. We'd shown the selected officer the Scudder pictures from Ammo and Emilee's picture from her driver's license. She was positive she would recognize both Emilee and the Scudders if they answered the door.

EOD rolled up to the Post Falls P.D at 1130 hours. Sergeant Hiwans left Fairchild AFB a little early. The truck with the large words BOMB DISPOSAL on the side would be a visual reinforcement of our ruse.

Coeur d'Alene SWAT rolled in behind them.

Post Falls had their street department standing by with the wooden barricades.

Our SWAT team had caravanned behind us from the office.

KXLY TV had a station in Coeur d'Alene. We had a close working relationship with them. They had agreed to make an eleven thirty announcement that an alleged bomb threat had been phoned into to Post Falls P.D. This would seem normal and if the Scudders were watching TV would give our ruse credibility. We agreed that they could have an exclusive of the results of any investigative outcome.

We had the Kootenai County Emergency/Disaster Command Truck positioned at the end of Emilee's street. Farm Garden Road was a short street. We had determined that we would only have to evacuate ten dwellings to make it look realistic.

SWAT teams would be evacuating the condos on the left, right, directly across the street, and directly behind Emilee's condo. This would get us in close with highly trained personnel.

Our team, Woody, Gunter, David and I would be in SWAT clothing complete with helmets, goggles, knee, elbow pads, and threat level four body armor (Level four is the most practical protective body armor an officer can wear. Anything else is too cumbersome to be practical. There are higher levels of protection that SWAT Teams wear for dynamic entry use, but you can't move easily in that type of armor.)

The plan was for us to follow the Sheriff's SWAT team inside when they entered Emilee's condo if she and the Scudders did not voluntarily leave when the Post Falls officers knocked on the door.

This was our 'Plan B' to be implemented only, if the very detailed "Plan A" fell apart.

The team gathered in a circle and all put our hands into the center of the circle. We grasped each other's hands and had a moment of silent prayer.

My prayer was for the team's safety and a sincere hope that we would not have to implement 'Plan B.'

Emilee lived in a condo complex that closely resembled one-story ranch homes. Every-other dwelling shared a common wall. The two-car garages were at the front of the condo. When the officer was at the door she was out of sight. We had to rely on her body transmitter to keep us advised of the events at the door.

We assigned the teams to the condos on the block. The Post Falls officer went to 898 Farm Garden Road. Our SWAT Team had divided into two segments. David and I were with one segment at 896. Gunter and Woody were with the other segment at 900. Coeur d'Alene had a team across the street at 897. We had placed a body transmitter on the Post Falls officer. Each member of the team had a special receiver to listen to the conversation at the door. We were on pins and needles as the officer went to the door.

"Good morning sir, I'm Officer Deanna Kinder of the Post Falls Police Department. I'm afraid that we've found a pipe bomb in the neighborhood. We have sniffer dogs combing the area for possible additional explosive devices. We have the Fairchild EOD here to handle the device we've found. They've requested that we evacuate the immediate area. We have an assembly point two blocks from here. We'd appreciate if you and every member of your family go to that area immediately. May I ask your name and how many persons are currently in this house? This is for our roster so we can account for everyone in the neighborhood."

"My name is Brian Fox, I'm here alone. My wife is at the grocery store in Post Falls. We're house sitting for a friend of ours. Would it be possible for me not to go to the assembly point and just drive into downtown Post Falls? I can call my wife on her cell phone. She could park her car in the store lot and get in my car with me. We have appointments in Spokane this afternoon. If we go to the assembly point, we'll be stuck until they declare the area safe. That would cause us to miss our first appointment. We're involved in a lawsuit and this is the only time we can meet with both our lawyer and opposing counsel. If we don't make the one o'clock appointment it will set our case back months. You understand don't you?"

Admittedly, we hadn't planned for this eventuality. We'd made plans for no answer. We'd made plans for Emilee to answer the door. We made plans for a Scudder to answer the door and the other Scudder and Emilee to be inside. Now Ronnie has said that he's alone and his wife is shopping. Now we don't know if Emilee is inside, captive or dead, or if Ronnie and Loni have split-up and he is saying that Emilee is his wife and is the one shopping.

We had done a complete work-up on Emilee when she drove Heidi to this address. We knew her vehicle make and license number. I immediately put out a BOL for Emilee's car. A 2008 Dark Blue Subaru Outback, License number K 471900.

Deanna was an excellent officer. She thought fast on her feet and asked, Mr. Fox what kind of car is your wife driving? We have established roadblocks to prevent anyone from coming into the neighborhood. She may be stopped at the roadblock. If she's three of four cars back from the officers she may not know what is going on yet and would worry about you. I can call our dispatch and have them reroute your wife to a rendezvous point out of the immediate area. We know what a hassle this is for everyone concerned and we're trying to lessen the inconvenience if we can."

There was a long pregnant pause before Ronnie answered.

"Officer Kinder, that's very nice, let me call her now to see if she still in the store or stopped at a roadblock."

"Actually Mr. Fox, we would prefer that you don't use a cell phone until the EOD has defused or safely detonated the bomb. We can't be sure that the bomb won't be detonated by a cell phone. I'm sure you understand. Our portable radios operate on a special frequency that has been determined to be safe."

We experienced another pregnant pause as Ronnie mentally worked out a plausible answer.

It was extremely nerve wracking for our team members not have a visual on the door where this was taking place. Officer Kinder was doing an outstanding job of thinking on her feet and improvising.

After what seemed like a full minute, Ronnie said, "O.K. Officer, I understand that you have my best interests at heart. My wife is driving a dark blue Subaru. I don't know the year or license plate. It belongs to the lady we're house sitting for. My wife was going to Super 1 and the Walgreens on Seltice. I expect her home any minute so she may be stopped at one of the roadblocks I'd appreciate it if you'd make the call. I'll grab my jacket and files and start toward Seltice and Spokane Street. If you reach her would you tell her that? Once I'm out of the area, I'll call her on my cell and repeat the message. You've been very helpful! Thank you."

Officer Kinder walked away from the door and once she was out of possible earshot, she began giving us details,

"The male who answered the door was Ronnie Scudder. He's dressed in a light blue dress shirt and dark blue slacks. His hair is a very light blonde and looks almost like an expensive wig. He only opened the front door partially. As if he wanted to prevent me from walking in. There was a light sheen of perspiration on his forehead. That might have been because he was nervous or the wig was making him sweat. He kept looking over his shoulder, but after the first few minutes of our conversation seemed to calm down. He began smiling and was almost coming on to me with his syrupy voice. It was almost as if he decided he'd pulled the wool over my eyes and won the battle. I'm going to the Command Post Van so we can discuss any details you might need."

Officer Deanna Kinder was a real professional. She had managed Ronnie Scudder as well as anyone could have. I had notified all three SWAT Teams to stand-by for a vehicle leaving the garage at 898. We didn't know what Ronnie would be driving, but apparently he and Loni had obtained some type of transportation. We had the EOD truck pull down Farm Garden Road and stop in front of the driveway leading out of the garage at 898. We had SWAT teams with body bunker shields milling around and the 'sniffer dog' was actually a patrol dog that would attack if commanded to do so. If Ronnie drove out of the garage, he would have a serious problem getting his vehicle past the EOD truck. We hoped it looked as if the EOD folks were unaware that he was attempting to meet his wife.

Our plan was to surround Ronnie's vehicle with superior firepower and hope that common sense prevailed. Seeing his escape route blocked with the EOD truck and SWAT officers with body bunkers shields on both sides of his vehicle, he should realize that he was caught.

The garage door started to roll up. A Cadillac STS rolled out of the door. Ronnie Scudder was driving. A SWAT Team member stepped in behind the Cadillac and two officers with body bunker shields stepped up to each door. Ronnie had about fifteen feet from the end of the STS to the EOD Truck. A reasonable man would have stopped and raised his hands in surrender.

Ronnie Scudder wasn't a reasonable man. He hit the accelerator jerked the wheel to the right and knocked the SWAT officer flat on his butt. Thankfully, the body bunker took the majority of the shock. He fishtailed the Cadillac across the lawn and slid onto to Farm Garden at about forty miles an hour smashing through the wooden barricade like it was balsa wood. The radio was instantly jammed with everyone trying to marshal a reactionary response. Sky One was hovering overhead and immediately began an aerial surveillance.

All of our vehicles were on the outer perimeter. Trying to run with all the SWAT gear on was cumbersome. It had been a while since I was on a SWAT Team. The intervening years were taking a toll on my ability to carry weight and jog. Maybe I should add a backpack to my morning jogs. Sky One asked us to go to Tac Two. I advised that it would be a couple of minutes until we got into our cars. Most portable radios don't have the ability to operate on scrambled channels.

Sky One advised that the suspect was heading south on Chase Road at approximately fifty miles an hour. It was possible that he would go to Seltice and turn east to arrive at Spokane Street. This was the location he said he would meet his wife. I was betting that he had placed a cell phone call and arranged an alternate meeting location.

We had arrived at our cars and shed some of the SWAT gear. I suggested that we keep on the threat level four vests. They might come in handy if Ronnie decided to attempt another dangerous escape.

Post Falls dispatch called to say that they had made a vehicle stop on Emile's Subaru at Seltice and Henry Street. The driver was being uncooperative, had locked the doors and would not roll down her window. Efforts to have her show identification met with no success. The physical description was of a mid twenties-early thirties white female with short brown hair. Since the driver was seated, further physical description could not be determined.

We were faced with a real conundrum now. Ronnie was running. A female was in Emilee's car and was being contained. We needed to split our team and identify the female. Part of the team would join in Ronnie's pursuit.

I advised Sky One we could go to Tac Two for Ronnie's pursuit. Gunter and Woody would go to Seltice and Henry to attempt to identify the female in Emilee's car. David and I would join in Ronnie's pursuit.

"Sky One on Tac Two. Suspect has turned west on Seltice. He's ramped his speed up to seventy. Erratic vehicle operation! He's passing on both the right and left side. If he hits traffic, he's gonna crash! If we can get some Washington State Patrol vehicles to set up at the state line, we can deploy some spike strips. The Seltice Bridge over the Spokane River is being rebuilt. He can't get on I-90 from Seltice. If he doesn't turn on Pleasant View, he can't get to I-90. He'll hit a dead end at the bridge and we've got him trapped.

Gunter and Woody advised they were monitoring both Post Falls and Tac Two as they rolled toward Seltice and Henry.

David and I were in separate cars and heading west on Seltice from Spokane Street.

"Sky One here, the suspect passed Pleasant view Road and is still heading west at seventy miles an hour. Delta Six, you boys better hurry! I've got Washington State Patrol set up on I-90 but it doesn't look like he's gonna get on the Interstate. Post Falls you better send some additional units west on Seltice. This guy's driving squirrelly! Once he hits the dead end. There's no telling what he's gonna do!"

"Delta Six, Delta Ten here, the female in the Subaru is Emilee. If she doesn't open the door or roll down the window, we're going to break the passenger side window and forcibly extract her from the vehicle. Post Falls has their Watch Commander enroute to our location. I think at this juncture we should send one of our units and a Post Falls unit to 898. Either Loni is in the house or she's hiding in Ronnie's car and we haven't seen her yet. What do you think?"

"Lets bring in Alpha One on this decision, you know me, I say do it! Boss are you on Tac Two?"

"That's affirmative Delta Six. It's also affirmative to send a unit to 898. I'm of the opinion that we have exigent circumstances to enter the house. I'm gonna check that with the D.A.'s office to make sure, but I'll start a unit that way. I'm with the Post Falls Chief. He says he has units rolling toward the west end of Seltice. He'll divert one unit to 898. He's of the opinion we have exigent circumstances also."

"Thanks Boss! We're rolling 'Code Three' trying to catch-up. The traffic is light and Ronnie has apparently spooked them with his erratic driving. They are pulling far to the right when we light them up.

"Delta Six, Alpha One here, Post Falls had Officer Kinder enroute to 898. I'm sending Lima Thirty, Deputy James to 898. This way we'll have two females on the scene. If the other Scudder is in the house, they may be able to convince her to talk. At least they can subdue her if necessary and hold her for the team."

Sky One again, suspect is about two miles from the dead end still at seventy. He's blown past multiple warning signs about the bridge being closed. We're turning on the loudspeaker and dropping down to one hundred feet altitude to try to get his attention. This isn't looking good! He's not slowing at all. We're going to move ahead and warn the workers on the bridge. If he doesn't stop, he's gonna launch off the Idaho end of the bridge but he's gonna land in the Washington side of the Spokane River about fifty feet below the bridge. There is a huge gap in the bridge. I'm telling the workers to get out of the way. He's not slowing!"

This was too weird! Nora drove the Jaguar into the North Sea. Now the person who is avenging her death is going to drive the Cadillac into the Spokane River. If crashing into the warning barricades doesn't stop him, the flight into mid air and resulting impact of hitting the river after a fifty-foot plunge, will surely kill him. The Spokane River is not very deep at the Idaho ~ Washington Line and the river bottom is strewn with rocks. Ronnie crashing into that river will surely end his life.

My hope now was that he didn't take some of the construction crew with him. At his speed they didn't have much time to get out of the way.

"Sky One to all units. He's airborne. I'm calling Spokane County Sheriff's River Rescue. This will be a body recovery, not a rescue operation. Chances of him living after that dive are slim. The Cadillac went in nose first. That's lucky, it probably won't burn. The rear end appears intact. The airbags deployed. Washington State Police are responding from the truck scales at the state line. They'll secure the scene until Spokane S.O arrives. If he survived, they'll pull him out of the wreck. He's on the Washington side so they have jurisdiction. O.K. Delta Six is there anything else we can do for you?"

"Sky One could we ask you to return back to 898 Farm Garden? We're still missing one suspect. Loni Scudder, the other twin has not been located. Our sheriff and Post Falls both have officers enroute to make a forcible entry if necessary. If Loni is in the house and attempts to flee, we might need you to do another aerial surveillance. We had SWAT units on the scene cleaning up from the bomb search. So the house has been under surveillance the entire time. We don't think she has had an opportunity to slip out with being detected. Air support would be a big plus."

"Roger Delta Six, Sky One enroute to 898 Farm Garden. We've got about one additional hour of fuel on board. If she flees, we can stay with her for the hour then we'll have to break off to refuel. Your officers better flush her out fast."

"Thanks Sky One, You and your crew can count on a huge steak with Liz as the chef. We'll keep you advised."

I called Gunter and Woody to ask them to bring Emilee to the house. My plan was to have her and Loni in the same room when the interview started. We were going to keep the fact that Ronnie had driven his car off the bridge from them. I was sure the media would be covering that crash as soon as they could roll their remote broadcast vehicles to the scene.

"Delta Six, Washington State Patrol on the scene has advised that your suspect is DOA. He wasn't seat belted. The air bags didn't save him. WSP and Spokane S.O are requesting one of your officers to make a positive I.D. They ran the plates. The Cadillac was a rental. Rented to Brian Fox. That was his alias wasn't it?"

"Affirmative Sky One. Ask them to stand-by. We're rolling toward 898. As soon as we can clear that detail I'll roll someone. Better yet, we have the suspect's British passport in our evidence room. I'll have one of our evidence techs bring it to the Spokane morgue for a positive I.D. The crash didn't mess up his face did it?"

"Don't know. I'll ask."

"Delta Six, nope! Face intact. Officers on the scene say the passport idea is excellent. Suspects body enroute to the Spokane County morgue. Spokane S.O. has a tow enroute to recover the Cadillac. They'll process it for forensics and make copies for your agency. Anything you're particularly interested in that they should focus on?"

"Nope! Just the usual micro search from bumper to bumper."

"Sky One we'll be out of contact for a few. We're at 898 and on portables. No Tac Two available. If you need us go to our Channel One. If our suspect rabbits, we'll alert you on Channel One and switch when we get to our vehicles."

"We'll monitor you on Channel One."

David, Gunter, Woody and I arrived at 898 at the same time. Deputy James and Officer Hinder had made entry. Post Falls SWAT had assisted in the entry. They had gone from room to room making sure that the condo was empty. One SWAT Team member had gone into the attic crawl space to verify that there was no one hiding there. The condos were built on concrete slab so there was no basement. We had no Loni Scudder in Emilee's house

I immediately called Sky One on Channel One and asked them to relay to WSP to closely examine the entire Cadillac to make sure there was no one in the trunk. I sent Woody and Gunter to rendezvous with Spokane S.O. on the Washington side of the river to be present when they brought the Cadillac out of the river. If Ronnie didn't survive the dive with the aid of air bags, I was sure that Loni wouldn't have survived without air bags if; she was hidden in the trunk of the Cadillac. I wanted Kootenai Detectives on the scene when the trunk was opened.

CHAPTER TWENTY THREE

David and I took Emilee into the house and sat her at the dining room table.

"Emilee we need to ask you some hard questions. We want your cooperation to help us solve this case. Ronnie was hiding here. Where is Loni? Ronnie got away. We have a BOL out for him and his Cadillac. Was Loni in the Cadillac with him?

"Detectives I've no idea who you're talking about. Brian Fox came by to visit for a few days. He told me Annalee was ill in hospital in Spokane. I'd gone to the store to get some cake mix to make her a cake. Her birthday is tomorrow. Brian asked me to pick up some Prilosec for him while I was out. So I went to Walgreens. Post

Falls Police pulled me over when I was returning home. I don't know any Ronnie or Loni. Brian was driving a Cadillac and it was parked in my garage. I haven't looked in the garage but I assumed it was still there. I was surprised when I came in the house that Brian wasn't here. I'm afraid you have the advantage over me. Why was I pulled over by Post Falls Police and brought to my home in handcuffs?"

As I was talking to Emilee, I noticed that she was wearing a Coeur d'Alene ring on her little finger. It was made of gold and silver. The small heart was pierced with an awl. It had to be an item created by Cheryl Burchell. Only Burchell could make something so delicate and beautiful. Based upon my observation and Emilee's statement, I motioned for David that I was going to terminate the interview. We weren't going to make any progress with her sitting in her own dining room in her comfort zone. If we're going to extract any information from Emilee, we're going to have to put her in a different environment. The best environment for that was our interview room at the sheriff's office.

"Emilee, I've just gotten a call on my radio that we're needed at a different location. We're going to have Deputy James drive you to our office. As soon as we can get there, we'll continue this conversation. For officer safety reasons, we're going to have to keep you in cuffs. That's a department policy if you're being transported in a sheriff's vehicle. We're sure you understand. It's uncomfortable, but necessary."

David called in Deputy James to take Emilee to her marked unit and secure her in the back seat. Once she had her secured, she should return inside the house to meet with us.

Deputy James came back to the dining room,

I said, "Shayla, we want you to take Emilee Lukin to Interview Room One and sit with her. Don't talk to her and don't answer any questions. Particularly don't smile. Just sit there as if you're both deaf and mute. Stare at her occasionally and make sort of 'Harrumphing' sounds. Don't show outright disgust, but border your stares and 'Harrumphing' on the edge of disgust. Cross your arms and occasionally jump up and walk around behind her and just stand. Then come back and sit with your arms crossed. David and I will be along in about fifteen minutes, so you don't have to worry about a civil rights lawsuit for not allowing her to go to the bathroom or give her water. We'll take care of that when we arrive at the interview room. Any questions?"

"No sir. Actually, I've a ton of questions, but I'll save them for later. Right now I'll transport her, put her in Interview One, and wait for your arrival."

"Shayla, you're a gem! Thanks!"

"O.K. David, we've got our work cut out for us. Emilee wearing the Coeur d'Alene ring is no small coincidence. Her trying to play 'Poor Pitiful Me' is cold and calculating. She's going to try to make us believe that she's an innocent pawn in the larger scheme of things. We've got to put her in a psychologically stressful posture to crack that cold exterior. At the moment, I'm thinking that we should do an 'Information Overload' style interview. I'll bet that Emilee has no idea how much we know about her, the Scudders, and Nora. We're gonna have to 'Baffle her with Bull' you know tell her so much that it appears that we know every answer. All we're trying to do is confirm what we know. This requires that we don't tell her an outright lie, if she catches us in an outright lie; we've lost the battle and the war. We'll have to walk a fine edge of being on the fence between whole truth and falling off that fence. I think with all the data we have it will allow us to walk the line. I almost sound like Johnny Cash don't I?"

"No partner to 'Ole David' here you sound like a cold calculating monster. Man you sure can come up with detailed game plans out of the blue. Why did you give those weird instructions to Shayla James?"

"I'm setting the scene for our ultimate entry into Interview One. By accusing her, without actually accusing her she should feel some relief when we enter the room and begin to talk to her. We'll start off slow and almost apologetic. As she loosens up, we'll toss in some occasional harder inquiries. We don't hit her with hard questions. If she begins to tense up, we back off. Drinks, snacks, personal needs breaks will happen as often as possible. We'll be unceremoniously interrupted to go to a crime scene. We'll put in a male deputy or detective. He or she'll repeat Shayla's performance. The polar opposites of us as a team and her 'captors' will make her really uncomfortable. Our second trip into the room will be a general discussion of family, vacations, sports, hometowns, good books, and music. No questions. No work related references. No display of badges, weapons, and no note taking, just a nice social gathering. We'll get a second call for a crime scene and we put a 'captor' back in the room. We can only do this for about two hours and then we're skating on thin ice.

If my training is on point, she should be ready to talk with us by then. Shall we head for the office partner?"

"O.K. Monster. I'm ready. Now that I know the plan, I'll try to make a contribution. I'm sure glad we're on the same side. If for no other reason, I'll be law abiding. I don't want to sit across the interview table from you. You're absolutely scary!"

David and I got in our cars and started the drive back to Coeur d'Alene and our office. We were still puzzled about Loni. Why would Ronnie keep her in the trunk, if she was indeed in the trunk, while he was making his escape? We had no marked units close behind him during his flight. Sky one was high enough that it wouldn't have been obvious. Did he think he could make it to Washington and be free of pursuing officers? I'm thinking that he was going to do another carjacking. Opening the trunk and having a female standing beside the open trunk would prompt a motorist to stop.

Woody called on Channel One.

"Delta Six, Delta Eleven here. Ronnie was the driver of the Cadillac. The trunk is empty. No Loni. Ronnie had thrown two suitcases in the back seat. They're dry. Spokane S.O. has seized them as evidence. We're going to their evidence lab with the lead detective. They'll process them for prints and we can witness the opening. He had the .380 in his trouser pocket. They ran the serial number. It comes back registered to Kirk Logan. His last listed address is in Priest Lake. I'm calling Morgan on my cell to see if he was related to Nicole. Did Emilee cooperate?"

"Negative Delta Eleven. She's enroute to Government Way with Lima Thirty. We'll keep you advised. Anything else of interest in Ronnie's pockets?"

"Wallet with the Brian Fox identity papers, eight hundred dollars in one hundred dollar bills, membership card for the English Chinese Alliance Club. Address on the card is for Oxford, U.K. He also had a small Buck knife and most interesting, a white handkerchief. The handkerchief is monogrammed with Chinese characters in red. We think it is the same Chinese characters as the signature on the note. Gunter took a digital and cell phone picture of the characters. He's sending it to our crime lab's email address for comparison. That's it."

"I'm anxious to see the picture. We'll stop by the lab and see what Jay's team comes up with. I'll send an email to Inspector Forbes to see what information he can gather on the club and its members."

David and I checked the CCTV monitor in Interview One. Emilee and Shayla James were there and not one sound was coming over the mics in the room. Shayla looked suitably grumpy and Emilee was beginning to look worried. So far the plan was working.

We checked with Jay Bass in the lab. He confirmed that the cell phone picture from Gunter was identical to the characters on the note pinned to Dr. Hardcastle's chest.

"Jay I've emailed Robbie Forbes in England. Ronnie had a membership card in his wallet from the English Chinese Alliance Club. The card had an address in Oxford, England. Maybe Robbie can find out some info on the club and its' members. Loni wasn't in the Cadillac. David and

I are going into Interview One to talk to Emilee Lukin. Maybe we can get a lead on her whereabouts."

"Deputy James, we'll take over now. Thanks for sitting in for us. Miss Lukin, we apologize for the delay. We can get down to business now. At your house you alleged that you didn't know Ronnie or Loni Scudder. The man at your house was known to you as Brian Fox and his wife's name was Annalee. Is that correct?"

"Why do you say alleged? That's the truth! I met Brian and Annalee here in Coeur d'Alene. They were also friends with Nicole Logan. We saw each other only occasionally. The last time I saw them was at the Fitness Center. They were staying with Nicole, but due to her murder, they apparently moved to a motel in Spokane. Brian was being recruited by a firm in Spokane."

Emilee's body language was not indicative of truth telling. Her emphasis on saying that she was telling the truth was too strong. She then filled in too much detail without being asked. All of my alarm bells went off.

"Emilee, I have to tell you that I've been in the police business for a long time. I've heard almost every story in the book. David here has also been in the police business for quite a while. He's heard any story I might have missed. What you're telling us is a bald faced lie. David and I have another case to handle right now. We're going to leave you with another detective for a short while. While we're gone, we want you to concentrate on finding the truth in your heart. If you don't change your story, we'll have no alternative but to charge you with being an accomplice to the four murders committed by Ronnie and Loni Scudder. Do you understand what we've just said? That is a serious charge. Not to be taken lightly."

I left the room. David stayed with Emilee. I contacted a detective and briefed him on the behavior we would like him to display with Emilee. He understood and agreed as long as he would not be liable for a potential civil rights suit.

David and I met back in the bullpen. Morgan had done the work-up on Nicole Logan. "Nicole's father's name was Kirk. He's deceased so apparently Nicole inherited the .380 from him. Ronnie apparently stole it from Nicole. I also took the liberty of doing a work-up update on Emilee. She made a cash withdrawal two days ago of one thousand dollars. Possibly that's where the eight hundred dollars in Ronnie's wallet came from. Emilee has made four withdrawals of one thousand dollars each in the past three weeks. She receives her normal bi-weekly paycheck from the veterinarian's office. She has a low balance on three credit cards that she pays in a timely manner. To my mind, four thousand dollars in three weeks is unusual. Did she have any money in her purse?"

"Shayla probably put her purse in the security locker when she placed her in number one. I'll go fetch that and her cell phone now. We weren't ready to do an "Information Overload Interview' quite yet, but her purse might give us some additional ammunition. David, would you grab our file and extract the email from Ammo where he details the info about the parties at Oxford. Copy only that part, not divulging the source or origin of the information. We'll do a little fancy footwork on Miss Emilee."

"Morgan, again you're a jewel in our crown. Where would we be without you and your computer skills? I guess that's rhetorical. I know where we'd be, stumped and ignorant!"

A close examination of Emilee's purse did yield some interesting items.

#1. Eighty three dollars and forty cents.

#2. A credit card receipt for Super One.

#3. A credit card receipt for Walgreens.

#4. A credit card receipt for Northwestern Travel Agency in the amount of two thousand dollars and nineteen cents for airline tickets.

#5. A membership card for the English Chinese Alliance Club.

#6. An Idaho driver's license in her name.

#7. Miscellaneous business cards. Two cards of interest, One from Liz's art collective. The second from Joanne Stebbins at Northwest Travel.

Emilee's cell phone also yielded some items of interest. Her contact list was revealing. A contact list is usually alphabetical unless you code your numbers to allow rapid access to frequently called numbers. Emilee had coded six numbers. Her code was pretty simple. The numbers were designated by a sequence of the letter "A."

#1. "A" ~ Office

#2. "AA" ~ Ronnie

#3. "AAA" ~Loni

#4. "AAAA" ~ Ronnie~Tosser

#5. "AAAAA" ~ Loni~Tosser

#6. "AAAAAA" Nicole's house

David and I discussed this revealing information. Emilee would have a difficult time denying knowing Ronnie and Loni based on her phone. I asked Morgan to call Joanne Stebbins to see what was the destination of the purchased tickets. I also asked her to see who the passengers were. David and I shared the series of "A's" I took numbers four and five. David took numbers two and three. I dialed the number associated with number three. The phone rang four times before it was answered with a gruff, "Hello"

I said, "Hello. I'm trying to reach Ronnie. Did I dial the wrong number?"

The man on the other end said, "No. Ronnie isn't available right now. Can I have him call you back? Give me your number and he'll call in less than ten minutes."

Every good investigative agency has what they call a "Hello" number. This is a 'cold' phone that is allegedly, untraceable. It's always answered with a simple, "Hello." This is the number used by informants and undercover officers to give to crooks to verify employment, an address, or for any other use. I gave the caller our "Hello" number. I was curious to see if the caller used Ronnie's phone or another. We would place an immediate trace on both phones and if 'Ronnie's Tosser' was a cell, I hoped it had a GPS so we could triangulate it and get a location.

While we were waiting for the return call, I dialed number five. That phone rang and rang with no answer and apparently the phone did not have a message center set up. After thirty rings I gave up.

David called number two. It was answered after the third ring. He got the same gruff "Hello." Again the man said the Ronnie wasn't available but would call him back soon. David gave him the "Hello Number" We might have a problem if the same man had received the same 'Hello' number. David and I immediately collaborated on a story as to why two different men were calling Ronnie.

In eight minutes our "Hello Phone" rang. I answered. The caller said, "Jake? This is Gunter. Spokane S.O. evidence folks were just opening Ronnie's suitcases when one of them began to ring. We were hoping it was Loni. When they showed Woody and me the number, we knew it was either you or David calling. Ronnie had two cell phones in his small suitcase. One phone, the first one called is a contract phone. You buy pre-paid minutes. This is a 'Throwaway Phone.' The second is a Verizon phone. We can probably check to see the info he provided to get the service. For a few seconds we thought we had struck pay dirt. How did you get the numbers?"

"Emilee's cell phone. She coded the phones in Ronnie and Loni's names. The 'Throwaway' is coded: 'Ronnie's Tosser.' So she knew it was a throwaway. I was thinking that she was using British slang. In the U.K. calling someone a 'Tosser' is an unkind label."

David had the same response to his call to number three. There was no answer to Loni's number and no message center set up. It looked as though either Loni was just not answering or had her phones turned off.

"Partner, shall we go back into One? I think Miss Emilee has stewed enough. I had wanted to do one more 'captor' session, but I think we can do the 'Overload' session now and achieve some success."

"Jake, I'll follow your lead. I've extracted the critical info from Ammo's email and have inserted it in the dummy case folder that we use for 'Overload' so let's go."

"Miss Lukin, again we apologize for the interruptions. David and I've been so busy that we almost meet our selves coming and going. I hope you've had time to reflect on our last conversation and have looked into your heart to decide to tell us the truth. I'll begin by saying that we have absolute proof that you know Ronnie and Loni Scudder. So continuing that attempt at deception is fruitless. David and I don't want to inform the District Attorney that you should be the subject of an indictment for four murders. It is a general rule of law that an accomplice is considered as guilty as the perpetrator. You know that we have four dead bodies in our morgue. Detective David and I, as a matter of fact the entire detective division, believe that you aided and abetted Ronnie and Loni Scudder to commit the serial murderers. This is the perfect time to clarify your position in these crimes."

"Detective Lowry, I have no idea what you're talking about. I know no Ronnie or Loni Scudder or what those names are. I AM friends with Brian and Annalee Fox! If they have another name, I'm unaware of it!"

"David, why don't you excuse yourself and go call the D.A. Tell them we have a suspect in custody for the four homicides and want them to come do a confirming interview prior to charging her."

David rose and left the room.

"Miss Lukin, based upon your insistence on lying, I have no alternative than to advise you of your rights. Emilee Tish Lukin you are being charged with four counts of first degree murder. You are under arrest for those charges. You have the right to remain silent. That is say nothing at all. If you decide to speak with me, or any member of this department, anything you say may be used in evidence against you. You have the right to an attorney, if you can't afford an attorney, one will be appointed for you free of charge. Those are your rights. Do you understand what I have just said? Having those rights in mind, do you want an attorney?"

"No. I don't need an attorney. I've done nothing wrong!"

"Since you have refused an attorney, do you wish to continue to answer our questions without an attorney present?"

"Of course. I have nothing to hide. Ask anything you wish."

David returned.

"I have a D.A. on the way. Mac is coming over. She should be here in fifteen minutes."

"Emilee, you just heard what may turn out to be a death knell. You have fifteen minutes to convince David and me that you don't know anything about these crimes. I'll tell you truthfully, so far you haven't done a very good job. We'll open the case file to show you why we can state that unequivocally.

David opened the file to the emails where they discussed Nora, Ronnie, Loni and Emilee's attendance at the American students living quarters in Oxford. I pulled her cell phone out of my trouser pocket and flipped the phone open to her contact listing. I then took the major gamble of the interview.

"Emilee, I called the numbers listed for Ronnie. He answered and we triangulated his location. Ronnie is now in custody of the Spokane Sheriff's Department. He has agreed to talk without an attorney. He has implicated you in all four crimes. This occurred, of course, because he was offered a reduced sentence if he cooperated with law enforcement. To put it succinctly, you're in 'The Trick Box.' Or as they say in England, 'In the Frame.' You now have less than fifteen minutes to convince David and me otherwise. You'd better start right now. I'll be quiet to allow you to collect your thoughts."

"Ronnie wouldn't do that to me! He loves me! You're lying! We agreed if any of us were caught, we wouldn't talk. Ronnie's lying! I'm innocent! That bitch Loni is the guilty one. Sure Ronnie and I helped her, but she did the stabbing. She and Nora were lovers. Everyone thinks Ronnie and Loni are lovers but that is so wrong. Ronnie and I were going to be married in Mexico. Loni was going to kill you and Detective David and then leave the country."

As Emilee was screaming these facts she was trembling and tears were flowing freely. She rose from her seat and David gently pushed her back down. Her head slumped onto the table and she sobbed uncontrollably.

It's never pleasant to see a person lose such complete control, but in this business we see it too often. A humanitarian would be prompted to console the person. A good cop would capitalize on the moment. I hope I'm a good cop and my partner and I can extract more information from the suspect.

"Emilee, we know you're upset, but we need more information from you to convince the D.A. that she could consider that you're marginally involved. You have to give us specific details right now. You just said that you and

Ronnie helped Loni. What did you do to help? Did you hold the victims down or anything?"

"No. Ronnie and I helped carry the bodies to the beach. I know that Rebecca Kunkle lives in Ken Kunkle's old house. Nicole had dated Ken many years ago and they still saw each other as friends. Nicole also knew Rebecca from the Susan G. Komen campaigns. They weren't friends, but Nicole knew them and also knew a lot about the family and the murder investigation. Extra details I learned from Garrett Reeves. He was so glad to date me. Ronnie was watching Rebecca's house and saw his patrol car. He followed him back to his office and then his home. I made arrangements to bump into him in the grocery store. He is such a wimp. But he's an excellent computer hacker. He hacked into the sheriff's computer and gave me all the names of the officers and witnesses. Ronnie was going to have Loni kill him next. The little creep thought I loved him. He'll do anything I ask. He was terrified that you knew he'd hacked into your computer when you brought him in for the tour of the department."

"Did Garrett provide you with any other assistance?"

"He loaned me a police radio scanner. Loni has it now. We would listen to all of your calls. This way we knew where your routine patrol vehicles were and when you and the other detectives were on duty. Loni really wants to kill both of you. She'll kill Detective Lenca and McNair if she gets a chance. Ronnie was going to hold Rebecca hostage for Loni if Rebecca had let him in the house after Loni killed the doctor."

The Spokane Sheriff's detectives say that Ronnie had a handkerchief with the Chinese characters saying Fahn Quai on it. Why is he called the 'White Devil?"

"That's not Ronnie's handkerchief. That's Loni's. We all belonged to the English Chinese Alliance Club. Loni adopted that Chinese name. Ronnie is called 'Buddha.' In Chinese his name is 'Fu Sa.' I'm called 'Angel.' In Chinese my name is 'Tin Shi.' I can write the names in Chinese characters if you like."

"That won't be necessary. Why does Ronnie have Loni's handkerchief?"

"We all had them made in England. Ronnie probably didn't look carefully when he picked up the laundry. He wasn't good at Chinese characters. Plus, they wouldn't embroider on women's handkerchiefs they're too flimsy. I have all six of mine in my cedar chest. I treasure them. It was a great time at Oxford. All of us loved the club. We had such great food at the meetings. Some of the members actually got to travel to Beijing. My Chinese is pretty rusty, but I hope to go there someday to see some of our fellow students from the Oxford vet school."

There was no chance that Emilee would ever see the light of day in China. I doubted she'd ever walk as a free woman for many years if at all. If she was convicted of all four counts of first degree murder, she could receive four life terms in prison. Her admissions thus far were enough to assure convictions.

David and I could ice the cake by continuing the interview. There were still many unanswered questions that she held the answer to.

David asked, "Emilee, who killed Nicole?"

"I told you Loni. She killed all four of them."

David again asked, "Why did you kill her?"

"She was getting suspicious. She had seen me with Garrett at a restaurant in Spokane. She knew that Ronnie and I were going to be married and also knew that Loni was a little crazy. Loni had come to see me here at my condo in Post Falls. She worked out with me and I mentioned Nicole was looking for some housemates. I introduced Nicole to her and they hit it off immediately. In one week Ronnie and Loni were living with her. I was sorry they had to kill her. She was a very nice person."

I asked, "Why were you withdrawing so much cash in the past three weeks?"

"Ronnie and I would need ready cash in Mexico. You know Traveler's Checks aren't generally accepted anymore. Ronnie said I should withdraw cash. He probably has it all with him in his wallet. He was keeping it for us. Loni has a private income from her husband's estate. She married one of the Chinese veterinary students two years ago. He was the son of a wealthy Chinese doctor. He died of mercury poisoning last year. It was a tragic freak accident."

"How and where did that accident occur?"

"I don't know all the details, but Loni said her husband was putting up a large outdoor thermometer on their house outside Oxford. The ladder slipped and he fell. Apparently he grabbed at the thermometer to try to regain his balance and it broke in his hand. Some of the mercury went into his open mouth. Apparently he was screaming from fear of the fall. The thermometer glass also cut his hand and he absorbed additional mercury through the cut. Loni was devastated."

"That truly sounds like a tragic accident. It seems like a lot of bad luck occurred at once." David said.

"Emilee, I agree with David. What a string of bad luck. How did you three find Cameron Haynes and why did you select him?"

"That was a string of good luck for Loni. Garrett had gotten us into the sheriff's mainframe computer. Detective McNair had just been promoted to her new job. She broadcast over channel One that she was out for a meal at G.W. Hunters in Post Falls. Loni, Ronnie and I had reservations at the White House. They just watched McNair come out and she was with Haynes. We followed him to his house. After that it was easy to get him alone and kill him. Loni said his murder would make all of you afraid to do anything. Loni didn't think you would link the murders so quickly."

"If Cameron was a streak of luck, why did you start with Lawrence Matile?"

"Lawrence just wasn't right for Heidi. He worked too much and didn't pay enough attention to her. Your police files said he was the one who led Detective David and you to Nora. That made Loni furious. She hates you, David, and that RCMP Sergeant Vecchio most of all. She knew you three would be too hard to get immediately, so she thought that she would kill as many people as she could until she could get close to you. I told her she should have selected you for the first, but she agreed with me about Lawrence and it sort of snowballed from there."

The hidden light under the edge of the table blinked to say we needed to take a break. We had almost all we needed so we took a break. I asked Shayla to come in and sit with

Emilee. This time I briefed her to be as pleasant as possible. I cautioned her not to ask any questions about the case. If Emilee asked any specific questions, Shayla should say she didn't know and would ask one of us.

Mac from the D.A.'s office had arrived. Mac had worked closely with us on a number of cases. She was an exceptionally skilled prosecutor and understood cops. Every detective in the department enjoyed working with her. David and I briefed her on the case and Emilee's involvement in it.

Emilee told us Loni was the primary mover in this criminal conspiracy, but her sentence construction and occasional word slippage convinced me that she was as deeply involved as Loni or Ronnie. I wasn't convinced that Emilee might not have been more involved than she professed. We would need additional testimony and forensics to prove that issue.

"O.K. Mac you've got the basics. Do you want to talk to her or shall we continue with our interview?"

"Jake, I'd like to speak with her. I know you have her softened up and are on a roll. But I need to get a feel for her mental state. I don't want some high priced shyster alleging that she was coerced. My brief intervention will destroy that defense ploy."

"Miss Emilee Tish Lukin, this is Assistant District Attorney MacDonald Laurence of the Kootenai County District Attorney's Office. As Detective David and I said, Miss Laurence needs to ask you some questions. As I said earlier, this is the time for truth. You'll get this opportunity only once. This is that opportunity. We'll leave you two to talk."

David and I left the room and went into the CCTV observation room. Mac told Emilee to relax. She asked if she had been advised of her rights and got an affirmative answer. Mac then asked Emilee to recount her involvement with Ronnie and Loni Scudder. We knew the narrative would be long and were interested in any deviation that might emerge.

True to our assumption, the dissertation was long and involved. There was enough deviation to make it sound plausible and unrehearsed. No major points of critical importance emerged. I tried to make notes of the sentence structure that belied her profession of minor involvement and also the word slippage. Mac and I would discuss this in detail after she concluded her interview.

Over an hour passed full of language and occasional arm waving. There were tears as she recalled fond memories and some bitter disappointments. Mac stayed the course and made the appropriate 'Ums and Aahs' to encourage Emilee to continue. At the end of the interview, Mac thanked Emilee for her candor and said that she would consider her cooperation and truthfulness when she made her recommendation to the District Attorney.

Mac came out of the interview room and we sent in Shayla again.

"Mac what do you think?"

"Jake I'm not as skilled as you are, but I agree that she's more involved than she alleges. What are your key points to make me even more convinced?"

"Mac, as you know, I'm a wordsmith and specialize in interviews. Here are my main sticking points from David's and my interview with Emilee. She professes that Loni was the killer. She implies that she went along due to her love for Ronnie. But during the interview she made these slips:

#1. When she mentioned Garrett Reeves, she slipped and said Garrett gave her all the names of persons involved in Ken's murder investigation. That shows me major involvement.

#2. She said Garrett gave her a police scanner. Not Loni or Ronnie ~ her.

#3. She said, "We would listen to the scanner," It seems to me she was fully involved.

#4. For later prosecution, you should contact Thames Valley Police to have Loni's husband exhumed. Her recounting of his 'unfortunate accident' stinks of murder. I would guess Loni killed him for his money. Emilee said that Loni and Nora were lovers. Maybe Loni married for the money. This is for use when we catch Loni.

#5. She was with them when they followed Cameron to his house. She said it was easy to get him alone and kill him

#6. Her opinion of Dr. Matile leads me to believe that she put Loni up to killing him. She said that Loni agreed with her about Dr. Matile's inattention to Heidi.

#7. This is a significant point. When you talk to her you will see she is wearing what I would call a 'Coeur d'Alene Ring.' You know the awl through the heart. I just don't believe that's a fashion statement. I believe it's sort of like a membership insignia.

Those are the major sticking points I've made notes on. Once we review the tapes, I can probably come up with some more."

"Jake you've got me convinced. I didn't catch all of those points, but I agree on the ones you've enumerated.

Those little slips tell a lot more than whole sentences. I think we have enough to charge her with all four counts of murder one. Thanks for the opportunity to work this case."

"Mac, we're going to bring in Garrett Reeves tomorrow. Based upon Emilee's statement I think we have enough to charge him also. He facilitated the trio's information gathering that resulted in four deaths. He's tangentially involved but enough to consider him an accomplice. David and I have established a bond with him. Now we're gonna wring him out. Do you agree?"

"Oh yeah! I agree. I want to see that young man wearing prison denims very soon. I don't see any deal in the offering for him. We can actually prosecute both Emilee and Garrett Federally as well as in the Idaho courts. They essentially did an illegal wiretap when they hacked your departmental computer. Let's do the Idaho violations first. If they don't get a long sentence in the State Courts, we'll let the Feds have a crack at them next."

"Before we send her to booking, we want to have one more shot at her to see if she'll tell us where Loni is. She didn't give that up to you and we need to locate her. I think I have one more piece of news she won't want to hear that may jar Loni's whereabouts from her."

Mac said, "You can tell her that any consideration depends on her disclosing Loni's location."

David and I reentered the interview room.

"Emilee, A.D.A. Laurence said that you were cooperative. But there is one piece of important information that you've not revealed. Where is Loni Scudder? Before you answer, there is one thing you should know. Ronnie only had forty dollars in his wallet when he was arrested. Where is all the rest of that money? Does Loni have it?"

"What do you mean he only had forty dollars? He was holding all of our money for our trip to Mexico. No! Loni doesn't have it. She has her own money. You're lying to me."

"Emilee why would David and I lie to you? We have been straight forward in all of our dealings. We got you an Assistant District Attorney who is sympathetic to your situation. We've been polite and concerned. We've given you information as we've received it, but when you said Ronnie had the money you took out of the bank, I called Spokane Sheriff's Department and had the detectives check Ronnie's wallet and search the entire car. He only had forty dollars. That makes us believe you aren't being truthful. A.D.A. Laurence told us to tell you that her thoughts about your case are dependent on you disclosing Loni's whereabouts. Now is the time to do that."

"Ronnie and Loni came to my house yesterday. He had the Cadillac and she was driving a little dark blue Honda. We didn't want a strange car sitting in my driveway so Loni said she would go to Garrett's house. We didn't think you would look for them there or at my house, but we wanted to be extra careful. If Ronnie doesn't have the money, it's in an olive drab metal container in my garage. I got it from an old boy friend. It used to contain army ammunition. It's just sitting on a shelf in the garage. My passport and other papers are in it. I got my passport out of the safe deposit box at the bank for our trip to Mexico. Ronnie said that it would be safe there. No one would suspect I had anything valuable in an old metal box just sitting on the shelf."

Emilee, may we have permission to search your house? We have a team of officers standing by from the bomb search. If you'll give us permission, we'll look for the metal box and notify you what's in it. Is that O.K.?"

"Of course. You have my permission. You've already searched it. You told me that Loni wasn't in the house. Why do you ask now?"

"We entered the house under exigent circumstances. Once that situation has been resolved, we didn't have legal cause to look in metal boxes. We were looking for people. We would violate your rights to look in drawers and boxes. Now we need to get a search warrant or receive your permission."

"O.K., now I understand. You have my permission to search my house. You can look in drawers and boxes and anything else that tickles your fancy. Is that what you want to hear?"

"Yes that's sufficient. If you'll excuse David now, he'll make the necessary calls to get the search started."

"I have one last question. I couldn't help but notice the very attractive ring on your little finger. The awl through the heart, Do you call that a 'Coeur d'Alene Ring'? I've never seen a ring like that. I know about Cheryl Burchell's shop. Did you buy it there?"

"No. Actually Loni bought it for me the first day she was here. She said it would have special significance as time passed. I had no idea what that meant at the time. It is beautiful isn't it? It's a combination of white and yellow gold. Ronnie had a necklace similar to it. I'm sure you know that. He wore it all the time."

I left the room to speak with Mac.

" Mac, we'll book Emilee now. Thanks Mac. We enjoy working with a genuine prosecutor. You're the best!"

We asked Shayla to take Emilee to the booking desk.

"David my boy, I guess we need to go to Garrett Reeves' house on Mississippi Street and have a little chat. We also need to have our SWAT Team reenter the house and search for the ammo box in the garage. We might also have them do an entire search for indicia. We'll have them look in Emilee's cedar chest for monogrammed handkerchiefs. We'll call off half the team from Farm Garden to meet us on Mississippi Street. If Loni's there, we may need backup."

Morgan stopped us with a sheaf of papers in her hand.

"You won't like this. I just talked to Joanne Stebbins at Northwest Travel. Yesterday afternoon Emilee Lukin came into their office to change her tickets. Instead of two tickets to Mexico, she wanted just one ticket to Beijing. They made the change, but the fare was an additional four hundred and eighty dollars. She paid in cash and took the new ticket. The plane left Spokane at six this morning for Seattle and the connecting flight for Beijing left Seattle at ten this morning. Emilee Lukin was onboard. They had an interim stop in Honolulu. It was a refueling stop and all passengers deplaned for the hour layover. Emilee did not re-board the plane. Joanne said that all of her previous discussions were over the phone and the Internet so she had never seen Emilee. She checked her passport and it seemed to be in order. I called Hawaii State Police and our local FBI to issue a BOL. I fudged a bit since you guys were on a roll and I knew you didn't want to be disturbed. I said I was Detective Lenca. We have a detective Lenca so you're covered. My brother will kill me if this goes wonky, but I knew time was of the essence. Is that O.K.?"

"O.K.? It's wonderful! Based on what you just told us, I'm sure that Loni Scudder or Emilee Lukin or Annalee Fox or some other alias she has cooked up, is lying on a beach in Hawaii smiling. If anything good has come of this she's not in Coeur d'Alene trying to put an awl in one of our hearts. I guess we don't have to go to Mississippi Street now. Let's leave Mr. Garrett Reeves until tomorrow shall we? This has been one interesting day! David, what say we go home and get some rest and hopefully some food?"

CHAPTER TWENTY FOUR

I didn't need to be coaxed into bed last night. I had a light snack and was asleep before ten. My jog this morning was a little slower paced than normal, but I did get in three full miles. Liz had red grapefruit and English Muffins on the table when I came back in the house after feeding. We had a new addition to our wild turkey population. A flock of fifteen had joined with my six toms and three hens. This was going to increase my feed bill substantially. It was interesting to see the interaction between the toms and the smaller hens in the new flock. There was definitely a 'pecking order.'

Driving in to work my mind was a little easier. Liz was pleased that she could also go in to work. We hadn't let our guard down, but had relaxed our vigilance a bit.

Loni would have to be very careful for at least two weeks if she attempted to leave Hawaii. Her three known aliases were on the Transportation Security Administration's watch list. We didn't know what her married name was when she married the Chinese student. Inspector Forbes hadn't gotten back to us last night when we left. That was due to the time difference between the U. K. and Idaho.

Perhaps we would have many questions answered this morning.

As usual, David's car was already in the employee's lot when I pulled in. My partner admittedly had a shorter drive, but he was compulsive about being extra early. I was usually the first one at any meeting. My years as a S.E.R.E. Specialist taught me the rule: "If you're not early, you're late." David was just compulsive.

"Morning Jake, I stopped by the Donut House on Kathleen and got some treats. No one else is here yet. You get your pick. I've already had two so don't be shy."

"Partner, you're trying to ruin me. I had a lovely English muffin and red grapefruit already this morning. I did my three miles and now you tempt me with chocolate. You know no reasonable man can resist chocolate. I'll have this chocolate old fashioned. I'll hate you and myself for the rest of the day. Do we have any news? Captain Nearing said he would have the IT boys completely go over our computer security system and recheck all the firewalls last night. Morgan was really spooked when we told her that Garrett had penetrated the mainframe. She said we should call Cal Davis. I don't know if Captain Nearing felt that was necessary or not."

"Jake, I've already booted up. There were no warnings on the boot up screen. Maybe we should go to dispatch and see if we can start making entries from yesterday's activity. I'll run down. I need a coffee refill anyhow. You know I make lousy coffee. Dispatch coffee tastes so much better than mine."

"I know they have a new dispatcher in training and the word is that she's single and cute. That's what I know. I also know you do like the coffee Morgan makes and you're a closet chauvinist. So go! See if they have paper reports from the search of Emilee's condo. I want to know if Loni stole all the money and Emilee's passport. That Loni is a real piece of work."

David was gone. In the interim, Woody, Morgan, and Gunter arrived at the bullpen. I asked they hold off on news until we're all present. Morgan started making coffee. She asked why David hadn't made it if he was already here. When I displayed the box of donuts, she smiled, selected a maple bar and was quiet.

David came back bearing a steaming cup of coffee and a wide smile. He had papers in his other hand.

"Morning everyone. I have paper reports from yesterday. The dispatch supervisor says our computers are safe and we can make entries. They did find a hole in the firewall and evidence someone had hacked us. Captain Nearing finally called Cal Davis about eleven last night to double check the system. Apparently he said that he trusted the County IT guys, but that we couldn't be too safe. That sure makes me feel better.

"What I do have is this: A search of Emilee's house found the forty five-caliber ammo box on the shelf in the garage, as she said. It did contain some indicia. Loan papers on the house, a warranty for the lawn mower, her Dad's discharge papers from the navy. No cash. No passport. Apparently: Loni strikes again.

The cedar chest did disclose six men's handkerchiefs with Chinese characters embroidered on them. There was a Chinese gown with matching characters embroidered on the left sleeve.

There were two contracts for Verizon cell phones in the name of Brian and Annalee Fox in the desk. Both cell phones have GPS in them. SWAT contacted the Verizon Office on Highway 95. They said if we can't locate the phones, the batteries must have been removed. SWAT didn't try to locate Ronnie's phone since we know where that phone is. They tried again for Loni's phone and had no luck.

Patrol was to meet Officer Garrett Reeves at eight this morning at Alpha Omega Security and bring him directly to a holding cell. We should expect him to be there as we speak. That's all the news I have except dispatch sure makes good coffee. Did Jake eat all the donuts or did he offer any to you all?"

Woody was the next to take the floor. "As you know, Gunter and I met with WSP and Spokane S.O. I may repeat what you already know, since we didn't make mainframe entries either last night. Ronnie Scudder was D.O.A. at the shallow, rocky, bottom of the Spokane River. I guess he didn't believe that 'seat belts save lives.' The airbags prevented him from flying through the windshield and saved him from also bleeding out, but the impact killed him instantly. The Cadillac was a rental. Thrifty car rental will write that one off for sure. The trunk was empty. His two suitcases in the back seat were barely damp from the splash of hitting the river. They yielded the two cell phones, men's clothing, a second blonde man's wig, a British driving license in the name of Ronnie Scudder and two pair of shoes. The car was essentially clean. You know he had eight hundred dollars in the wallet. Gunter took the picture of the monogram on the handkerchief. Jake you told us last night that the handkerchief allegedly belongs to Loni. That's it from the liaison team."

"I guess we're up to speed. Our next target is Garrett Reeves. I spoke with Mac yesterday. She says that she'll prosecute locally first and then hand him over to the Feds if our courts are too lenient. We don't have the sheriff's views on our security breach, so we're unaware of how hot he is. I'm betting that he's pretty hot. I wouldn't want to be in Garrett Reeves shoes."

David asked, "Shall we go interview Garrett now or do you want him to sit in the holding cell for a while longer?"

"Let's let him sit for a while and ponder why he's here. We want him docile and anxious to please when we bring him in for his interview. Holding cell time is good for reflection. We want to clean up from yesterday and do our report writing. Garrett can wait. He'll be here for quite a while after our interview. As backed up as the courts are he may not go to trial for months. I'll bet that Garrett isn't expecting the type of interview we're prepared to subject him to."

The four of us sat at our computers and began writing about yesterday's events. Morgan brought coffee to the other's desks and tea to mine. Morgan was a real treasure. I got a call from Robbie Forbes. He said that the English

Chinese Alliance Club was a social club that had a good reputation at the University. He had requested their membership roster and expected it later today. He was having marriage records researched to attempt to learn Loni's married name. He had contacts at the University. They were asking around. Until that was learned, the prospect of exhuming her deceased husband was on hold. You can't dig up all dead Chinese in the U.K.

Almost two busy hours had passed when the sheriff walked into the bullpen. Everyone sat a little straighter. He stopped at my desk.

"Morning Jake. How are things going? I see that the entire team is using their computers. That's a good thing. That hacker could have done some serious damage to our system if we hadn't fixed the firewall. Captain Nearing tells me you know who the hacker is and that he's in custody in a holding cell. I assume that you haven't interviewed him yet. When are you boys planning on doing that? I'd kinda like to either sit in or at least watch that on the CCTV."

"Sheriff our plan was let him sit a while in holding. We're doing our mainframe entries so we can catch up on yesterday's activities. We thought that would be doubly productive. He's been alone in holding since before eight hundred. He should be really ready to talk to someone now. David, if you'll set up interview room number two, I'll go fetch Mr. Garrett Reeves. Sheriff you're welcome to sit in or monitor from the observation room."

"Jake I've heard talk that you're a specialist at interviewing. I don't want to cramp your style. I'll just slide into the observation room and watch the fun on the CCTV monitors. You go and eat this boy up. I'm pretty mad at him, particularly after we gave him such swell treatment."

David signaled that the room was ready. I walked over to detention side of the building to get Garrett out of the holding cell.

"Detective Lowry why was I arrested? I've been in that solitary cell for hours. I thought we were friends. I've already made my application to become a member of this department. I'm scheduled to participate in the next testing cycle. Detective, you're not talking to me. Where are we going?"

I walked Garrett into room number two and sat him in the hot seat. David was already in the room

"Garrett Jack Reeves you have been arrested for the first degree murder of four persons. Doctor Matile, Cameron Haynes, Doctor Hardcastle, and Nicole Logan. You have the right to remain silent. That is not say a word. If you decide to talk to Detective David and me, Detective Jake Lowry, anything you do say can be used as evidence against you in a court of law. You have the right to an attorney. If you can't afford and attorney, one will be appointed for you free of charge. Those are your rights. Do you understand what I have just told you?

"Yes sir. You don't have to advise me of my rights. I know them. I haven't done anything wrong. I don't know what you're talking about. I've never killed anyone."

"Garrett, we understand that you may know your rights, but this is a serious matter. If you understand your rights, do you waive your right to an attorney?

"Yes sir. I'll be glad to talk to you. I want to straighten this thing out."

"Garrett, there comes a time in every man's life when he has to stand up and admit his mistakes. That time is right now for you. David and I have treated you with respect and kindness. You've been a guest in our most sacred place. We inducted you into the brotherhood of the badge. We saw potential and tried to cultivate it. That gesture isn't extended to any Tom, Dick, or Harry. Now what did you do? You threw all that away! You violated our trust. In your crass and unfeeling way penetrated the department's computer system. That penetration and your subsequent collusion with three deadly and dangerous persons caused four good people to die. Now you have the gall to sit across the table from my partner and me and lie. Garrett, that is intolerable! Now I want you to sit there and contemplate all that I have said. Detective David and I are going to go outside and cool down and try to calm our emotions. We're deeply hurt! You have hurt us! Truthfully, we don't know quite how to deal with this betrayal. We'll be back in a while."

David and I left with our heads hanging down, shoulders slumped, and shuffling our feet.

With a hardened criminal, this act would have drawn gales of laughter. I had an idea that Garrett Jack Reeves would be almost in tears when we returned. If he wasn't, my plan was to throw in his violation of the 'Patriot Act' by engaging in wiretap violations, sheltering a Federal Fugitive and aiding and abetting her escape. David grabbed a cup of coffee and I had a nice cup of Earl Grey tea. We took our drinks into the observation room to chat with the sheriff.

"Jake, I was almost in tears when you told Reeves of his putrid behavior. I don't know if the tears were from sadness or laughter. This is the most unusual interview approach I've ever witnessed. May I be bold enough to ask where you're going with this when you go back in?"

"Sheriff, Garret Reeves, underneath his criminal behavior, is a devout 'Wanna Be.' Deep in his heart he's hoping that a full confession will absolve him of any guilt and he can still join the brotherhood of the badge. He'll ask that question midway through his confession. If we say no, he may shut up and lawyer up. David and I are going to have to not tell him yes, but have him believe that it might work. You know that cops can lie, but a defense attorney would try to eat us up if we told him we'd forgive his sins to extract a more complete confession from him." That's my plan. You know what they say about plans? 'The best laid, must eventually go awry.' Keep your fingers crossed that I've figured Garrett Reeves out."

David and I finished our drinks and re-entered the interview room. We kept Garrett under observation with the CCTV. He was slumped in his chair and staring at the ceiling. That was a good sign. His feet weren't moving and he was squared in facing the table. If he had been turned toward the door, I'd have been worried.

"Garrett, we hope you've had time to search your heart for the right thing to do. We both know that you are, deep in your heart a very good man, a good man that wants to do the right thing. My partner and I want to give you that opportunity to do that right now. I want to remind you that you don't have to say anything without the advice of an attorney. If you choose to do so, whatever you say can be used in evidence against you. You do understand that don't you?"

"Yes sir I do, but I do want to do the right thing. You were right! I did hack into the Sheriff's Department computer. Initially, I did it to see if I could get an advantage in the testing. But, Emilee Lukin and I met by accident in the grocery store. She's so beautiful. I didn't think I had any chance with such a beautiful woman. We fell in love. Then she introduced me to Brian and Annalee Fox. They asked me to open the Ken Kunkle murder investigation file. Emilee assured me that it was O.K. She said they were friends with one of the victims. I made a CD of the file and gave it to them. A couple of days ago Annalee came to my house and asked if she could spend the night. I let her use the spare bedroom. Annalee told me that Brian was in Seattle and since Miss Logan was killed they didn't have a place to live. I don't know anything about any murders."

"Well Garrett, you were played for a sucker. Unfortunately, ignorance of the ultimate purpose of the conspiracy is not a defense. Brian, Annalee, and Emilee conspired to murder the four people I named earlier. Your computer hacking furthered that conspiracy and facilitated the selection of the victims. Garrett you are as guilty as the person who stabbed the victims in the heart. We're sorry, but you're going to have to stand trial with the other suspects. If you did anything else, now is the time to cleanse your heart of guilt."

"I didn't really see a prowler like I said. Brian asked me to do that to see how fast you guys responded. I didn't know what he was planning, but I thought I was doing the right thing for Emilee. You guys busted me for firing my weapon, but Emilee said she would hire me a good attorney and get me off. I go to trial next week. I guess I better call Emilee to find out my attorney's name."

"Garrett, before we make arrangements for you to meet Emilee in person so you can discuss the attorney. We have one last question. When I picked you up from the holding cell, I noticed in the envelope containing your personal effects, that you have all your keys on a 'Coeur d'Alene' key ring. I call it that because it is the traditional awl through the heart. When we booked you for discharging your weapon, you had a conventional round metal key ring. When did you acquire this beautiful key ring?"

"Actually I love that key ring. I got it at the special party that we had at Emilee's house a few days ago. Emilee called me and asked me to come over on my day off. I had to arrive at twenty three hundred hours. The house was dark except for the special black candles that were burning in the garage. Emilee and Ronnie were dressed in black trousers and turtle neck shirts. Loni was wearing a long black dress with a kind of Chinese writing embroidered in red on the back. There were other people there. Emilee gave me a really potent drink when I came in. The rest of the evening was kind of fuzzy in my mind. I know we went into the garage and there was a white circle in some kind of powder on the floor. Everyone stood around outside the circle. Loni was in the center of the circle. There was a little table in the center covered in a red cloth. The key ring was on the table. The people standing around were humming some kind of weird tune. The next thing I remember is Emilee walking me to my car. She pressed the key ring in my hand and told me it was a token of special significance. I was to keep it always."

"You're going to arrange for me to talk to Emilee? Boy you guys are great! When can Emilee and I get together?"

"How about in fifteen minutes?"

"Do you mean I can go? My explanation cleared me. Wow!

"No Garrett, I guess my mean streak just came out. Emilee is also in custody. We'll put you on one side of the glass and Emilee on the other side. You can talk over the phone. We just told you that you're going to be charged with four counts of murder. Your unlawful discharge of a weapon complaint will probably go away. I also don't think that Emilee will be fronting the money for your defense to any charges. Garrett when we put you back in the cells, you have to do some serious introspection. You were played by Emilee and her fellow conspirators. If you have any financial resources, you better collect them and look for a very good criminal defense lawyer."

David took Garrett to booking. I went into the observation room.

"Sheriff, I lost it in there. I never should have said that to Garrett. I was just so mad that I had to zing him at least once. We did get his partial confession. We have enough for the D.A. to charge him. If you want, we can call the FBI to do a follow-on interview for violation of the Patriot Act."

"Jake, I'd have been kicking him around the interview room way before you zinged him. I admired your restraint. You sure didn't show you were mad. I also admire your technique. You read him like a child's book. We'll wait on the FBI. If our D.A. doesn't get four consecutive life sentences, we can call in the Feds. For now, we'll see if Hawaii turns up anything on Loni. Where are you going from here?"

"Boss, We still need to collect the reports from Spokane S.O. Robbie Forbes called this morning from the U.K. he's got his sources working on Loni's married name. Once he has that, we suggest that they exhume the husband's body and check for signs of murder. Emilee's story was reeking of murder, not an unfortunate accident. We're going to meet with Mac at the D.A's office to see if she needs any additional investigation on our part. I want the evidence folks to go to Emilee's house and look for the white circle in the garage. If someone cleaned it up, there may still be traces. I hate to bring this up, but Garrett's recounting of the special party sounds a little like Black Magic. Loni's black dress may have had the 'Fahn Quai' symbol on it. Based on Garrett's story, we need to reinterview Emilee. 'Miss Goody Two Shoes' is obviously more involved that she would have us believe. The entire team will attend both Dr. Hardcastle's and Nicole Logan's funerals. If on the off chance, Loni is able to return to the U.S., she may attend the funerals. Serial killers, just like arsonists like to admire their work. We'll have some other officers on the perimeter with video cameras. We know Ronnie had spare wigs to modify his appearance. Loni was able to pass through passport control as Emilee.

"That sounds like a viable plan. How did you come up with the idea that the party involved Black Magic?"

"Oakland had practioners in Black Magic, Santeria and Voodoo. We had storefront 'chapels' that offered to remove hexes and bad 'Ju Ju'. During my career it was necessary to do some intense library research on those arts. Aleister Crowley, "The Most Evil Man That Ever Lived", also lived in the Bay Area. Although he was born in England, he practiced his belief system in that area. You know the old saying, 'Know Your Enemy.'"

"Jake, sometimes you amaze me. Now we have to be concerned that Loni in addition to being just plain evil may dabble in Black Magic to further her goals."

Sheriff, I didn't say that, but I may come to that conclusion after we do the search of Emilee's garage."

David returned as I was finishing my conversation with the sheriff.

"I heard you say we're going to search Emilee's garage. What are we looking for? I thought the SWAT guys found the metal ammo box. No one commented on a powder ring on the garage floor. I agree what Garrett told us is kind of spooky, but what can you hope to find now that we've had boots all over the garage?"

"During our initial search we were looking for Loni. The second search was looking for the ammo box. This time we need to take the evidence folks. We're looking for Sea Salt. If we're lucky, we might also find some black candles with Loni's prints on them. I agree, it's not much, but it'll solidify my suspicions about what may have transpired at Emilee's Condo"

"I'm going to call Mac and see if we can get her to walk a search warrant through for us. I believe that a reasonable judge will sign it."

My call to Mac went smoothly. David and I drove over to the courthouse and I swore to the information as the 'Affiant' for the warrant. I called Jay on my cell and he agreed to bring the evidence van and meet us in Post Falls at Emilee's condo.

898 was quiet. The crime scene tape was gone and the neighborhood appeared to be resuming their normal day-to-day life. The arrival of the evidence van didn't draw anyone out of their condos. We entered using Emilee's keys that I'd secured from her personal property envelope. She wasn't happy we were going back into her house. I didn't tell her why. I just said that a judge had issued another search warrant and we were going back in. I told her I was taking the keys so we wouldn't have to make forced entry.

David and I would search the condo proper. I briefed Jay, Sherry and Ron on what I was looking for. Jay wasn't hopeful for an unblemished discovery. We walked into the garage. Jay took a black light, lay on the floor and shone the light on the floor. A very faint image of a lighter circle was visible. Sherry attached a special filter and took videos. Ron tried a couple of filters and did get a faint image. Jay then used a special LED light to see if the circle would be brighter. We got a slightly better image. Once we had the video and photos, Jay began carefully sweeping the floor. At the edges of the garage there were small white crystals that had apparently been missed by whoever had cleaned up the circle. Jay also detected small smears of what looked like candle wax in five separate locations around the circle's edge. He scraped the smears and crystals into separate evidence bags.

David and I began our search. We were looking for five, black, pillar candles. Hopefully they would have Loni's prints on them. At least we could compare the prints from the candles with prints we'd collected in Nicole's house. We now had Ronnie's, Emilee's, and Nicole's prints for elimination. Logically any prints on the candles would be Loni's.

"Jake I've gone along with you on this search, but I have to ask why we're looking for the candles?"

"Well partner, I have two goals. You remember that Garrett said there were black candles at the special party. In Black Magic Ceremonies five candles are placed at the points of the pentagram. In some belief systems that star is also called the 'Star of Solomon'. We saw the smudges on the garage floor I believe an analysis will show that those smudges are candle wax. That'll confirm what type of ceremony was conducted here. The second reason is to see if we can identify Loni's prints. Normally the person conducting the ceremony would be the person to place and light the candles. If luck is with us, we will only find one set of prints on the candles if we find the candles. Loni has thus far not left much for us to collect evidence from. We may extract DNA from some of the clothing, but that is not guaranteed. Anything we can get is a plus."

We both began our search. Opening drawers and cupboards you get a view of the home owner. You learn if they're neat, obsessive about have their jars all facing one way, or the jars are in the cupboard in alphabetical order. I've done search warrants and found copious numbers of bugs in the cupboards and even in dresser drawers. I've been thankful for nitrile gloves many times. Emilee's cupboards and drawers didn't reveal much. She was neat but apparently not obsessive. David found the five black candles in the dining room buffet. They were in a fitted cardboard box. All five had been burned. David called for the evidence team. They videoed and took digitals. Jay placed the box in an evidence bag. I made entries into the log. Subsequent searches didn't reveal anything. We wrapped up and returned to the office.

Woody and Gunter had finished their computer entries. David and I sat at our desks and worked on finishing what was interrupted by the sheriff's arrival this morning. Jay promised that he'd do a rush analysis of the crystals and smudges from the garage floor.

Mac called to say she had some questions but she'd rely on the District Attorney's Investigators to find the answers. That was good news! That freed up our complete team. We could use a little free time. Crime hadn't stood still while we focused on the Coeur d'Alene Murders.

Three hours passed before Jay called.

"Jake bring your team to the evidence lab. We have some results."

All five of us walked down the hall. Morgan was first through the door to the lab.

"Jay, hurry and tell us. I've been on pins and needles since Jake and David came back from the search. What was the circle made of?"

"Oh Morgan! You'll all be mystified by our results. The white crystals were Sea Salt, as Jake said. Prior to collecting the smudges, we measured the smudges. If you drew straight lines from point to point you would form a five-pointed star or pentagram. The smudges were candle wax. The smudges match wax taken from the five black candles David found. We did recover fingerprints from the candles. They match prints recovered from Nicole Logan's bedroom. An interesting note is that when we were working on the circle, I noticed some light stains near the center.

I collected what I could. Those stains tested positive for human blood. It was so deteriorated by cleaning solvents that we won't be able to get DNA from the samples, but we might have located the murder spot for our four victims. I called Spokane S.O. They found a Coeur d'Alene necklace in the lining of Ronnie's suitcase. ISP and CDA P.D's labs are working up the DNA collection from the clothing in Nicole's closet. I've contacted Mac to ask her to request a warrant to draw blood from Garrett and Emilee. Getting a warrant for blood will be iffy. Judges are very hesitant to penetrate a body. I want the blood draw to see if we can detect Rohypnol in their blood. Garrett said that the evening of the special party they gave him a drink and the rest of the evening was 'fuzzy.' Depending on the elapsed time there may be some traces remaining. We know that there were traces of Rohypnol in Matile, Haynes, and Hardcastle. The autopsy for Nicole is not done yet and the labs will be awhile. There's no health risk to Garrett or Emilee. This would be an information gathering request only. We'll see if Mac can float the warrant. That's all the lab news for now. Any questions?"

"David and I are going to the sheriff right now and see if he agrees that we can pull off the protective details from everyone. Gunter, you and Woody go bring Heidi home. Then we're going personally to Husam's new house to meet his family. If the sheriff agrees, we will bring Michelle, Lori and Kim out of the motel and tell them they can return to work. We don't want them to get sloppy with their vigilance, but they can relax a bit. Loni would have to be a master of disguise and also capable of obtaining false identity documents and passport to return to our area this quick. That's the plan. Any questions?"

Woody asked, "Can Gunter and I rendezvous with you before you go to Husam's? We'd also like to meet his family."

"O.K. That's a good plan. Morgan, do you want to ride with David and me? I'm sure the boss will understand. As I said earlier, we all deserve some free time. You put in so much overtime that wasn't on the books. We owe you!"

David and I walked down the hall to the sheriff's office

"Good morning Patti. Is the boss free? For a change, this isn't a crisis. We just want to ask him if he agrees that we can pull off our protective details."

"David, Jake, you two are going to be surprised one day when I say no. This one time I'll tell him you're here and I'm sure he'll be glad to concur. The overtime bill for those details is taxing our operational budget. He's free go on in."

The sheriff agreed with our plan and we swung back by the bullpen to get Morgan. Husam had located a nice house in an older neighborhood not far from the North Idaho College Campus. The house was about two blocks from the lake. We didn't know what to expect from his family. Husam was completely Americanized. He spoke without any noticeable accent. He was a devout Muslim and strictly adhered to the tenants of the Koran. We hadn't had any in-depth discussions with him about his family's dedication to Islam. We expected his wife to wear a head covering, but young girls normally don't. Young men dress in western clothes. Only on special occasions would they wear a Thobe (*Long white dress like garment*) and Kafieh (*Head scarf worn by*

Arabic men). I had called Husam to ask if we could come by. We didn't expect the reception we received.

Woody knocked on the door. We all were standing behind her. Husam opened the door and was dressed in the traditional Thobe and Kafieh. His Thobe was a brilliant white. Complete with French cuffs, cuff links, and black onyx studs. His Kafieh was the traditional red and white check. Red and white indicated you were Jordanian. Black and white indicated you were Palestinian. Husam's son was also dressed in Thobe and Kafieh. The ankle length Thobe gave both males an appearance that was foreign to our culture. Husam's wife, Nadia, was dressed in a black Abaya (*Black long sleeved, dress won by Arabic women*). She wasn't wearing a veil, but did have her head covered.

"As Salamu AlayKum, Husam"

"Wa AlayKum As Salamu, Jake, Morgan, Woody, Gunter. Welcome to my home. I would like to introduce my wife, Nadia and my son Nayef."

Nadia shyly shook each of our hands. Husam and I exchanged the traditional hug and kiss on both cheeks. He was beaming.

When I lived and worked in Saudi Arabia meeting the wife of a colleague was a very special event. My Saudi counterpart introduced me to his ten-year old daughter and both his sons. I had tea at his home on three separate occasions. I never met his wife. Jordan was a little more liberal. I had the honor of meeting three colleagues' wives as well as their children. We drove out of Amman to a farm that had been in my colleague's family for four hundred years. He had a metal detector and we searched a large portion of the property for buried treasure. It was a family legend that in times past an ancestor had buried large amounts of gold to protect it from marauders. The family had collectively bought a very expensive detector. A fellow International Police Officer and I had been invited to assist in a focused hunt for the treasure. We searched all possible locations the family folklore indicated might be the spot. We did find a crushed soft drink can in one spot. It was buried about three feet deep. When the detector pinged on that spot there was great anticipation. All the young boys in the family joined in digging. Discovery of the soda can failed to bring universal jubilation. The detector was swung over the spot with the can removed but no signal was forth coming. The disappointment was palpable. There was a grand picnic after the search was concluded. We cooked over an open fire and had grilled chicken, lamb, koefte, falafel, and fresh baked pita bread. My colleague's father brought both of his wives. The interaction was a cultural study in pecking orders.

Nadia had laid an elegant table for us. Grilled lamb chops sliced so thin you could almost read a paper through them. This offering is not done to imply frugality, but elegance. In Turkey, you order these at fast food restaurants and at roadside stands. They are called 'Pirzola.' They come in groups of four, apparently this dish was an Ottoman remnant; Falafel, homemade and piping hot. Fresh homemade pita so light and fluffy that it would almost float off the plate; homemade hummus; the pungent garlic smell was tantalizing; Farmer's salad; chopped tomatoes, cucumbers, celery, green onions, garlic, parsley, cilantro, lemon juice olive oil and salt; She also made what the Turks call 'jedge jik' in the Turkish language it is spelled Cecik. The letter 'C' in Turkish changes to a 'J' if the 'C' is normal on the lower portion. A 'C' with a lower tail has the 'ch' sound. Cecik is made from fresh yogurt, garlic, and cucumbers. This is well mixed, just prior to serving, you pour a small dollop of olive oil on the top.

You're expected to tear your pita into sections and dip into the hummus or Cecik. My taste buds were dancing. Husam gestured for us to take a seat. Nadia bustled to assure that everyone had drinks. She asked if we would like coffee or chai. Husam knew I didn't drink coffee and asked for chai for me. Jordanian coffee, like Turkish and most Baltic Country's coffee is served in tiny cups. It's so strong you can stand a spoon in it. As you near the bottom there is a thick sludge. Coffee in a Jordanian house is not for the weak of heart. Chai on the other hand can assume many disguises. Black tea is a popular variety. Other varieties can be apple, cherry, mint, or herbal. I'm a straight black tea fan.

We all joined hands while Husam offered thanks for the gathering and for the safety of his family.

Just like Maria's meals at the Kunkle compound, Nadia was a superb cook. My stomach felt just like I was back in Jordan again.

We offered our sincere thanks. Bid Maa Salamu to Husam and his family and refocused our minds on work.

Woody and Gunter offered to contact Lori Larson at her job to make any necessary explanations. David, Morgan, and I would go downtown to check on Michelle and verify she was now moderately safe.

Michelle was dressed in a trim pin striped business suit, black stockings, and patent leather heels. David stammered a faltering hello. Morgan grabbed Michelle and spun her around.

"Lady, where did you have these clothes made? They're gorgeous! You look fabulous! I want the name of your tailor. Rebecca must be paying you a lot more than Ken paid me to do this job."

"Morgan, my tailor's name is Kohl's, Macy's, and on very rare occasions, Nordstrom's Rack. Thank you for the compliment! I looked at the last audit. I'm drawing the same salary you were when the sheriff's office stole you from this desk."

"Well you must be a very savvy shopper. We'll have to get together and go shopping some time. I need the help. Actually, we didn't come here to discuss fashion. I'll be quiet for a few minutes and let Jake tell you."

"Michelle, Loni Scudder has fled the country. Emilee Lukin is in jail. Ronnie Scudder is dead unfortunately. We think that the immediate danger to all concerned with the Ken Kunkle investigation is safe for the time being."

"I'm so glad to hear that. I've been so scared for the entire time. I could hardly sleep at the motel. Every time the door opened, I knew I was dead. How did Loni escape?"

"You would have to ask! She stole Emilee's passport and changed Emilee's ticket to Mexico for a ticket to Beijing. She got off the plane in Honolulu. They held the plane for an hour making announcements. Then took her luggage off the plane and left without her. The FBI and Hawaii State Police have a BOL out for her. We hope to bring her into custody soon."

My cell phone buzzed. I excused myself.

"Detective Lowry, dispatch here. You have a long distance call from an Inspector Forbes in England. Shall I put him through?"

"Yes please."

"Robbie, Jake here. This must be important. I figure that it must be close to eleven in the evening there."

"Jake you're absolutely right. It is eleven here. I have some news that I didn't think should wait. I got the results on our search for Loni Scudder's married name. Miss Loni Scudder married Michael Chin in a civil ceremony in Oxford. That's news, but the real cracker is that she formally renounced her British citizenship and filed for a Chinese passport in the name of Loni Quai Chin. Her Chinese citizenship was granted and a passport issued. She swore under oath that her British Passport was stolen. A formal notice was issued to void that passport, but apparently that notice fell through the cracks. She was allowed to leave the U.K. using that passport. It would appear that your BOL in Hawaii should now also include the name Loni Quai Scudder using a Chinese Passport. I'll email you the number so we don't have any phone confusion. How do you like that?"

"I don't like it at all! As a matter of fact, it's horrible! We all know that these things happen. You can't point a finger, but you hope it won't happen again. Robbie, that's a vital piece of information. Anything else?

"No. That's it for now. I guess that's enough. Good luck on the pursuit. I hope the new info is of assistance. My preliminary inquiries don't indicate that we'll be able to exhume Michael Chin. Queen's Counsel doesn't think the wigs will approve. You know that the wigs are what our judges wear. Sorry! Until I gather more supporting data, we're going to let him lie. I guess that's gallows humor. Cheerio!"

"Thanks Robbie. I'll call Hawaii and give them the update. We'll see if this closes the net. We're also sorry about Michael Chin. Here in Idaho, we're convinced that Loni killed him."

I called Hawaii and the FBI. They were pleased to have the additional information. I was assured that they would add the new information and publish it immediately. In thirty minutes, the FBI in Honolulu called me back and said they had bad news for me. Loni Quai Chin had caught an Air China flight from Honolulu to Beijing the previous day. Since she wasn't on the watch list, she passed through customs and passport control without any problem.

"Folks, Robbie advised that Loni married Michael Chin in Oxford. She has a Chinese Passport in the name of Loni Quai Chin. The FBI office in Hawaii advised that Loni Quai Chin flew to Beijing the day before yesterday. Our spider has escaped the net."

We all went home mildly frustrated that Loni was 'in the wind.' Assuming that the Chinese government would be able to find Loni in a city with eighteen million inhabitants. Making another assumption that they would even care.

We were also hopeful that our lab reports would confirm that Rohypnol was in Emilee and Garrett's blood. We knew that DNA reports would not be available for at least two weeks.

The next day the sheriff called us all in for a meeting.

"Detectives, I want to congratulate you all for the work you've done on these Coeur d'Alene murder cases. You did an excellent job. We have two of the four suspects identified and in custody. The third is unfortunately dead at his own hands. The fourth has momentarily escaped our net. We'll have to rely on the assistance of the Chinese Government to bring her to justice. I don't believe that we could have done anymore than we did to apprehend her.

I can't think there is anything else we can do on these cases. Until we get more positive evidence, these cases are wrapped up. Let's focus on the crimes that are now affecting our citizens here in Kootenai County. Make your final entries into the mainframe and forward your reports to MacDonald Laurence at the D.A's. office. Her D.A. Investigators will take over from here. Now let's go hit it!"

PROLOGUE

Two weeks passed and the DNA results showed that Ronnie had indeed owned the clothing found in Nicole's house. Residual DNA on the ammo box belonged to the same person who wore some of the women's clothing left in Nicole's closet. Elimination led us to believe that we had Loni's DNA.

Three months passed. Emilee Lukin went to trial. Pled not guilty, was convicted on four counts of first degree murder. She was sentenced to four consecutive life terms. Her earliest possible parole date was fifty-five years in the future. Garrett Reeves was brought to trial. Made a deal with the prosecution by pleading guilty to four counts of accessory to involuntary manslaughter. Was sentenced to four consecutive fifteen-year terms. The earliest parole date was thirty years in the future.

The Chinese Government provided continuing lip service they were actively pursuing Loni, but had been unsuccessful in all of their efforts.

Nicole Logan had no surviving relatives. Her possessions reverted to the state. They sold her house and car at auction.

Heidi Matile was given total control of Emilee's possessions. Any money earned from the sale of her possessions would revert to the Victim's Assistance Fund. Heidi kept

Emilee's condo. She hired Ken Kunkle Management Inc. to handle the rental of the condo. Rebecca and Michelle became the property managers of that dwelling.

David started dating Michelle Keller on an intermittent basis. The entire division was rooting for him.

Woody McNair met a Coeur d'Alene Police Officer who seemed nice and wasn't threatened by a woman who carried a gun and had a challenging job.

Liz and I invited the entire team to our house in Kingston for an end of summer barbecue. We prepared Santa Maria Tri-tips on the outdoor grill. Liz prepared her famous potato salad. She got rave reviews. John Preston brought his entire Sky One Team and righteously strutted since they were the only non-Kootenai sheriff's employees invited.

Mac was celebrated for her aggressive prosecution of Emilee and the deal she struck with Garrett.

The FBI agent assigned to Beijing, wasn't present but was vilified for his apparent inability to encourage the Chinese Government to actively pursue Loni.

David and I had a large number of cases to occupy our time. No matter how busy we were, Loni was always present in our minds. Our security awareness relaxed but was never forgotten.

We knew Loni would be back!

ACKNOWLEDGEMENTS

Again the MRU (Monkseaton Research Unit) has come through with extensive knowledge about all things English. The MRU is personified in my very best friends, Jean and Ron Rushbrooke. They are as usual founts of knowledge, diligent fact checkers and during my visits to the U.K. gracious hosts.

My readers and unparalleled editor are worthy of loud and exhaustive praise. Kimara and Sharron were relentless in doing the initial proofing of the raw manuscript. Joanne Stebbins is a gift any author would treasure. She eliminated critical errors that hopefully will make this novel more enjoyable to read

Finally I must again offer my heartfelt thanks to the wonderful people who have populated my life. Special and wonderful folks that allowed me to use their names. John Preston's guidance on the technical aspects of helicopter enforcement made my writing easier. A thank you to the crooks, con artists, thieves, junkies, and wanna-be's, I encountered during my thirty–two year law enforcement career. You added a realistic flavor to this book as you did to "THE TANNING BED MURDERS" and "THE SEARCH FOR NORA WALLACE."

DISCLAIMER

This novel is a work of fiction. The locations named are real. The Coeur d'Alene area is truly beautiful and the surrounding country is magical. Any comment made about a retail establishment is the author's opinion and is not meant to be slanderous or libelous. It reflects the author's experience with that establishment or location.

Jake Lowry is fictitious character albeit slightly autobiographical, some editorial license has been taken.

JOHN EISLER EXTENDED BIOGRAPHY

I have lived a very interesting and adrenaline filled life. My first thirteen years of professional life were served as a Survival, Evasion, Resistance, Escape (S.E.R.E.) Specialist. I served at the main USAF School in Reno, NV and Spokane, WA. I also commanded my own schools in Thailand, Germany, and New Jersey. While in Reno, I was honored to be selected to provide training in Survival for the Mercury and Gemini Astronauts. At Fairchild AFB, I taught the initial Apollo Astronauts. While in Reno, I also worked as a stagehand part time and became the # 2 Elephant Trainer/Handler at John Ascuaga's Nugget.

Realizing that I was getting a little long in the tooth to jump out of airplanes, I became a Special Agent in the Office of Special Investigations. I served as Team Leader of the Narcotics Interdiction Team at Cam Rahn Bay, Vietnam. Upon completion of my tour there, I transferred to Germany and was the Commander of the Narcotics Team for Western Germany, Holland, Luxembourg, Austria and West Berlin.

I returned to California and retired on March 31, 1976. On April 1, I entered Civilian Law Enforcement as a Narcotics Inspector for the Bureau of Narcotic Enforcement.

In 84, I returned to my SERE roots to serve in Saudi Arabia training the Royal Saudi and Jordanian Air Forces in Desert and Sea Survival. In 85, I returned to the U.S. and back to Law Enforcement. I served with Vacaville and Oakland, CA Police Departments until 99. In 99, I was selected to assist in the opening of the "New Democratic Police Academy" in Kosovo. I returned to Kosovo in 2000 to serve as the Commander of Investigations in Rahovec, Kosovo. I returned to Idaho and joined the Fort Sherman Academy as a consultant and instructor. Fort Sherman teaches "Personal Safety" to persons who are at risk while traveling or living abroad. In 2004 I was selected to join the Jordan International Police Training Course in Amman, Jordan. Our mission for the U.S. Department of State was to train Iraqi Police Officers in the fundamentals of "Democratic Law Enforcement."

I'm now home in Idaho and again a member of the Fort Sherman Academy, where I teach on a part-time basis.

"Adrenaline Junky" is an apt term for my life. I hope I have not bored you with too much detail. I also hope you enjoy: "THE TANNING BED MURDERS", "THE SEARCH FOR NORA WALLACE." And "THE COEUR d'ALENE MURDERS."

Any question that you may have, I would be delighted to answer. My primary email contact is through: cop2tor@ hotmail.com.

Author's Cover Photograph by: www.silvervalleyphoto. com

WALL TO WALL MURDERS

This is the fourth in the Jake Lowry Mystery Series. The first: "THE TANNING BED MURDERS, The second: "THE SEARCH FOR NORA WALLACE" The third: "THE COEUR d'ALENE MURDERS" All three novels are available at: www.amazon.com.

This is a short excerpt from "WALL TO WALL MURDERS"

I have a 'Bucket List.' As I've aged, my list was becoming more important. Jogging on the Great Wall was pretty high on my list and had suddenly become possible. The Coeur d'Alene Chamber of Commerce had advertised a guided tour to Beijing and Shanghai. They advertised five star accommodations, excellent English speaking guides, air conditioned tour busses and all meals. The price was reasonable. I had vacation time on the books. Liz could arrange for a replacement at the Art Collective.

The China trip would also provide an opportunity to personally liaison with the Chinese National Police to see if I could light a fire to have them more aggressively look for Loni Quai Chin.

Loni had murdered Lawrence Matile, Cameron Haynes, Lionel Hardcastle and Nicole Logan. All four victims were killed by stabbing an awl into their hearts. She escaped by stealing Emilee Lukin's passport and flying to Honolulu. It was learned from Inspector Robbie Forbes of the Whitley Bay, England Police, that Loni also renounced her English citizenship and secured a Chinese Passport and citizenship. She flew from Honolulu to Beijing using her Chinese Passport. Since arriving in Beijing, she apparently vanished into thin air.

The tour group, including Liz, and I, were staying at the Beijing Sun Palace Crowne Plaza. The Crowne Plaza was a real five star hotel. The Great Wall visit was scheduled the second day of the tour. The first day, Liz and I rode with the tour group to the Jade Factory. An excellent guide explained the uniqueness of jade and its place in the Chinese culture. Liz selected a beautiful jade bangle bracelet as a memento of the trip.

The Chinese say Jade is a living organism. Overtime it will change colors. Jade is given as a good luck omen. A new bride receives a significant piece of jade from her new mother-in-law. The bride's mother also gives her departing daughter a jade bangle. Once this custom is observed, the new bride must kow tow (bow) three times to her new mother-in-law. This shows she has sublimated herself and will be obedient for the remainder of the marriage.

After the jade factory, we visited Tian' Anmen Square and The Forbidden City. Our guide said that over one hundred thousand people were there the previous day. Liz and I opined that maybe two of them didn't come out today.

One thing was obvious all over the city; there were literally thousands of police officers visible. In addition to police officers, there were thousands of soldiers. They stood at attention in full dress uniforms complete with white gloves. They all looked to be about fourteen years of age. I'm sure they're older, but if I conducted a line-up, it would be hard to find six possible persons that didn't look identical.

Tomorrow after The Wall, I was meeting with the Beijing President of the International Police Officer's Association (IPA). Chief Inspector Patric Sean Lee was assigned to the Tourist Police Division.

I've been a member of IPA for over twenty years. We have chapters all over the world. If you're traveling to a foreign country, you can contact the National Secretary and they will make a contact for you in the country and frequently the city you desire to visit. This entrée allows you to contact a local officer who'll usually grease the wheels for you if you want a departmental tour or need some very personal liaison.

I was hoping for a lot of grease!

The trip to Badaling, the closest point to encounter The Wall was only about forty-five minute drive from the hotel. I was excited to see the actual wall. It was even more impressive than any picture I'd previously seen. Liz and I climbed the first set of stairs from the parking lot to the rampart above the highway. This section of the wall went almost directly up the side of a small mountain. My jog was going to be short and tiresome, but at least I was jogging on The Wall. A major check-off on my 'Bucket List.'

I was sweating and puffing when I returned to the rampart. Liz had walked down the stairs to an outdoor coffee kiosk. She was enjoying a cup of coffee under a paper umbrella. She smiled broadly and clapped her hands.

"Jake, honey, I'm so proud of you! You did it. That was a super big hill. How high did you go?"

"Much higher than I thought possible. I'm getting old. Years ago I would have sprinted up that hill. Today I took it nice and slow. The sweat shows how much I've aged. But it is honest sweat and I love it."

"I'll have time to shower and get into some decent clothes before I meet Inspector Lee. I hope he is ready to get some work done. We need the Chinese National Police to seriously focus on trying to apprehend Loni."

I was to meet Chief Inspector Lee in the lobby of the Crowne Plaza. I wanted to impress him, but also put him at ease. The hotel was way above my normal pay grade. If I book lodging, it's usually a Best Western or Holiday Inn.

Chief Inspector Lee arrived punctually. He was dressed in a navy blue suit with striped tie, black wing tipped shoes and a crew style hair cut. Not quite matching my mental picture.

"Detective Lowry?"

"Yes sir. Chief Inspector Lee?"

Chief Inspector Lee's English was flawless. No accent. A slight British intonation on some words, but he could pass for a native born English speaker easily.

"Detective Lowry, please call me 'Patric' although it sounds like the conventional spelling, it lacks the 'K' at the end. My father was of Irish extraction and my mother was born in Shanghai. In my family we call each other 'Chirish.' That's a combination of Chinese and Irish. May I call you Jake?"

"Please do. I'm sure the National Secretary informed you that I'm on the Coeur d'Alene Chamber of Commerce Tour. I'm really here for three reasons. Do you know what a 'Bucket List' is?"

"Yes I do. I've one also. What does Beijing have to do with your 'Bucket List'? I'll bet Beijing is only ancillary. My guess is The Great Wall plays well into your list."

"Patric, you and I'll get along well. You're 'spot on' as the Brits say. I wanted to see it in person and also to take a short jog. I accomplished that earlier today. My second reason for being here is to hopefully meet with some National Police Officers and impress upon them the urgency to actively pursue Loni Quai Chin. She is also known as Emilee Tish Lukin, Annalee Fox and Loni Scudder. Are you aware of her involvement in the serial murders that were committed in my jurisdiction?"

"As a matter of a fact, yes! I read the notices and have spoken with the FBI liaison agent at the American Embassy. I do have some news for you. Although it appears the Chinese Government and our National Police have done nothing to pursue and or apprehend Mrs. Chin that's not the fact. We've been actively looking for her. First of all to hopefully cement our excellent relationship with the United States and secondly, because we have had two murders here in Beijing where the victims were stabbed through the heart with an awl. This method appears to be identical to the modus operandi used by Mrs. Chin in your city."

"As a matter of policy, we require every tourist to register their visa and passport when they enter the country. Since Mrs. Chin was not a tourist, but a Chinese citizen, she passed easily through customs and passport control. We know exactly what day and at what time she arrived in Beijing, sadly little else. She stated that she was staying at the home of her father-in-law, Doctor Eason Chin. We have contacted Dr. Chin. He was unaware of Mrs. Chin coming to China and obviously wasn't aware of her impending visit to his home. He denies any contact with Mrs. Chin."

"We've placed alerts at every reputable hotel and lodging facility in the city. That task alone was no small accomplishment. I'm sure you're aware that our population is estimated to be over eighteen million inhabitants here in Beijing. It's easy to disappear. We're trying to establish a common link between our two stabbing victims. So far, no identifiable link."

"Patric, I have to ask. Were the victims locals or tourists?"

"Both were American males. They were on an extended six months student visa. They'd been in the country for five months. One lived on the north side of the city, the other on the west. Both were teaching English as a Secondary Language in Chinese grammar schools. One victim was from Texas, the other from Oregon. They attended different universities in the U.S. The information collected thus far shows no common link between them. The only thing they both did in common, was swim in the Olympic Water Cube in the center of the city. This has become a real attraction for both residents and tourists here in Beijing. Our District Commander has officers stationed at the Cube during every hour that the Cube is open. They're questioning every swimmer, trying to see if anyone remembers either victim. This has been ongoing for three weeks. Thus far we haven't encountered anyone who remembers either victim. We have your picture of Mrs. Chin that the FBI Liaison Officer furnished with the BOL. We've also been showing her picture to the swimmers and no one remembers seeing her at the Cube.

"Patric, do you have any members of the police force with an extensive knowledge of Black Magic?"

"Jake, you have to understand; mysticism is an integral part of the Chinese culture. We have spirits, genies, ghosts, demons, angels, and other things that as they say, "go bump in the night' as part of our culture. We do have a section devoted to splinter groups that exploit our citizen's beliefs. We try to identify any organized criminal groups that attempt to extort money with false claims of unorthodox or extraordinary skills. Why do you ask?"

"Loni in addition to her fatal skills with an awl also practiced Black Magic. Is an autopsy a routine practice here in China?"

"Yes. We do autopsies on all murder victims and for any unattended death to assure that there was no foul play. Again, I must ask. Why do you ask?"

"All four of our victim's toxicology screens showed traces of Rohypnol in their system. Rohypnol is also known by slang names of 'Roofies' and the 'Date Rape Drug.' Are you familiar with that drug?"

"Jake you, like so many other people who are not familiar with China think we run around in silk pajamas with small black caps on our heads and a long braid of hair called a queue or pigtail trailing behind. Actually China is a very progressive country. We have Internet access, International television, and read papers and magazines from many nations. In addition to the IPA, I'm a member of the Tactical Officers Association, The Police Training Officer's Consortium and was also an International Police Officer serving in Indonesia. So your misconception although commonly shared is just that; a misconception."

"Patric, I didn't mean to offend you, but I'm admittedly, not a student of China and Chinese culture. Your previous statement hit the mark. I apologize. When will you get the toxicology reports on your stabbing victims?"

"Based upon your disclosure, I can ask for a speeded up response. We could possibly have it in two days. Would you like to speak with members of the, what we jokingly call, 'Spook Squad?' that's a play on words because they deal with spirits and such."

"I have eight more days left on this tour. Could you arrange for that to happen within that period?

"How about tomorrow? We can do that if you don't mind missing some of the tour's attractions. This might be a mutually educational experience for the 'Spook Squad' and for you. You most assuredly will learn some interesting fact about Chinese culture and they will learn about the American view of 'Black Magic' as you call it."

"Tomorrow sounds good. What time shall I plan for?"

"Jake if I may take another liberty, my wife, Lily, and I would like to take you and your wife, Liz to dinner this evening. As you know Beijing was previously known as Peking. We still call our most famous dish 'Peking Duck'. A large number of restaurants offer this delicacy, but few prepare it in the old tradition. We'd like to take you to the most popular restaurant in the city for that dish. The owner is a cousin of mine. I can get us a nice table on short notice. Tomorrow morning at nine, I'll pick you up here and take both you and Liz to our Hutong Substation. That Substation is also the office of the 'Spook Squad.' I'll bring Lily with me. She and Liz can explore the Hutong Alleys while we talk to the 'Spook Squad.'"

"The Hutong Alleys are on our schedule of things to see. Liz, having a personal guide would be a real treat for her. I'm embarrassed to ask, but does Lily speak English as well as you do?"

"Sadly no. Her English far surpasses mine. Lily is also 'Chirish.' She is reversed from me. Her mother was an Irish nurse working here and her father was also a Chinese Police Officer. They met in the emergency room. Her father had shot an armed robber and took him in for emergency surgery. The rest is 'History,' as they say, or as Lily and I say the outcome was my beautiful wife, Lily."

"I don't want to monopolize your free time, but if Liz and you are amenable, after dinner we can drive over to the Water Cube so you can see the venue with your own eyes. It is a remarkable sight."

Patric and I agreed to meet in the lobby again at seven this evening. Liz had caught up with the tour at the Cloisonné Factory. She returned to the hotel a little before six. I brought her up to speed on the day's events while she showered and shared some of my thoughts with her.

"Liz, Patric Sean Lee is an enigma. I didn't mention your name, but he knew it. It may have been a slip for him to mention it, or it may have been a very subtle display of power to show that we may be 'free' but 'Big Brother' does know who we are and probably quite a bit about us. I didn't specify in my email to the National IPA Secretary I would be accompanied by my spouse. I figured since we were on the tour, I'd try not to interrupt your sightseeing schedule unless absolutely necessary. Secondly, he said, he was also an International Police Officer who served in Indonesia. I never mentioned that I served in that capacity in Kosovo or Jordan. But he knew I had also previously been an International Police Officer. That comment may have been an effort to establish a bond, or another subtle indication of the power of knowledge. His wife's name is Lily. She, like Patric is considered 'Chirish.' That is they have one Chinese and one Irish parent. Patric says Lily's English is better than his and his is near perfect."

"After dinner tonight we're going to see the Water Cube. You remember that fantastic building we saw during the Olympics. Beijing has two stabbing victims that were killed by having an awl thrust into their hearts. The only thing they have in common is they swam at the Cube. Patric suggested that tomorrow while he and I are talking to a special division that handles esoteric crimes, you and Lily go to the Hutong Alleys. The tour was supposed to go there, but you will have a special bi-lingual guide."

Liz was toweling off and said, "I'll be the envy of the rest of the tour. The buzz is that Hutong is such a quaint spot. They discourage vehicles and use bicycle powered rickshaws to go down the narrow alleys. This'll be a real adventure."

Dinner was a truly remarkable event. The lines outside and inside the restaurant were both long and wide. It appears that entire families come for Peking Duck. Patric walked us past the lines and spoke quietly to the hostess. We were whisked to a small elevator and it creaked slowly up to the fourth floor. A Maître'd in a well tailored tuxedo greeted us and took us to a private room. Patric ordered Peking Duck. Both Liz and I had previously eaten this dish numerous times. None of our prior meals equaled the duck we had. It was exquisite!

Patric drove us to the Cube just as it was getting dark. The Cube is capable of changing from one vibrant, intense color to another. It does look like a very deep ocean when the blue color is present. Patric parked in a reserved spot, very close to the main entrance. A credential flash and quiet conversation and we were inside the cube. The noise of swimmers and the smell of chlorine brought back memories of many hours spent in pools as a young man.

I guess when you really come down to it; cops are the same the world over. Patric greased us into the restaurant and the cube. I wasn't sure if this was the standard IPA treatment, or he and his department were truly interested in apprehending Loni.

Liz and I thanked Patric and Lily for a wonderful evening. We confirmed out meeting time the next morning.

We jumped into the elevator and were quietly whisked to the seventeenth floor. Quite a contrast from the creaky elevator in the restaurant. We watched a little BBC TV and were under the covers by ten.

An hour in the fitness room on the weights and treadmill then a stinging good shower and we were ready for a grand buffet breakfast. The Crowne Plaza catered to everyone's taste in the buffet. You could have traditional Chinese Dim Sum, Full English, Continental, or regular Ol' American. We both opted for Continental and had crispy German Brotchen, sliced prosciutto, goat cheese, fresh fruit, tomatoes and cherry jam. I could have tripled my consumption it was so good. Liz tried the Turkish coffee. I wasn't so brave and opted for Earl Grey tea.

Patric and Lily were waiting when we stepped off the elevator. We went to his car and he drove us through early morning traffic that reminded me of the Bay Area. When we arrived in Beijing, our guide said, "We have a forty five minute drive from the airport to our evening restaurant unless there's a traffic jam."

I think that what they call a traffic jam in Beijing is "Normal Traffic." It reminds me of the current TV Weather Prognosticators. They say, "Our temperatures are above average. They've been above average for the past ten years." That indicates to me that our NEW Average is what the last ten years of temperature have been. So any estimate of driving time in Beijing is based on an old ten year estimate. Well before the influx of millions more inhabitants.

Patric pulled up to a flat roofed grey building. It had no multi-lingual sign or indication that it was a Substation. There were two uniformed police officers standing beside the door. They saluted Patric and he spoke quietly to them and they also saluted me. He'd let Lily and Liz out at what I would consider to be a rickshaw terminal.

The hallways were bustling with people. There were telephones ringing and keyboards clicking and conversations all round. Even without the sign, this was a police station. We walked to the end of the hall. Patric knocked on the door.

We heard a melodious, "Come in please" in perfect English.

Patric opened the door and sitting on the edge of an old wooden desk was a girl dressed in all black 'Goth' clothing. Her coal black hair was straight and appeared lifeless. Her black 'Black Sabbath' 'T' shirt was at least four sizes too large for her petite frame. She was wearing black combat boots and black opaque tights. Her lips and fingernails were also black. She would have fit in perfectly on any high school campus in the U.S.

With a casual wave of her hand she said, "Hi guys! Make yourself at home. The rest of the team is at the cafeteria getting a cup of tea. They'll be here in a minute. Patric who is your American friend? I know he's a cop, but that's all I know."

"Jake, may I introduce Susie Wong? That's not her real name, but that's the name she uses on the street. I think the irony is lost on the people she deals with."

"Susie, how do you do? I'm Jake Lowry. You're correct. I'm a cop. Actually I'm a Detective with the Kootenai County Sheriff's Department in Coeur d'Alene, Idaho. Are there many 'Goths' here in China?"

"Amelican you know Goth? Wow! Gee! I no know Amelicans know bout Goth. We make Goth in China and think we invent. Wow! Gee! You Amelicans sure smart."

This short tirade was done with a heavily accented voice and a mincing manner. It was very convincing and if I hadn't met her in this Substation, I probably would have fallen for it.

"Would it be in poor form for me to applaud? Miss Wong that was a superior performance! If you hadn't invited us in with such perfect English, I'd have bet your English was limited at best. Patric said this is your street name. Am I to assume that you work undercover?"

"Yes sir. I do. I'm part of the Street Crimes Unit. We work against pick pockets, thieves, and con artists. Beijing has recently become even more of a tourist destination. We've had to form specialized units to combat the criminal threat. I'm glad I impressed you. Particularly since you have such a reputation for outstanding interview skills. Thank you for the compliment. I believe that most of our Street Crime Staff are ham actors at heart. We love to perform and fool people. It's particularly satisfying when we fool crooks."

The door opened and what I could only graciously call, the weirdest assortment of people came into the large office. I felt that I had come to a weird costume party but they had failed to advise that I should also wear a costume. They were a wide assortment of ages and builds. The clothes ranged from two men in rags complete with offensive body odor. Another young male 'Goth.' Two men and two women dressed in Saville Row business suits, very chic and probably expensive. From those two extremes the others had on a wide variety of Chinese and Western clothing.

Patric stood and introduced me. He said that he would not offer their names as they may have changed overnight. He did say that everyone was anxious to hear my experience with Black Magic. I was really on the spot! I asked how much time I had and they told me I had all day if necessary, they had come off the street to listen to me.

I told them about Ken, Nora, and went into detail about Loni. That was a natural lead-in to Black Magic. I gave them my background in Oakland and was asked about the Raiders and Athletics. After I gave them the basics they also asked about Santeria and Voodoo.

Before I knew it, I've been talking for three hours. Patric suggested a break for lunch. He'd call Lily so we could meet in the Hutong.

We went into the station's cafeteria and sat at a large table with a glass Lazy Susan in the center. Food was placed on the Lazy Susan and slowly rotated. You chose what you wished to eat and took a portion. You could sample everything or be selective.

Midway through the meal, Patric's cell rang. He blanched slightly and motioned for me to leave the table. I met him at the door.

"Jake, we have a murder. This time the victim has a note attached. It is written in English but does have a Chinese chop signature. Loni Quai Chin knows you are in Beijing. She has sent you a message."

The message is, "**Jake welcome to the Great Wall. Hope you enjoyed the jog.**" It's signed by '**Fahn Quai**'. The chop is the signature of '**Fahn Quai**'

"Patric I'm overwhelmed! Who was the victim and where is the body located? Can we go there? I'm sorry to be so inquisitive, but this is worse than horrible!"

"The body of another male American was left in a taxi parked in the parking lot of the Great Wall. The parking attendant became suspicious when the taxi didn't try to respond to his whistle for the taxi to move forward to accept passengers. We have a forensics team on the scene as I speak. This is the first murder on the Great Wall in many years.

Made in the USA
Charleston, SC
30 April 2011